# JOSHUA GAYOU
# COMMUNE

## BOOK ONE

AETHON
BOOKS

**COMMUNE BOOK 1**

**©2017 JOSHUA GAYOU**

Print and eBook formatting, and cover design by Steve Beaulieu.

Published by Aethon Books LLC.

# ACKNOWLEDGMENTS

To my wife, Jennifer, who did so much to improve my writing and helped to make Amanda more real,

To my good friend, Scott Brandt, who saved me from making several stupid civilian mistakes,

To my friend, Brittany-Rose Tribulski, who helped me to understand that each person in the world must have their own Voice,

And to the rest of my friends, who assured me that this was a story worth sharing,

Thank you all.

# THE FLARE

## Jake

"It's amazing how everything breaks when you don't have an army of people staring at it."

This is where Jacob Martin (who we all know as Jake) decides to start his story: at the fall of everything. I would love to have him start further back than this. We would all love to hear it, truly. We have all lived with him now for various periods of time, spanning from several months to at least two years. The realities of day to day life have made him familiar to us, but the fact remains: we know essentially nothing about this man's origin. I suspect some of the others in our community may have a pool running—the person who comes closest to guessing the details of Jake's former life takes the pot! This is all contingent, of course, on me wheedling the details from him. Hope springs eternal.

Those of us who have asked him directly about his life well-understand the fruitless nature of this pursuit. No one ever asks a second time or, at least, not often. He's not mean about it (I don't think I can even remember him ever raising his voice). He simply favors you with a flat, emotionless stare. I've gotten it once, and I can tell you: you don't want a second helping after the first taste. It is not a look that telegraphs danger; rather, it is a betrayal of Jake's inner workings. There is clearly something happening inside him during these times. He is also clearly expending a great force of will to hide this. It is unnerving to see a face you associate with familiar warmth assume an aspect of reptilian disregard. Having been a part of the commune for over a year, living close with the people in it, struggling for survival alongside them, and looking along with them to Jake for leadership, the thought that Jake might be more Stranger than Friend is terrible.

My name is Brian Chambers. My job, within the context of this document, is to write down everything that Jake and the other members of the commune care to share. I was "awarded" this position, despite my best efforts to protest against it, primarily because I am familiar with shorthand (a skill left over from my college days). This skill combined with the fact that Jake is unable to write (or at least he cannot write in a way that makes sense to others) means that this appointment was a foregone conclusion.

We must assume that Jake can read, after a fashion; he has taught himself many things from the books in Billy's library. This fact notwithstanding, I have witnessed him attempt to read through some bit of text while others stand by awaiting him. There is a certain charm to these events; he always tries to read the item handed to him. We all know he will stare at the page for a few seconds, shake his head with an exasperated grunt, and then hand it to one of the onlookers and ask them to explain. This is one of his behaviors that have endeared him to many here. He never betrays frustrated anger during these interactions nor does he express embarrassment. To my knowledge, he has never attempted to hide his condition from anyone. My best personal guess is that he has some form of dyslexia. He can bull through reading things, mostly through patient willpower alone, but he is not willing to make us wait for him (his advice is usually being solicited on these occasions, anyway). I am almost certain that writing coherently is beyond his ability. Despite all of this, he never utters an angry word. He only offers a sheepish, apologetic grin and asks to be helped. It is odd what things might strike a person as brave, yet this has always seemed to me like one of the bravest things he does.

In summation, I am gifted at taking rapid dictation, and Jake writes nothing at all. Some of our other members who have fallen naturally into the position of "Elder" have determined that we should begin to keep records for those generations that come after us (I would add that concerns for such concepts as "legacy" and "posterity" naturally become the province of the aged. However, tact restricts me from saying this out loud). It is certainly possible that this record is found useful by some unknown reader at a later time—I honestly think it just as likely that this is our way of leaving something behind. This is the evidence of our existence. The Census, public records, and the sum total of all digital human knowledge are lost to us. We must be our own historians.

Jake is the first of us; the first surviving member of the Jackson Commune. Additionally, everyone else who lives here follows his lead. It is natural and right that the record starts with him.

At the time of this writing, we believe Jacob Martin to be in his mid to late thirties. We have made our guess based on small details the most astute of us have managed to glean in conversation with him. The current estimate of his age is attributed to the earliest movie he has admitted to seeing in the theater: E.T. His memory of this event is spare, limited only to sitting in his father's lap. Consequently, we estimate his age by adding five years to the film's release date. Attempts at uncovering more information from this memory resulted in an emotional shutdown, effectively ending the conversation until a later time. With practice, one discovers what subjects to avoid.

Jake's appearance is an odd combination of remarkable and unremarkable factors. Physically, he is incredibly strong. Another of our members, Blake Gibson, has reported personally seeing Jake lift a barbell loaded with over five hundred pounds from the concrete floor of the garage (a set of barbells, plates, and a rack are among the many items with which Billy had outfitted his property years ago). Despite his overall strength, Jake resembles a strongman competitor more than a bodybuilder. His shoulders, legs, trunk, and back are tremendously thick; however, he lacks the giant pectorals and biceps of one who focuses on physique. He has far more physicality in common with the great apes of Africa than he does with any Olympian.

He has a mashed-in nose from a previous fracture with a jaw and neck that makes his head look slightly undersized which, Amanda assures me, was far less noticeable when he was not shaving his head. The hair that is visible (in his beard and in the stubble of his scalp) is brown with patches of grey. I have asked him why he goes to the effort to shave his scalp, which must be a burdensome undertaking in a world free of abundant electricity. His reply was that he was once nearly killed by a man who was able to grab a handful of his hair. Oddly enough, his beard appears to be thick enough to present the same weakness; I assume someone will have to make the mistake of attempting such a gambit before Jake maintains a clean shave all over.

The evidence of his age is hidden from his face until he smiles, a rare enough event under any circumstances. At rest, his face is smooth with the exception of the forehead, which is always lined with worry or concentration. When he smiles, his cheeks and eyes explode in wrinkles like a fireworks show. The rest of us sometimes think we have underestimated his age when he smiles.

I ask Jake to start at the beginning of the Flare, knowing that any attempts to push back further will run the risk of ending the narrative before it has the chance to begin. He leans back in his chair and settles against the table with his blocky chin cupped in his hand, thinking.

Finally, he says, "You know, it's amazing how everything breaks when you don't have an army of people staring at it."

———

I'm not speaking of when the Flare hit, of course. I mean after that. The Flare was what it was; what we all remember. One day you step outside (if you were lucky enough to be outside when it occurred) and saw what I can only describe as The Northern Lights on steroids. The dead of night and there's enough light to read by with some of the wildest colors dancing across the sky that you've ever seen, making everything all around you take on this other-worldly, ghostly appearance. This goes on for days, and you get used to it, of course. There was nothing on the news but coverage of the event; I saw more of Neil DeGrasse Tyson's face on the TV in those few days than years' worth of wasting time on the Internet.

Those few days of remaining twenty-four-hour cycle coverage became pretty interesting, if not outright fun. Suddenly everyone was an amateur cosmologist weighing in on what they thought was coming next. The conspiracy theorists came falling out of the woodwork, like they always do, and blamed it all on everything from space-based weapons systems to aliens. The "journalists" on TV ate all this garbage up (because what the hell else are you going to do with a twenty-four-hour news cycle?) and hit their expert guests with unceasing, breathless questions. "What comes next?" "What of the rumors we're seeing on Reddit?" "What should our viewers at home be doing?"

At first, all the experts were very soothing. They almost fulfilled the role of Hyperbole Goalies, catching each idiotic or leading comment from the news anchors and pulling them (and everyone else) back down to reality. In the first day, all we heard were the few lines of calming mantra: Solar Flares and Coronal Mass Ejections (CMEs) are two different things and don't always occur at the same time; it's incredibly unlikely that a CME would be directed right at Earth given the distances involved; the Earth has this really neat thing called a Magnetosphere in place to protect us from this kind of activity; and so on.

A couple of days into the dazzling skylights, we started to notice the narrative change. The experts became less placating. We heard less and less about the likelihood (or lack thereof) of an impact to day-to-day life as a result of the solar event. We heard more and more side stories about disaster preparedness kits, how much water you should have stashed on hand, knowing the location of local community crisis management centers. Various local news stations started to broadcast the possibility of rolling brown-outs as a mitigation tactic just in case something really gnarly was coming our way. I actually don't know if anything ever came of that; it seemed the officials had only just begun to discuss mitigation when all the lights went out.

This was no normal outage either; I recall sparks jumping out of some of my wall sockets and a few of the homes up the street burned down completely. We had already been living with the idea that something like this could happen for at least a few days by this point, so many of us started to filter outside from our houses (usually you'd just stay inside, light a candle, and wait for your WIFI to come back). It was evening, and I was standing around outside discussing the possibility of a block-wide BBQ with a neighbor when we all started hearing the crashing of the cars up and down the highway. Later on, some of us figured out that it probably wasn't every car that started crashing; just the newer, fancier ones that had fully electronic braking systems. Turns out those few were enough to create a massive pile-up for miles on the overcrowded California freeways.

It was a little after that when planes started falling out of the sky; again, not all of them—just the really unlucky ones with electrically controlled hydraulic systems. Sometime later (once the news slowly started coming back online and being distributed through old-fashioned means—in many cases military personnel in old-school jeeps), we learned that the Flare, as it was being called, was the single greatest solar flare/CME ever encountered in history with a magnitude several times greater than the event recorded in the mid 1800s (I don't recall what that one's name was anymore or when it was, exactly).

All in all, it was a massive, crippling blow to an overburdened power grid running at capacity. This wasn't just localized to North America either; apparently, the only countries that hadn't been greatly affected were those of the third world with little to no infrastructure to speak of. Slowly over the next few days, chaos bled quickly into mass insanity. At first, when everything went down, it was a nice change of pace. Many of us commented on how nice it was to unplug from the stupid TV for a few hours. By the second day, it was less like a nice little diversion and more like an unplanned camping trip; still not so bad. After a week, water and sewage began to be a serious problem. The Flare had effectively killed all of the satellites (which we were informed were now also on a slow, plodding collision course with the planet) so all but the slowest, courier-based communication was offline. Supplies and relief were non-existent. You may or may not be old enough to remember Hurricane Katrina but if you are, picture that times ten, only spread out across twenty or thirty percent of the planet. We were informed that we were collectively looking at about a six month recovery period just before the riots broke out and Martial Law was declared. This was also the same time that all news just stopped coming. It isn't that they weren't trying to get us information; the military in our area and the military couriers remained friendly with those of us who weren't behaving like fools. There just wasn't any new information to speak of.

Life became very different over the next couple of months. We adapted to it (you'd be amazed what you can adapt to when you have no choice). One of the things we had going for us was that the Flare really only affected large electrical systems spread out over a great distance. Basically, the generation plants, the distribution systems, and the structures connected to them. Instances where smaller, self-contained systems were destroyed (such as airplanes, autos, boats, and personal electronics) were the rare exception and not the rule. Smaller scale electronics that were either not connected to the grid or behind circuit breakers were still functional, which meant that a lot of our gadgetry could still be used provided a backup generator was available. In the meantime, work crews scrambled to replace the blown components of the underlying grid. Over time it seemed as though we were making some traction towards clawing our way back to dominance over the planet. All of the riots had been put down. Those of us who were still lucky enough to have homes, worked with the military to set them up as supply distribution points or other critical facilities (it was very much in our interest to do this as it resulted in a Strategic Importance designation, which basically meant your house got its own detachment of armed guards—not a bad deal). I remember tent cities set up all along the streets, fenced off between checkpoints and so forth. It seemed a little off-putting at first, but you got the idea real quick that it was just what it had to be. Once things had calmed down, we heard some rumors here and there via the border of how things were going on down in Mexico and the rest of South America. Just those rumors were enough to make us grateful for what we had at home, tent cities and all.

It seems the world has a way of delivering the second part of a two-punch combo at the time when you can afford it the least. For us, that second punch was the Plague.

It's been some years since that time, and I still don't know if anyone figured out where the Plague came from. We're not even sure what species of virus it was. There was some word that it came out of Arkansas, but the lines of communication were so confused by that point that it might as well have come from Mars for all the good that info would do. We learned plenty about it over time through experience and exposure. It started out acting like a common cold, only it held on a lot longer. You could operate anywhere from three weeks to a month with nothing more than an annoying cough or sniffle. At some point, depending on how strong you were I guess, the virus would turn the heat up on you, and you spent the next three days or so going from cold to flu to super flu. After that, you eventually suffocated and died.

The most discouraging aspect of that time (for me) is I'm almost certain that if it had just taken us a little longer to start recovering from the Flare, the virus (a lot of us were calling it the Plague by then) might have stayed local to wherever it came from and burned out like Ebola would tend to do. Instead, the military was making some real progress into getting air travel back online. When you consider that the virus would just sit and gestate inside you for weeks until it finally ramped up to kill you (combined with its high communicability rate), it's easy to understand how a localized epidemic quickly blossomed into a pandemic the likes of which we had never seen.

We know it was airborne. We at least managed to figure that out before it killed most of us.

We also learned that even the Plague doesn't have a one hundred percent communicability rate or a one hundred percent mortality rate (even though both numbers were so close to one hundred percent that it didn't matter on the macro scale). We figured out that immunity could be hereditary; if a mother was immune, it always meant that any of her offspring were immune. If the father was immune, offspring had maybe a fifty-fifty chance of being immune. I'm not sure if there have been any instances of offspring being immune while both of their parents contracted the Plague; there have been so few cases of intact families beyond two or three people that we just can't say for sure. Anything is possible, I guess. I think I heard that a handful of people actually survived contracting the Plague, but their respiratory systems never recovered; think emphysema symptoms for the rest of your life.

I can't really give you a percentage of people who died due to the Plague (because the Flare/Plague one-two combo killed all statistics too), but out of my whole neighborhood, I'm the only...

———

Jake's narrative trails off abruptly at this point. I know what has happened, of course. The look on his face tells me all I need to know.

"I think we'll stop there tonight, Brian. It's late. There is a long day ahead of us," Jake says quietly as he gets up and moves to the door. I know there will be no discussion on this. I carefully collect my papers into a neat bundle, wish him goodnight, and walk quietly out into the evening.

# 2

# CEDAR CITY

## Amanda

A manda Contreras is a single mother in a world where all parents from before the Plague have been rendered single by default. She is a compact 5'5" woman, twenty-six years old, with naturally brown skin and hair from her Hispanic heritage. Her eyes are a striking light-grey with sharp cheekbones. Her daughter, Elizabeth, is nine years old and favors her mother's appearance. If there is still such a thing as a helicopter parent in this world, Amanda is of the Apache Longbow variety.

I am sitting with Amanda on the porch of the small, three-room cabin that she built with the help Oscar and some of the others who live in the commune. Her daughter sits a short distance off from us on a stump, happily making cordage by twisting together the shredded leaves of cattails. She hums a tuneless song to herself as she works in the dying light of the day. There is already several yards of the strong coil at her feet. Her feet are bare; she uses her toes to control and coil the rope as it is produced.

Amanda has served us both a cup of tea, a rare delicacy. It is possible that someone somewhere is still cultivating the crop, but the resurgence of the beverage is not something we anticipate seeing any time soon in Wyoming. She has produced some scavenged bags of Lipton and boiled water over a fire. There is no sugar to spare for this treat ,but it does not matter. It is delicious, and I feel myself invigorated by the caffeine almost immediately.

I inform her that we can take as little or as much time for this as she would like and that I am at her service for as long as she is willing to go. She smiles at me, sips at her drink, and watches Elizabeth a while. Finally, she says, "That little girl is the only reason I'm still alive, you know?"

———

The plague took everything from us. I mean more than just the people it took. It took our certainty. I've been thinking about this a really long time, now, and I think I have a good idea what it was that made it so horrible besides...the obvious.

I got pregnant with Elizabeth when I was seventeen with my boyfriend, Eddie. Before that, I wasn't certain about anything. I didn't know what I was going to do or where I was going. Everyone around me from my parents to the counselor at school, all my teachers; everyone told me I had to get ready for college, but I had no idea what I wanted to do. I didn't really have any hobbies besides hanging out with girlfriends. I was just a kid, anyway.

I wasn't certain about Eddie. He wanted to be a Marine. He told me we were going to get married and all the rest but I knew how that went. He goes off to Basic, then training for his MOS. At some point, he ships out on a boat, maybe spends time in the Philippines. The whole time I'm back here being *not* with him. Not a recipe for a strong marriage. I knew where I was going to be in a week, but I didn't have any idea when it came to a few years later. No matter what, the smart money said I'd still be stuck in Beaver, Utah.

Then Lizzy happened, and things started getting "certain" real fast. I certainly wasn't going to college, for one thing. I was certainly keeping the baby, though my dad pleaded with me to "take care of it" when I told him about it. I also learned that Eddie was certainly the man I was going to marry, as you'll see.

I was afraid to tell him the most out of anyone—even more than my mother. I had seen this happen before (Beaver is a small town with not a lot of privacy). The boyfriend always gives the same lines. "Yes, I'm going to be involved. I want to be a part of the kid's life. I'm going to contribute. Do my part." All that. They're gung-ho during the pregnancy and maybe a few months after but that all dries up once the whole situation becomes more work than fantasy. I loved Eddie, and he was always good to me. He said he loved me, but I was terrified to put his future as a Marine up against my need. A part of it was that I didn't want him to have to give up that future but, in my secret heart—that place I don't like to admit exists—I was mostly just afraid to see which would win out: the Corps or me and the baby. I really, really didn't want to know what it felt like to be discarded. Not telling him at all was tempting but also not possible. At some point, he was going to notice something different about me.

I told him before anyone else. We were over at his place (actually, his parents' place) in the backyard sitting on his little brother's swing set ("I never got a swing set, the little shit," Eddie used to joke while messing up the kid's hair... Dillon was his name). There were a lot of things I admired in Eddie, but there were none so much as how he reacted to the news. Keep in mind: he was seventeen like me. The plan was for him to head down to the recruiter's office in Saint George on his birthday to enlist and, if I remember right, that was coming up in something like three months. He'd been talking about this for years— for as long as I knew him—like some people would talk about a guaranteed spot at MIT. I was a part of his planning too, but the way he talked was always that the Corps was something that happened first and then he could have me (like I was the prize at the end of the ordeal or something). I liked that he included me in his future, but I also knew that a lot happens on deployment; I had spoken to some military wives on the Internet and what I heard made me feel scared. And honestly, I wasn't so sure that I wanted to sit around waiting for a husband I rarely saw to come home and spend short stretches of time with me before shipping out again.

I told him straight out. I didn't try to soften the blow or make a little joke or anything. I tried really…really hard to keep the panic out of my voice but I don't think I did the best job. I just wanted to be straight with him. He was such a good guy; he was always straight with me. He never jerked me around, and I just wanted to give him that same kind of respect.

I'm never going to forget the look he had on his face. I think I counted about five seconds where he looked like the wind was knocked out of him. Like, just literally knocked out of him and he couldn't breathe or even move. Then, he sucked in air sharply, let it out, and finally nodded his head once. And that was it. That was all it took for him. Five seconds, a breath, and a nod to completely re-plan his whole life trajectory.

He reached out across the swings and took my hand in his (his hands were one of my favorite things about him; they were strong, a little scarred on the backs from the ranch work he did to earn extra cash, and big—big enough to disappear my hands when he held them) and asked, "Will you keep her?"

Not "him" or "it." "Her." I didn't even have any idea what I was having yet—I was only something like six weeks in. It was like he knew, though. She was already a person to him. So I said, "Yes."

He squeezed my hand and said, "Thank God. Will you marry me, then?"

I started crying. Not hard or hysterical…just some tears and some effort to keep my voice steady. "I don't know if I can be a Marine wife *and* a single mom, Eddie."

"Oh, that shit's over," he scoffed. "There are more important things to deal with now."

That was when I started to lose it. "Oh, no, no, no, no. You can't," I said. "That's your dream. You can't. You…baby, you can't." I was starting to blubber. He made all the soothing noises you're supposed to make when your girlfriend falls apart (he was probably also afraid one of his parents would see what was happening out the window and come interrupt).

When I finally calmed down, he said, "Look, baby. Yes, I wanted to do that and, yeah, it sucks. But this is a big deal. You were always going to be a part of my life. After the Marines, you were still going to be there. You're the thing that's most important. And now, with this, well… I'm not leaving so you can deal with it on your own. I'm definitely not missing the birth of my kid. Fuck that."

And on that note, he asked me again to marry him, and I said "yes." Not exactly the way I expected my proposal to go but, all things considered, I still felt pretty great about it. We said a lot more to each other out there on the swing set, but I'm keeping that conversation for me.

He insisted we tell my parents first, maybe because he wanted to get that part out of the way. I was dreading it but having told Eddie, I felt like this would be easier and it was. My parents did and said all the things you'd expect. I *will* say that my dad never tried to get physical with Eddie. He didn't have any illusions about us; he knew we'd been sleeping together. There were no big blow-ups. But there was the shock, the disappointment, the usual run of unhelpful and pointless questions. My dad tried to talk us into terminating, and we both told him that wasn't happening.

"I want to marry her," Eddie said. "I want to take care of her. I want the baby to have a dad."

"We'll see," my father said, and Eddie showed him.

He saw, alright. We had a couple of months to finish high school, but Eddie started taking all these night classes and got himself set up in an apprenticeship to become an electrician. He got a job up in Sandy along with a little two-bedroom apartment. We got married at the courthouse in this tiny, non-event. Both of our mothers moaned over our lack of big, traditional wedding but they calmed down after I explained that we needed to save money and, given my childbearing condition, the whole big-ceremony-thing with a pure white gown seemed kind of ridiculous. My one concession to my mother was a veil. A veil with a faded, old English Beat t-shirt (I loved my ska), some jeans, and a pair of Chucks. I still have the picture from that day back inside the cabin, here.

We moved up to Sandy together, Elizabeth came shortly after, and we did okay. We weren't rich, or even really comfortable, but we kept getting better. Eddie was relentless with his work. He was serious and focused. He plowed through his apprenticeship and, by the time Lizzy was three, he was making enough money that I could quit my job at Starbucks and stay home with her. As soon as Eddie made journeyman, he was right back into night classes getting all these specialized certificates. Certificates in fire alarm systems, national code, you name it. Anything he could get a slot in that was relevant. He knocked them down one after the other like he was bowling and, over time, his take-home pay showed the results.

He wasn't getting so much that we could buy a house, but he was making enough that we were able to save money. All of our needs were handled and even some of our wants and, though it was some time out, our own home was on the timeline.

I didn't notice it while it was happening but, one day, I realized that everything had become certain. Don't get me wrong, there were still plenty of question marks, but I was at least certain of my place in life. I was certain my husband would be there. I was certain we loved each other. I was certain Lizzy would be okay and that she'd have everything she needed. I was certain I could go to the store whenever we needed something (whether it was food, clothes, or other things) and, when I swiped my card, there would be money in the account to cover it. I was certain our cars would run and, if there was a problem with them, I was certain Eddie could fix it. I was certain the bills were always going to be paid on time. Things were very, very good.

When the Plague took Eddie, Lizzy and I had to leave our apartment and relocate to one of the quarantine tents just outside the city. Losing him was…hard. I'm a strong girl. I've been a strong girl for a long time. But I was mostly strong because I knew he'd be there behind me. Eduardo was the love of my life. I didn't want to continue to "be" without him. And they wouldn't let me bury him or anything. A couple of soldiers came in, gave me a bunch of "Yes, ma'am" and "No, ma'am" and hustled us right out of there. The last time I saw my husband alive was over the shoulder of someone named Sgt. Alvarez as he picked me up and carried me out of my own home, saying, "I'm sorry, ma'am. I'm so sorry," the whole time.

We were told we'd be safe in the quarantine tents; what was being called Cedar City (not to be confused with the actual Cedar City further south) because it was just off the 73 on the way to Cedar Fort. But we weren't safe. Or actually, most of us weren't. The flu rolled through Cedar City just as hard and fast as it rolled through Sandy. Lizzy and I watched as everyone around us died off in a period of weeks, no longer than a month and a half at most.

How can I describe what it was like sitting there waiting to get sick? There was something like eighty thousand or so people living in Sandy. I know that probably doesn't sound like a lot, but it was one of the bigger cities in Utah. Sandy was also stacked right next to other cities like South Jordan, Draper, and Riverton, plus it was just south of Salt Lake City itself. Cedar City had to be big enough to support the people from all of these areas (it wasn't, of course, but they did the best they could to keep up with the number of infected). I don't know how many people passed away before Cedar City was constructed, but even half of all the cities just north would have required a massive amount of area and staff. None of us ever got an official count; communication had been reduced to nothing in those days.

By the time the Plague was all done killing us off, there were just little pockets of people left, mostly on their own but in some places they were in two's or three's.

The soldiers who were out there with us were all kind, but they weren't helpful in any way. The best you could get out of them was "I'm sorry, we'll update you as soon as our command tells us" or "I'm sorry, we're expecting new supplies to arrive any day now." Everything they said to us always began with the words "I'm sorry." Despite my situation, I felt bad for them. They all looked like they were just a few minutes away from panic. They all had this universal deer-in-the-headlights look when you talked to them. All they knew was what they'd been told which, from what I gathered at the time, was to guard the camp, distribute food and medicine, put down looters, rioters, or resistance, and await further orders.

The actual medical staff seemed to be a lot better off in this regard. There were any number of Army combat medics and nurses in constant motion between the cots; they had all been either bused in or flown in while Cedar City was being put together. At least, they were all there by the time Lizzy and I arrived on our school bus. They all moved from place to place with purpose. They looked like they had a mission. In those days when there were still many of us to care for, there was always one more thing to do, one more task to accomplish, one more battle to wage by the bedside. They had it together and spoke with certainty. They were resolved.

Then, as people kept dying at the same rate despite their best efforts and especially when the soldiers and medics themselves began to find themselves on their own sick cots, we all saw that certainty and resolve erode away. Despite everything that was going on, despite the never-ending fear I had in waiting for Lizzy to get sick, watching the medics and the nurses crumble was heartbreaking. We all loved them —loved them for how hard they fought for us. When they finally found themselves down on the cot among the sick, it was the sick who were reaching their hands out between wracking coughs to soothe and comfort them. Those medical people who were still on their feet began to carry the same expressions as the soldiers and the rest of us understood: there wasn't much left to do but wait to die.

We left long before everyone died off, of course. Lots of the survivors did. Once we figured out that the soldiers were no longer confining us to the quarantine area, folks just started slipping away in little pockets. In my case, we stayed a bit longer because I was still terrified that Lizzy was going to get sick. I didn't want to take us too far away from where all the medical supplies and people were. I didn't spend a lot of time thinking about my health, though, or what it might mean that both Lizzy and I remained healthy long after everyone else gave out. It's like I said: she's the reason I'm still alive. If she hadn't been with me at that time, I think I would have just laid down on a cot and waited for my brain to turn off... or maybe grab one of the rifles from a dead soldier and turn my brain off.

So, when all the medics started dying off, I was left with a load of medical supplies that I didn't know how to use and no one to show me. It didn't make any sense to hang around anymore. The staff stationed with us had dropped off to a minuscule degree; I mean there were maybe one or two people left for every five sick tents. You could literally walk along column after column in the grid and not run into anyone official or in charge. More often than not, you could see people who used to be in charge lying in sick cots. There was no one running the place.

I led Lizzy to one of the supply tents (you had to lead her everywhere by that time; all she did anymore was sit quietly and stare off into the distance or just sleep) and got what seemed like plenty of supplies at the time. I grabbed a bottle of Ibuprofen, a first aid kit, and so on. I saw a bunch of other drugs and what I guess must have been antibiotics (they all had names I didn't recognize and couldn't pronounce, all ending in "-l-i-n"). I saw one bottle that said "Broad Spectrum" so I grabbed that. A couple of sleeping bags, a ruck from one of the soldiers that I stuffed with some MREs and a couple of bottled waters, and finally one of the soldier's rifles. I didn't even get any extra magazines for the rifle; I just took it with whatever it had loaded in. I didn't know about survival or self-reliance or even bug-out bags back then. A backpack with some waters and some food seemed like it was enough.

I didn't have much of a plan at the time outside of getting away from all the dead and dying people. Lizzy and I went back into the city to see what we could find. In the weeks that we had been restricted to the tents, Sandy and the areas around it had changed more than I would have thought possible. The quarantine was set up far away (I think twelve or fifteen miles) on the other side of the mountains from the city, so the most we ever really heard or saw was the occasional *pop pop pop* of gunfire at night, or perhaps a plume of black smoke rising into the sky from some undetermined place in the distance past Latimer point. It was like a whole different city when we came back to it. There

were abandoned barricades everywhere and vehicles in between them, also abandoned. Shop windows all over were broken out with merchandise lying in the street. It was pretty obvious what had taken place, but I still remember how hard it was to accept what I was seeing. Riots were a thing that happened up the 15 in Salt Lake City, and they were always confined to a block or two. I couldn't think of a single riot ever taking place in Sandy. I didn't think our people were like that, but then I started to look closer at the businesses that had been hit, and things started to make sense. I saw the occasional TV or appliance on the sidewalk but, for the most part, grocery stores and pharmacies were gutted without exception. Other places like outdoor and sporting goods stores were also ripped wide open.

We walked through the streets for hours. Sometimes, we ran into little knots of people that looked as confused and lost as we must have appeared. We never said anything to each other. It seems crazy, but you have to understand the situation: the only supplies any of us had were what we could carry on our backs. Most of us were armed in some way. If we didn't talk to each other, if we didn't join up, it meant one less challenge we had to deal with. Other people meant risk. You risked getting involved with crazy or violent people, or you risked joining up with people who would need more help or more supplies than you were willing to give. You just didn't know who they were going to be. And this was universally understood by all of us, so when we saw each other across the street, all we did was make momentary eye contact and then look down and move on in another direction.

Eventually, we came to our old apartment. The door hung open with a few strands of orange colored biohazard barricade tape trailing from the jam. I don't know what I thought we were going to find there. The place was as ripped apart as the rest of the city. All of our things... the things that made the place our home were destroyed. The couches were ripped up. Picture frames pulled off the wall and smashed on the floor. Every cabinet and drawer in the kitchen had been upended. I picked up a chair that had been knocked over and sat Lizzy down in it. "Stay here, Mija," I told her. She nodded and then turned her head to stare out the front door. I went down the hall to our old bedroom.

I don't know what I thought I was going to find there. Some piece of me was expecting or hoping to find Eddie lying in our bed, perfectly preserved in the state he was in when I left him, so I could finally say goodbye. He wasn't there, of course. He had been bagged up and taken out to the mass grave where they burned the remains of the infected. Whatever was left of my husband—my best friend who had always been there for me, had always protected and provided for me, who had loved me without fail for as long as I knew him—all that was left were ashes in a pit that I didn't even know how to find. I collapsed into my bed and had a complete breakdown. I sobbed for I don't know how long, jamming my face into the one remaining pillow out of fear Elizabeth would hear. She heard me anyway, I guess, because she was there a few minutes later, climbing into the bed behind me and wrapping her arms around me. We fell asleep in the bed that way; her holding me, me holding the rifle.

We woke up with the sun the next morning. I began moving around our home mechanically, cleaning a little here, straightening some furniture there. I was mentally numb and trying to come up with some idea of what to do next. I think a part of my brain was operating under this assumption that if I could just clean the place up enough, we could hunker down and survive there until whoever was still in charge figured out how to fix everything. I'm sure I would have figured it out eventually once it was clear that the water was never coming back on, but Lizzy had two and two added way ahead of me.

"Can we go get Lelo and Lela?" Lizzy asked me. I didn't have much hope that my or Eddie's parents were still alive, but it was at least a plan. Things might be better down in Beaver. It was something to hold on to.

I went through the apartment and collected some things that I couldn't live without: several pictures from before, our wedding rings, and Lizzy's old stroller. I hadn't been able to donate it to Goodwill yet, and I had always dreamed that Lizzy might have a brother one day, so it was easier to just store it under the stairs. It was one of the huge ones that you get when your baby is newborn; a mother's rolling toolkit, complete with fully reclining bed, lower shelf space for diaper bag, toys, and doo-dads—even a cup holder. It wasn't exactly a pack mule, but it helped me to get some of the weight off my back. I found some canned food that had been missed in our pantry, so I threw that into the stroller, plus some kitchen matches, extra sweaters, and blankets.

It was at this moment that I really started to realize what we had lost. The concept of certainty had not just been ended; it had been completely erased. Forget being certain about next year, we couldn't be certain anymore that we'd have enough water to drink in a couple of days. We didn't know if we'd have shelter over our heads tomorrow. We couldn't be sure of our health or security—a simple toothache could become terminal now. My inner scavenger was born that day as we rolled out of the city. Anything that caught my eye as we left that looked useful was thrown into the pile including old batteries and books or loose paper (for starting fires). At one point I hit the jackpot and found a half-empty gallon of water. Anything that looked like it might be helpful was tossed into the stroller. That thing could haul some serious weight, too. God bless Eddie Bauer.

Since it was only a little bit out of our way, we went back by Cedar City on the way to Beaver. I knew for sure I could get more food and water there and I knew we would need to bring a lot with us to make a walk down to Beaver. I wasn't looking for any cars at the time because the roads were completely jammed with abandoned cars. I had an idea about keeping my eyes open for bicycles, but I didn't think I could find one much less two—especially one that would fit a seven-year-old. On top of that, Lizzy was not one hundred percent comfortable on a bike yet. There was no such thing as hospitals or ambulances or casts for broken bones anymore, as far as I knew. Because of that, a bike suddenly became a nerve-wracking proposition. The most popular method of transportation in the world had been downgraded to feet. I had no idea how long it was going to take us to walk all the way to Beaver, but it was a little over a two-hour drive. It wasn't anything I was looking forward to.

We loaded up on more of everything at Cedar City. I grabbed more bottles of pills ending in the letters "l-i-n." I got what I hoped would be enough water to last us a week and stuffed the baby compartment of the stroller full of MREs. Now that I had a chance to think about what I was doing, it also occurred to me to get more bullets for my new rifle (which I still hadn't the first clue how to operate). I didn't want to screw it up, so I found more rifles that looked like the one I was carrying and (after fiddling around with one of them for several minutes) found the button that dropped out the magazine. I pulled the magazine out of my rifle to compare the bullets against what I had found and saw that they looked identical. I put the one magazine back into my rifle and then threw three more that I was able to find into the ruck, which I hung off the stroller's push handle. I had no idea how many rounds a magazine held at the time, but I couldn't imagine needing more than whatever four magazines could carry. I didn't know any better back then.

After topping off, we turned around and headed back up towards the 15. I hated taking the time to do it and wasn't excited about looping around Utah Lake but sticking to the 15 seemed to be the best way to go. I was afraid of getting lost and losing time on all of the backroads, and the direct approach along the freeway just seemed to be the safest way to go. We didn't know about marauders back then—hadn't heard of any or seen any yet.

———

"Lizzy, honey? It's close to dinner time. Go inside and wash up, okay?"

Lizzy flashes an angelic smile at her mother and hops up off her stump. She says, "Okay, mom," while collecting what has become a sizable coil of twisted rope as well as a much-diminished pile of leaves. She heads into the cabin, still humming to herself as she passes us.

"I don't want to talk about the next part while she's around," Amanda tells me in hushed tones. "She has Survival tomorrow with Gibs after her math and reading lessons. You can come back around then if you have the time and get the rest from me."

"Yeah, that's probably a good idea," I agree. I do not know the details, but I have some inkling of how Jake and Billy found Amanda and her daughter—I know it was not pretty. I know there was killing involved, at least.

"Look, are you sure you want to cover that?" I ask. "I don't want you to have to relive anything better left behind for this book. A lot of that doesn't need to be anybody's business, as far as I'm concerned."

"No," she says. "I want to. The things that happened to us—to me —happened because I was ignorant and unprepared. If this is going to be a part of the new history books, I want it to be perfectly clear what the unprepared can expect out of their fellow man. We all built up a lot of bad habits when everything was easy. We forgot how to survive when *easy* stops. I want to help prevent that."

# 3

# PRIMM

## Jake

I ran into Billy somewhere between California and Nevada. Well, maybe "ran into" isn't the right expression. "Slowly collided with over a period of days" would be a lot more accurate. We were going in the same direction, you see, so it took me some time to catch up with him.

When I first spotted him, I wasn't even sure what I was seeing. Between hauling my gear and maintaining awareness of my immediate area, "dead ahead" was not a direction I was spending much of my time with. As far as gear was concerned, essentials like food and water were piled up in one of those... wheeled tent/buggy things that you used to see people stuff their toddlers in and drag behind them when they went on bike rides.

That's actually funny. This is the first time I've given any thought to what you might call those things. A "bike trailer" I suppose.

Anyway, among some odds and ends like a flashlight, extra batteries, a spare change of clothes, and so on, was a good-sized pile of food (canned food, mostly, but also some freeze-dried rations that I found at an outpost) and several jugs of water. The water was the worst of it. You never think about this when water is plentiful, but it really is the limiting factor in everything you do. I can go for several days without food before I start getting into trouble (I've done it). Going just a few days without water is *bad news*.

Before this all happened, water was the least of anyone's concerns. You could always get it from somewhere. In fact, all you had to do was lift a magic lever in your kitchen and water just fell out of a pipe *and* it wouldn't stop until you pushed the lever down again. I mean… it *wouldn't* stop. It would just continue—hundreds of gallons could pass by, unused, until you hit that magic lever. When I think about what we all lost in the fall, I don't think about all the distractions. I don't think about the televisions or the cell phones or the ludicrous social media or any of the little gadgets that we thought we needed but really didn't. I think about a kitchen faucet. I remember water being so plentiful that it was literally the last thing on anyone's mind.

As we all learned, water is actually the first thing you consider in a truly natural world. It doesn't matter what task you're about to embark on; water is always your first consideration. Where can it be found? How are you going to transport it? How will you protect it from evaporating? Does it need to be purified? How will you purify it? Do you have the equipment necessary to purify it? How much of it can you carry? I've since learned from reading one of Billy's old survival books that a full-grown human needs to consume two quarts of water per day to stay healthy. If you're in deep trouble, you can ration that down to maybe one quart per day but you need to be really careful about how you take it in and limit your level of physical activity, or you'll run into severe issues.

So, four quarts to a gallon, yes? That means if you're being good to yourself (and the supply is abundant), you'll be drinking one gallon every two days or (again, if the situation is dire) one gallon every four days. Now, where this produces a problem is in weight. One gallon of drinkable water weighs a little over eight pounds. This means if you have to make a trip that will take one week you need to haul thirty pounds of water.

It is possible, of course, to get more water on the way and you always keep your eye out. It can be scavenged, certainly. It can also be found out in the wild (the human race did survive for a period without utilities or irrigation, after all) but unless you find a safe, swift-running source, the chances are you need to treat it properly, or you run the risk of becoming deathly ill from bacteria or other contaminants.

Clearly, you could boil the water, given you have a receptacle that will stand up to the heat necessary to boil water for the time needed— about twelve minutes. But then, you need the ability to make fire. You also can't drink water that has just been boiled, unfortunately, because you'll burn yourself terribly. You need to sit around and wait for it to be cool enough to consume. This means that if you find yourself having to treat water in this way, roughly half of your usable daylight travel time is eaten up in the process of gathering enough fuel to run a fire long enough to boil the water, not to mention finding water to boil, waiting for it to cool, and so on and so on. Additionally, you don't know if you're going to find any water to process on the following day.

Given all of that, you always need to know the total distance you'll be traveling, you need to know what kind of terrain you'll be running into so that you can estimate average distance traveled per day, and some means to carry all of that heavy water you'll need to survive.

I knew none of this when I ran into Billy. The only thing that really saved me was that I'd traveled most of the distance to Primm in a car. The main roads inside and around cities were all completely unmanageable. In the places that weren't blocked off or barricaded, the streets were clogged with those cars that had survived the Flare or those cars that had been repaired since the Flare occurred.

The sequence of events to which we had been subjected meant that all of the major cities had undergone a double pileup. First, there was the initial traffic jam created by everyone trying to escape the riots that broke out after the Flare hit. When things became bad enough, the military came in to establish some kind of order. They weren't there to win friendship medals, so the first thing they did was bulldoze all the vehicles off the major arteries for the purposes of securing supply lines and aid distribution networks.

The second pileup came after the Plague began to burn through what was left of us. The military personnel were just as susceptible as the rest of us and, as they started dying off in larger numbers, the unwatched roads began to bind up again.

A lot of people in all of the crowded areas where trying to get away. It's kind of funny... or maybe ironic is the word. As long as society is intact and everyone understands that there's some sort of system in place to ensure we all play nice, we'll all cram together in one place like we can't get enough of each other. As soon as those support systems start to fall apart, we can't get away from each other fast enough.

Once you get a ways outside cities or towns and into the big empty of the open highway, it becomes possible to drive if you can find a vehicle. I had found one just outside of Hesperia, only slightly used with the owner still in it. I pulled him out, set him aside, and then went through the car (it was a sedan) to see what it had in it. There wasn't much gas in the tank; however I couldn't be too choosy. Any cars behind me were all blocked-in bumper to bumper, and I didn't have any way to get gas out of them and into this car. There were other cars in sight further up the road, but I didn't want to spend a lot of time shopping for transportation. This car had gas and, because a driver was still in it, it had keys. I was grateful for that.

Whoever he was, he was less of a survivalist than I was. There was a roadside emergency kit in the trunk that looked as though it had been cannibalized, anything useful having been pillaged with the exception of the jumper cables. I also found a flimsy plastic parka in a clear plastic pouch. I opened the parka and pulled it over the driver's seat. The previous owner of the vehicle hadn't started to go all runny yet, but he had still been out there long enough to get rather foul, especially in that hot California sun, and I wasn't excited about settling into what-ever he may have left behind in the seat (visible or otherwise). I threw my rifle in the front seat, my supplies in the back seat, and folded up the bike trailer and tossed it in the trunk. I settled in behind the wheel, turned the key, and the engine started up with no complaints (most cars would still do that in those early days if you could find them in an un-fried state). I pulled the column shifter down to "drive" and proceeded on down the road, rolling all the windows down as I went to try and air out the evidence of the previous owner.

I didn't realize it at the time but finding that car probably saved my life. I made it all the way to Primm before the engine finally gagged and died from a lack of fuel. This would have been days' worth of travel on foot, requiring water that I didn't have with me. Not realizing this, I shrugged, set the brake, and went about the business of removing all of my things from the vehicle. Once all was re-situated, and I had my rifle slung over my shoulder, I gave the front tire a light kick (*see yah 'round, partner*) and continued on my way. The sun was low in the sky, and it would be evening soon so I wanted to see if I could find somewhere in Primm to settle for the night.

I had my eyes peeled for anything that might be useful as I walked into the little town (the larger cities had been swarmed thoroughly once things like "rules" and "manners" had fallen apart—though you could still get lucky—but I had hope for the smaller places with small popu-lations). What I found would disabuse me of any hope. In Primm, I would find yet another example of the complete and total faith we had devoted to our society. There was nothing else for miles in all direc-tions (with the ridiculous exception of a golf course) in this desert, and yet here in, Primm there was nothing to be found that was conducive to living out in the desert. There was an outlet mall packed full of clothing made in India, China, or Taiwan that would fall to tatters after only a few weeks of hard living. All of the restaurants…the Subways and Carl's Juniors and Taco Bells—all of those were filled with rotting food, if any of that could have been called food at any point. The restaurants did have water but no real way to carry it as it was distributed in cups via a filtered Magic Lever.

I did get lucky at a gas station I found right next to a Starbuck's (those places where just everywhere) and found non-perishable food in the form of pretzels and beef jerky. The water had been cleaned out by those who had come before me.

The good news was that since I was now on the Nevada side of the border, there were already hotels and casinos available that had been positioned on the utmost extremity of the legal limit to entice those lunatic gamblers who couldn't restrain themselves from waiting the extra hour or so to just drive into Vegas itself. For me, this meant that lodging would be plentiful. I had not needed to use my sleeping bag under the stars by that point, and I wasn't looking forward to doing so in the Nevada desert.

I opted for Whiskey Pete's across the way from the gas station. Crossing the highway, I approached what I can only describe as a hideous attempt at a castle tower slapped onto a tall, hive-like hotel building ("See Bonnie and Clyde's Getaway Car!" advised a sign out front). I had no idea what castles have to do with either Whiskey or gentlemen named Peter, but then, searching for any kind of logic in a gambling town isn't exactly the *done* thing.

The hotel (which I had started thinking of as The Hive) was around the back of the casino itself. I wasn't interested in navigating my way through the casino. Casinos usually smelled like a stale, wet ashtray even before the world ended. I was in no rush to see what the experience turns into when you mix in desert weather, dead people, and a lack of ventilation. I veered to the left through the parking lot and swung around the back.

What I found was a little swimming pool oasis populated by plants that had seen better days; the pool itself was drained. Ringing this "oasis" were rooms accessible either via doors or large windows, should I decide to break them, which I decided would be my last resort if I couldn't find a way into any of the rooms. I wheeled my trailer to one end of a line of rooms, parked it, and checked the chamber and safety of my rifle. I approached the first room; saw that the door was wedged open. I slowly pushed it open with my left hand while the rifle was awkwardly shouldered with my right.

As the door opened, my eyes registered frantic movement before they adjusted to the dim light and I noted a man somewhere in the area of my own age but looking far worse off than me. His clothes were filthy and torn, his hair couldn't decide which direction it wanted to stand up, and his skin was so caked in dirt and grime that I couldn't be sure of his pigmentation. He was leaned over, reaching for something on the table.

"That'll do right there," I said.

He froze, arms stretched out in front of him. He grimaced, and I saw him mouth the word "fuck."

"Hey, ease up, okay? I'm not here to hurt you. I'm just looking for a place to spend the night. Go ahead and straighten up—you don't need to stay hunched over like that."

He straightened into a more comfortable position and turned towards me, keeping his hands where I could see them, which I appreciated. "Kind of hard to accept with you pointing that at me," he said, eyeing the rifle. His voice was nervous and hesitant.

"I know, and I'm sorry about that," I told him. "But you have to admit: can't be too careful anymore."

He nodded and swallowed. "So, now what? What is it you want?" he asked.

"I told you. I'm just looking for a place to sleep. I'm going to back out of your room here and find somewhere else to sleep. I'll just leave you alone, right?"

"Just like that?"

"Just like that," I nodded and started to move backward.

"Hey," he called. "You have any food or water with you?"

I stopped and tried to center the barrel on his chest without looking like I was trying to center the barrel on his chest. "Nothing I can spare," I said. "Sorry."

"Oh. Alright," he muttered.

I backed out and let the door swing shut. I collected my cart and started walking backward by the line of rooms while pulling it with my left hand. I kept the rifle leveled at the door of his room as I went while attempting to watch all directions at once in case he had friends covering me from another angle.

I spent the next few seconds thinking furiously about my new problem. My first instinct was to just leave the whole area entirely and go find a new place to shack for the night, but I discounted that as soon as it occurred to me. My new friend knew there was someone else out here now, and he had the advantage of having spent more time in this area than me. I didn't know how long he'd been here, but I had to assume he knew all the tricks and secrets of the terrain. He knew I had supplies—he at least knew I had a nice military grade rifle. I didn't want to continue on with a possible stalker, but I also didn't just want to kill the poor man outright.

So, though it may sound crazy, the plan I came up with involved staying right where I was. I figured on finding a vacant room, settling in, and giving him a night to see if he would behave himself. If he did, I reasoned he was probably safe enough that I could at least help him collect some provisions together from the surrounding area.

I found another vacancy with a busted door handle perhaps six or eight rooms down from where I met the human flea colony. Pulling my rifle up tight to my shoulder, I entered into the room hip and barrel first with eyes squinted against the change in light level. These rooms were not big or complicated, and it didn't take long to clear. I pulled my supply trailer into the room behind me and shoved it into a corner.

Hurrying now, I moved to the back of the hotel room to poke my muzzle into the bathroom to confirm that it too was empty. It was, so I came back into the main area, righted a chair that was knocked over by a writing desk, and set it up in a straight line across from the door. Following that, I gathered what was left of the bed comforter (it had been ripped to shreds) and piled it into the chair in order to make its appearance even more irregular. My thought was that anyone barging into the room would be distracted by the unexpected and confusing sight of a nebulous mass lying in wait before them. It might be worth a half second or so, but I wouldn't need much more than that.

I moved to the window and arranged what was left of the curtain such that my little slice of heaven couldn't be spied into unless that hypothetical spy mashed his face right up to the bottom corners of the window. Having made these preparations, I got on the other side of the bed so that it was between me and the door. I sat down in the space between the bed and the wall behind me, propped my rifle on the bed with the muzzle pointed at the door, and settled in to wait.

I was just about to give up on my new friend when he finally came around (I saw his movement as he crept by my window, shadowed by the moonlight on the curtain). At first, I thought I was only dreaming as I had been drowsing in and out of sleep for what felt like hours, but I realized very quickly that it was real when I heard his feet scuff outside. There were several moments that felt like minutes to me as we both struggled to make decisions about what would come next. I could almost hear him arguing with himself out there, and I came very close to saying, "Just go away, okay? Just go away, and we can pretend you never came by." I didn't. It wouldn't have mattered.

Having apparently decided, he pushed the door open and slunk into my room, hardly breathing. He saw the chair and blanket almost instantly gasped and dropped into a crouch. Almost as quickly, I saw the silhouette of his head cock to the side as he uttered, "...the fuck?"

I shot him three times in the chest, and he dropped straight down onto his rump like he had been cut from a noose. He continued to breathe deep, slow, and ragged for a few remaining moments while the knee of his left leg flexed in and out rhythmically—two seconds to bend, two seconds to straighten, and so on. I think whatever was left of his conscious mind was still trying to run away as he died.

I got up from my spot and moved over to him, groaning as I went (my legs and back were killing me from all the time spent on the floor); checked his neck for a pulse. There was none.

"God damn it," I muttered. "You couldn't just give it a night?" Silence was my response.

Sighing, I shouldered the rifle and cautiously left the room. I know now that he was alone and so I feel a bit ridiculous now to think of myself creeping back down the line of rooms like some Recon guy out of a war movie, but this is what I did, looking for anyone else who might be there to jump out at me. When I made it to his room unchallenged, I loosened up.

I pulled a small flashlight from my back pocket and had a look around. I was able to actually focus on things now that my attention wasn't completely occupied by a half-crazy transient reaching for a gun. He wasn't exactly sitting on a survivalist's gold mine, but there were several useful items stashed away including several boxes of protein bars. Additionally, he had a hand ax, some clothes as nasty and ratty as he was, and a partial box of hollow point 9mm rounds. The ammunition had my interest—there was no gun to go with it, but I had a good idea where I could find it. I rolled up the protein bars, ax, and bullets in a tattered sweater and headed back to my room.

I patted him down and found the pistol a foot away from his hand just outside of a spreading ring of blood. Shining the flashlight on it, I saw that it was a Glock 19. After fiddling with it, I was able to discover the button to extract the magazine, which I pulled from the grip and inspected. At the time, I didn't understand that many magazines will actually show you how many rounds they hold if you know where to look. It was dark, and that was a detail I missed, so I started spitting bullets out onto the carpet with my thumb, counting fourteen. I then pulled back on the slide and was rewarded with a fifteenth round popping out of the gun and dropping onto the carpet next to the others. With the chamber emptied, I pointed out toward the door, and dry fired to confirm that the mechanism functioned.

Finally, I started loading the loose rounds back into the magazine. I was able to get all fifteen in, though my thumb took a real beating towards the end. I slid the magazine back into the pistol and then examined it all over looking for some sort of safety mechanism, which I obviously didn't find. This made me a little nervous as I intended to stash the gun in the back of my jeans waistband like you see in the movies, but I didn't want to shoot myself trying to haul it back out again. Understanding the reality of the situation, I opted to not chamber a round and placed the gun in the small of my back, shifting it around until it sat comfortably. The goods wrapped up in the sweater were placed in my bike trailer.

Finally, I pulled the jumbled blanket from the chair and used it to cover the body. I collected my things and left the room in search of a new place to pass the night.

———

The morning found me well quit of Primm and headed North again up the I-15. I wasn't having any luck finding another ride despite my best efforts (well, in this case, "best effort" means I was checking anything in my immediate path) so it looked like another full day of walking, which it very much turned out to be.

If you have ever driven through a long desert, you probably know how boring the activity can be when there is nothing to occupy your attention. I was fast learning that walking through a long desert is psychologically demoralizing. The horizon simply does not move. You walk for what feels like hours and, as far as you can tell, you haven't made any real progress. Nothing moves. All the waypoints that you pay attention to out on the horizon just stay where they are, refusing to come any closer as you labor on. If you focus intently on objects far away, you'll begin to get the sense that you're not actually moving. I found this to be unnerving and began to put my attention only on those things that were close to me as I was able to perceive their change in position relative to my own. The problem with this, though, was that whenever I looked up again to the far away things, they were always exactly where I left them. All in all, the two realities from which I had to choose were to look up and never make progress or to look down so that I could perceive progress only to look up later and discover that progress was an illusion.

It was at one such transition from looking down to looking up towards mid-day that I first noticed the speck on the road at great distance ahead of me. I couldn't even guess at how far away it was; once a distance is great enough, the best a human eye can usually do is tell you "it's *waaaay* over there."

At first, all I could tell was that it was *something* and that, over a few hours of steady walking, it seemed to be maintaining its distance from me (I was using landmarks like hills and so forth positioned laterally to the object to determine that it was not stationary). It was at this time that I began to suspect that I was looking at a person. I mean, I guess it could have been a howler monkey, but another person on the road seemed the most likely explanation.

You will more than likely call me a fool (I certainly kick myself every time I think of this) but it never once occurred to me to use the scope on my rifle to get a better look at what I was seeing. I was not uncomfortable around firearms at the time but I also certainly was not familiar with them either; the optic on that rifle was the first one I had personally ever looked through. I thought of it only as a mechanism used to sight and shoot at a target. When I realized later that it would easily stand in as a replacement for binoculars, I was so embarrassed by my own stupidity that I actually cringed.

My suspicions regarding what I saw on the road were more or less confirmed when night fell. I kept walking into the evening. Far, far away in the distance, I saw the light of a campfire off the road.

I resolved to keep going. There was still a pretty good moon up in the sky, so I had plenty of light by which to see as long as I kept to the road. I only had a sleeping bag with my gear and no tent, so I didn't have much to set up when I finally decided to stop for the evening. I wanted to catch up to that howler monkey, and this seemed like the best way to do it. By the time I quit walking I'm sure it was into the wee hours of the morning. I pulled my cart a short ways off the road, pulled out the sleeping bag, and bundled up. I must have fallen asleep almost instantly despite how uncomfortable the ground was. Given the lack of sleep I enjoyed at Whiskey Pete's, and the long, miserable day of walking, there wasn't much left in the tank.

I jolted awake the next morning, afraid that whoever I was following had gotten a head start on me and eroded any ground I was able to gain the night before. I frantically jumped up, voided my bladder, collected all my gear, and got back on the road. I was relieved almost as soon as I did; I could see him out in front of me, and he was close enough now that I could definitely tell it was no monkey. It was a person—a man judging by the shape of the shoulders.

Now things were going to get touchy. I wanted to catch up to him, but I didn't want to scare him or get myself shot if I could help it. I couldn't tell for sure if he had a weapon at this distance. I could certainly see that he had a large burden hanging off his back, but it was impossible to make out fine detail.

It's hard for me to explain why I wanted to catch up with him so badly. My reasons didn't come out of a feeling of loneliness or boredom at my environment. Mostly I think that the guy I shot at Pete's was bothering me and I felt like I wanted a do-over. I told him I didn't have any food because I was trying to avoid him attacking me to get it, but it must have been obvious to him that I was the better outfitted of the two of us. Wouldn't my refusal to share food have driven a starving man to desperate behavior? What if I had just said, "Yeah, man, here's a pack of chicken curry," and tossed him one of those god-awful MREs?

I couldn't know, of course, but I was in the process of figuring out that I wasn't terribly interested in living that way; killing whoever I came across because they might be dangerous. It didn't sound like much of a life worth holding onto as far as I was concerned.

The day passed very much like the previous one. I maintained a steady pace, and he maintained a static distance. As the evening came on, I was just able to make out his figure leaving the road. I continued walking. Shortly after, I saw the dim evidence of smoke rising from behind some hills. I realized that he was doing to me what I had done to the man at Whiskey Pete's. He was choosing his ground and waiting to see what I would do. If I'm being honest, I was rather curious to see what I would do myself.

As I approached the small swell of hills just off the road, I unslung my rifle and threw it in the bike trailer and continued on. As I came around a bend, I saw him sitting calmly on the ground and facing me, with the fire just to his left. His back was propped up against some-thing (I later discovered it was a massive hiking backpack). He had a shotgun laid over his knee like it was a bipod and pointed in my direction.

I stopped and put my hands out to my side. "Hey, there," I said.

"Eve-ning?" He pronounced it as two words and framed it as a question, as if to say, *"What do you want?"*

"Uh, yeah. Well, I saw you on the road," I offered as a lame answer.

"Yap. I seen you too."

"Yes, well, I was just curious and thought I'd poke my head in. See what's happening." I was wracking my brain for something that sounded better but anything that I could have said that made sense was a little complex for the current situation. This was not going well.

"Curiosity can be a dangerous thing, these days."

This was really not going well at all. Deciding to cut my losses, I said, "Okay, look. I'm not here to start anything or bushwhack you or any such thing. Just saw another human on the road and thought I'd see about...seeing about you, I guess. I'll move along and leave you to it." I turned to leave.

"You thirsty?" he asked.

I turned back. "Well, thanks but I have my own water. I'm not here to beg for supplies."

"Water..." he scoffed. "I said 'are you *thirsty*'?" He emphasized the last word and swirled a large glass bottle half filled with a rich, brown liquid.

"Ah," I said.

"C'mon, Whitey," he said. "It's just chilly enough out here that we can pretend we're drinkin' this shit to stay warm." He had a deep, hollow voice. It had an almost hooting quality, like he was speaking from inside the chambers of some massive, dead redwood. There was an accent that was nearly Hispanic in flavor, but he shaped his words differently, clipping the hard sounds off in ways that I was not used to.

He lifted the shotgun up off his knee and laid it on the ground beside his leg; gestured to a spot by the fire beside himself. I pulled the bike trailer a bit closer to the fire and then circled around it to sit down. I remembered the Glock just then and stopped before lowering myself to the ground.

"Hey, listen. I have a pistol in the back of my jeans, here. I don't want to forget about it and have you see it later. Don't want you to think I'm being shady."

"I figure you're probably okay," he said with a grin. "And if you're not, I'll put money on my 870 versus your pistol. Sit down, Whitey. Don't shoot your ass off."

I was starting to like this man. I pulled the pistol from my back and laid it in my lap as I sat down. There was nothing to lean against, so I just sat cross-legged in the dirt. As I did, he reached over to a man-sized pile of dried brush (I'm pretty sure it was dead sagebrush) and pulled out what once must have been a complete plant. He tossed it onto the fire, where it flared up almost instantly.

"We won't have a fire for very long tonight," he said. "There's not much good fuel out here. There's plenty of this dead brush around if you're willing to walk a bit for it, but it burns up fast. It'll go down to ember pretty quick after we pass out."

"It'll be okay, I think," I replied. "It wasn't so bad last night, anyway."

The man held out his hand to me, which I shook. "My name is William," he said. "Everyone has always called me Billy."

"Jacob. Jake," I offered in return. He took back his hand and then sent the bottle my way. I wasn't much for hard liquor, but I took a knock to be polite. There was a bit of a burn and a hint of charcoal to the flavor. I guessed it was whiskey.

"Well, Jake," he began before taking a swig himself, "what brings you out this way? I can't imagine it's the Craps tables."

"No. I have some family out this way, just North of Vegas. I want to see if they're still there."

"I see. Siblings? Cousins?" he asked.

"Parents."

"Oh. Well then…" he muttered and handed me back the bottle.

I got a good look at him in the dying light as he passed the whiskey my way. I'd learn later that he was a pretty high-up tribal elder in one of the Mission Indian bands out of Southern California—Cahuilla (assuming I'm pronouncing that right). He didn't look Indian at all to me, though. His skin was rather light in color, and he didn't have what I had been conditioned by movies to think of as "Native American" features. He looked a lot more Spanish than anything else. He had several days' growth of facial hair like all the rest of us, but I could tell that he had cultivated a mustache before things like daily grooming became a luxury. He was somewhere in his sixties, with hair almost entirely gray. Between his fair skin and white hair, the only color in his face was in his eyes, which were brown. His face itself was inviting and friendly.

He was not fat, but he had run to portliness in his old age. He carried his fat like most men; big barrel chest with the extra meat slapped around his gut and back. What could be seen of his legs through his pants was well-formed and muscular even for a man of thirty, never mind a man old enough to be a grandfather. His hands were massive, nearly enveloping mine when we shook—I judged from this, and his legs stretched out in front of him that he was rather tall.

I threw back a drink, coughed, and shivered a bit as I passed it back. Billy politely made no mention of this though I'm sure I could see his eyes twinkle as he took the bottle.

"How about yourself?" I asked. "I haven't run into many people out here."

"Ah, but you have run into people?" he responded (ducking the question a bit, I noticed).

"I have."

"They're not with you now, I see."

"No."

He scratched his chin; hesitated a bit. "Are they with us at all?"

I looked at him straight on. "You know how it is now," I said, gesturing to his shotgun.

"Yeah, okay. I guess I do," he said, nodding. "Fine. I'm making my way up to Wyoming. Have a patch of land up there with some supplies laid by. I think I can settle in up there and either wait for the rest of the world to pull its head out of its ass or at least live the rest of my days peacefully without being bothered. What?"

I must have telegraphed surprise on my face. "Wyoming is a pretty good distance from here. You plan to walk that whole way?"

"Naw," he said, smiling. "I plan to walk into Vegas, spend some quality time shamelessly looting the place for anything I can find, and then throw what I do find into a vehicle and drive the rest of the way."

"Oh. Well, that makes more sense, certainly," I said.

"What about your plan? What comes after you look in on your people?"

I took another drink. Billy was right: it was warming me up rather well. "Hadn't thought much about that, honestly. I don't really know. I suppose I'll solve that when it comes."

"There's always another problem to solve in this world," he agreed and threw another brush on the fire, illustrating the point.

"That fuel isn't going to last much longer at that rate," I said, getting up. I was a little shocked at how I felt once on my feet. I didn't think I had drunk so much. I could feel my teeth buzzing.

"Oh, better not go out looking for more, Jake," he said as I moved over to my trailer.

"It's fine. I have a flashlight here somewhere."

"Sure, but you don't know what's out there," he warned.

I stopped and looked back at him over my shoulder. "What's out there, Billy?"

He threw his hands out. "Well, how the hell do I know? Coyotes and shit, maybe. Point is: neither of us knows. Could be people out there drawn to our fire and waiting to see if one of us does something silly like walking off into the distance looking for firewood. Could be nothing, I guess. Hell, you could put a foot wrong and twist or break an ankle in the dark."

I couldn't help but smile at him. I was just getting to know who he was, but I got the impression that he tended to get agitated when people resolved to engage in what he considered to be "foolish behavior."

"I'll keep to the road. You can usually find trash along the highway. I might get lucky." I pulled the flashlight and rifle out of the trailer.

"Say," Billy said, "where'd you get that AR?"

"Is that what this is? I took it from a friend who passed away back home. He was a soldier."

"Oh? Would you mind if I had a look at it?" he asked. He seemed pretty interested.

"Sure," I said. I took the rifle by the barrel and stock and passed it over to him.

He took it and looked at the grip closely by the firelight. "Damn. This is an M4. You know this thing'll fire full auto?" He pulled the rifle into his shoulder, looked through the optic, and whistled softly. "ACOG," he whispered. "Nice."

"I suspected but wasn't sure," I said, crouching down next to him to look. I hadn't been much of a gun person before and knew next to nothing about modern weaponry. It had taken me longer than I care to admit to figure out how to extract the magazine when I acquired the rifle.

"Yeah, it's the safety selector here. Lever-back is safe, straight down is normal single fire. All the way forward in this direction will shit a whole mag before you know what happened."

"Huh," I said. "I've always just been leaving it down."

He looked at me with a blank face. His Disapproving Face was always a blank stare. "I'll have to show you a few things, it seems. For now, keep the lever back if you're not planning on going to work, okay? I'm not interested in being shot."

"Gotcha," I said. I took back the rifle and set the switch as instructed.

"How many rounds do you have for that?" he asked as I straightened up.

"I have six magazines for it. They each had twenty-eight rounds. I have a number of loose bullets in the trailer here, too, in a box."

"Pretty good," he said, nodding. "You certainly lucked out with your choice of rifle. The Stoner platform ended up being just about the most popular rifle in the country before the world shit itself. We should be able to find you plenty more rounds in Vegas."

"You think a hundred and fifty or so isn't enough?"

"One hundred sixty-eight," he said promptly, "and, no, I don't. They're not making bullets anymore, and you're always going to run out. The world is such now that you want to be looking for bullets as much as you're looking for water. It's a challenge because everyone else will be looking too. 5.56 is a popular round though, like I said. We should be able to find some even if we have to go door to door to do it."

"What about yourself?" I asked. "I don't know very much, but I know a 12 gauge when I see it. Any reason you have one of those instead of one of these?" I gestured to my rifle.

"Yeah, there are a few," he nodded. "I'll tell you about them later. For now, you better go looking for that fuel if you're going at all. I'll start heating us up some food."

"Sounds good," I said. "I have some edibles in my trailer as well. Feel free to rummage around for anything you think you might want to eat tonight."

He pinned me with that blank stare again. "You know, some asshole's going to kill you if you don't exercise a little more caution."

I was sure now. I really liked this guy. Smiling despite myself, I said, "Are you an asshole, Billy?"

"I am," he responded without hesitation. "I'm not a murdering asshole, though. Even so, you can't know that."

"The fact that you even bring it up gives me a pretty good idea. Besides, suppose someone does kill me because of a lack of caution? God forbid I miss out on a moment of this veritable paradise we've all inherited!"

"Wiseass…" I heard him mutter after I turned my back to leave.

I wasn't searching along the highway very long before I got lucky and found an old wooden pallet on the roadside. I hauled it back to the fire where Billy still sat with a couple of cans of food cracked open and sitting near to the embers. The look on his face was rather priceless.

"The hell did you find that?" he exclaimed.

"Further North up the 15. I told you: you find a lot of garbage by the roadside."

"Huh," was all he said. The wood was old and dry, and there wasn't much holding it together anymore. There was a moderate amount of effort with the flat end of the hatchet to knock the thing apart. When I was finished, I threw a couple of planks on the fire. They didn't flare up like the sagebrush, but they did get burning fairly well in short order and continued to do so evenly for much longer.

Billy and I sat back to eat the canned food (beef stew, in this case—he advised waiting to eat the MREs until we had a situation where no fire was available). We talked about more things as we finished off the whiskey, some important and some not. We laughed from time to time at our own nonsense and pretended for the evening that the world was still sane. When the whiskey was gone, we set down sleeping bags close to the fire, put some more planks on, and turned in for the night.

# 4

## SELF-RELIANCE

### Jake

We were up just before dawn the next morning, which was actually a lot easier than you'd think. Dry desert ground is quite uncomfortable when you have nothing but a sleeping bag. This all took place a couple of years ago now, but I remember that morning vividly. I had been so exhausted the night before that getting to sleep had been easy—I don't think I could have stayed awake if I had tried. On the following night when I met Billy, I had a hard time drifting off due in large part to the novelty of having company again. That and the hard ground meant that I only found sleep in brief, thirty-minute stretches before parts of my body started aching enough to wake me up and force me to move.

The Nevada sun was just coming up over the horizon, turning the blue-black sky blood red, when we were rolling up our sleeping bags. I was stuffing mine back into the trailer and Billy was strapping his back onto his hiking rig; a massive backpack that hung lower than his back-side and peeked up over the top of his head.

He looked to the sunrise and said, "Dawn stretched out her finger-tips of rose."

"How's that?" I asked.

"It's Homer," he said, standing up and setting his hands on his hips. "The Iliad. It was just one of those lines that always stuck with me. The phrase is used in the story almost every time a sunrise is described."

"What, you mean over and over? That's a pretty flowery line to go around repeating all the time, isn't it?"

Billy chuckled; pushed his fists into the small of his back and leaned into them, growling as he responded. "Yeah, well, Homer didn't actually write the Iliad. He composed and recited it. It was an epic poem, and he was a famous poet of the day, sort of the equivalent of a big-time actor or rock star. People like him would be invited to entertain important people. Kings, wealthy landowners, you get the idea. The performance was the recitation of sections of these heroic poems that were kept memorized. All written down, the things span hundreds or thousands of pages, but Homer kept it all in his head."

"Man..." I muttered.

"Yeah," he agreed. "So in order to make it easier, you see a lot of the phrasing in these works take on a formulaic quality. Whole passages turn into a kind of mnemonic device. People like Homer must have kept whole paragraphs in their heads and shuffled them about at need to make a meaningful story in the same way we use words to make a coherent sentence. It suggests an incredible amount of genius."

I didn't quite know what to say to this. Up until now, Billy had shown a simple, easy manner that almost bordered on "backwoods bumpkin." His speech and pronunciation suggested a blue collar education, but when he started talking about a nearly-three-thousand-year-old poem, it was like listening to a different person. His demeanor changed to that of a professor. His elocution became precise and clear —nearly musical.

I said, "Billy, go ahead and say this is none of my business if you like, but what exactly did you do before things went south?"

"I was involved in the casino business. Indian gaming." That twinkle in his eye again.

"There a lot of call to read ancient Greek poetry in your line of work?"

Billy leaned in conspiratorially and said in a low voice, "You know, the Greeks *loved* their games..." He gave me a light slap on the shoulder and moved by me to walk over to the bike trailer. *Right*, I thought. *Take the hint.*

"So, we'll make it into Vegas today," Billy started. "How did you want to run this? We can push straight through and check on your parents, but I had planned to take some time moving through the area, keep my eyes out for supplies, like. What kind of a rush are you in? Also, how far north of Vegas is their place?"

I decided to answer the questions in reverse order. "It's not that far, just on the north edge. It's up Decatur, if you know the area."

"I do, and that's good news, I think. That's close to the shooting range. It would be good to go through there; we might get lucky. They always sold range ammo in those places."

"That sounds fine," I agreed. "Aside from that, if you have places in mind that you want to check on, let's do that. Just about anywhere you'd want to go would be on the way to my folks' place. We might as well handle your scavenging on the way."

"Okay, deal," said Billy. "So let's run through the gear you have so we can figure out what you need. Put a shopping list together, see?"

"Right. So with this trailer, I have the rifle and the ammunition that goes with it, obviously. Then I have the canned food, the MREs, and the protein bars and those water jugs, there. Spare clothes with jeans, sweater, some socks, and underwear. I have this little flashlight here with some extra double A's to go with it. Aaaand, I guess all that's left is the sleeping bag, hatchet, and the pistol with however many rounds are in that box."

Billy didn't say anything for a few moments after I finished speaking. He just stood there next to me with his hands on his hips, staring at the open flap of the bike trailer, and nodding.

"What?" I prompted.

"Oh, it's fine," he said, making a shooing motion at me with his left hand. "You're missing some important items, but you kind of make up for your lack of gear with this trailer thing. I don't know why the hell I didn't think of it; it's pretty smart. We'll keep our eyes open to round out your kit. There should be plenty of room to carry it all, I think."

"Well, what am I missing?" I asked. "I know there could probably be more food, but the gear seems pretty okay."

"Okay, where's your trauma kit?"

"Uh…" I hesitated. "You mean like first aid?"

"No, I mean like trauma. First aid kits are good for sprained ankles and paper cuts. I'm talking about a serious trauma kit. Kind of thing you can use to treat gunshots or sucking chest wounds."

"I wasn't aware there was a difference, but I don't have either anyway."

"Yap," Billy agreed. "Either way, we'll keep our eyes open and find you something—either ready-made or we'll get some stuff together to cover all the bases. We need to beef up some other things as well. You and I could probably both use a tent if we can find something small enough to haul around. We'll get you a rain fly at the least. We'll want fire-making tools, a good knife for you, and some better clothes for when the weather goes to shit. We'll see if we can find some medicine like Tylenol, Aspirin; if we get really lucky, we can find some antibiotics, maybe."

He trailed off as he saw me staring at him while he rattled off the list. "Will we be able to haul all that?" I said.

"Just trust me," he said. "You keep your eyes open for anything that might be useful. No one is making new stuff anymore, Whitey, and if you find yourself needful of something you can't just pop off down to the store to get it. Most things have been picked over already so we'll get lucky to find even half of what we'd like. You'll see. The new basis of short-term survival is going to be defined by our ability to loot like it's 1992."

"Short-term survival, huh? What will be the basis of long-term survival, then?"

Billy pinned me in place with a sober, serious gaze. "Long-term survival will depend on our ability to wean ourselves from the dependency on that loot."

———

The 15 became more clogged with stalled and abandoned vehicles as we came closer to the edge of the city. Weaving my way through became an exercise in patience as I was forced to zig-zag back and forth with the bike trailer. Billy never commented on this; he just patiently moved along next to me. I noticed that his head was always moving. He was always trying to see all directions at the same time, always had his hand on his shotgun. If we got into tight areas where visibility was reduced, he would even hold it in a high ready position (presented out in front of him with the butt down and barrel up on the level with his eyes). Despite his apparent focus on our surroundings, he was still perfectly happy to chit-chat as we made our way in. This was absolutely fine with me as it felt less like he was standing around waiting for me to get a move on, which he was.

"So you were going to explain the superiority of shotguns to me..." I prompted.

"Oh, I don't think they're superior," Billy said. "They're just the right tool for the job when you're close-in or in the city. That M4 is outstanding when you need to reach out and touch someone at distance, say four hundred yards or so. You have to aim and take your time, but you can do it reliably with some practice. When you're in the city, you don't often get uninterrupted stretches at that distance. Everything becomes a lot closer."

"Okay," I said, struggling around a bumper with teeth grinding, "but you're not spending all your time in cities, right? What happens when you're out in the open on the road?"

"Everyone that I've run into so far has been in a city or on the outskirts of a city. Everyone is gravitating to them doing the same thing we're doing right now: looking for supplies. You're the first guy I've run into out on the open road. You actually had me sweating a little—I didn't know you had that rifle, but I knew you had some kind of long gun. I kept waiting for a bullet to hit me. Damned unnerving."

"Sorry about that," I muttered. "I guess I could have raised my hand up in a salute or something. Give some kind of indication that I wasn't out to get you."

Billy straightened up at that, looked directly at me, and raised his hand up in the air, palm out, and said "How," in a voice even deeper than his natural rumble. He then bugged out his eyes, reversed his hand, and flipped me the bird while sticking his tongue out, surprising a belly laugh out of me.

"Forget about it," he said. "There was really nothing you could have done at the time to settle any nerves. We're both walking and talking right now, which indicates that everyone did everything correctly, more or less."

I don't remember saying anything in response to this, but I may have grunted.

"So, yeah," he continued, "Having both the shotgun and the carbine would be nice in a perfect world, but you have to make choices when you're traveling light and on foot. My experience has been that the carbine has been required a lot less than the 870 out here, so shotgun is what I went with. It's not just the weapon, you know. You have to carry the ammunition to support it. Shotgun shells are, unfortunately, about as big, nasty, and heavy as it gets for small arms but I can still lug quite a few around with me. It would be a lot worse, though, if I had to lug both 12 gauge and 5.56. I'm getting too old for that shit."

That earned a look out of me. Though not old, I wasn't exactly in the prime of my youthful vigor, and Billy had at least another twenty years on me. Even so, his physical strength was easily apparent. You could see leg muscle through the denim of his jeans, which you'd maybe expect from a twenty-year-old gym rat. Likewise, he was wearing a bulky jacket that looked like a cross between a military-style utility jacket and camping or hiking attire (despite the fact that we were just entering into the warm part of the year) that was incapable of masking the breadth of his shoulders or the stability of his back. It's true he carried a bit of a gut under that barrel of a chest, but it didn't bother him in any way I could see. He certainly didn't breathe heavy or even huff carrying his own weight plus all that gear on his back. He could certainly joke about his age, but I wasn't buying it.

He continued on oblivious to my appraisal. "There's more call to fight in the city than there is out on the open road, therefore I stuck with a shotgun, which was my choice for home defense anyway, okay? This Remington was mine before the shit hit the fan; I didn't lift it after the fact. It was just ready to go."

"So what is it that makes it better close up? I'm guessing you just don't have to aim it due to it firing shot?"

"Oh, no, you still have to aim it," he said, extending his hand in a "slow down, tiger" gesture. "It's true that the shot spreads out as it flies but not massive like you'd think. The pellets might spread out to the size of a fist at fifty yards. That's a pretty big pattern, but you still have to aim to get that to hit your target. It's just that it's so damned fast to put it on target. Here, look at this sight…"

He held the shotgun out to me; pointed in the direction we were walking and rotated it so that I could see a small, brass nub out on the tip of the barrel.

"That's a bead sight. That's all you get on your average shotgun. No rear sight component. So you put your cheek on the stock, put the bead on what you want to hit, and pull the trigger. You don't have to spend time lining up the front sight with the rear sight, making a perfect little picture and all that shit. Close up, it doesn't matter so much if you're not one hundred percent perfect because what you're shooting at is up close. Two or three inches off of center mass still hits center mass. And, the nature of the shot tends to correct for a lack of accuracy at a distance because the pattern spreads out. It's pretty forgiving."

"So how far can you reliably shoot that thing?" I asked.

"All depends on your ammo. This is the other reason I'm such a fan of shotguns. Assuming I can find it, there is a long list of ammunition types I can fire that are all useful for different things. I can load birdshot into it and go hunting for small game. If I'm fighting someone, I can load buckshot, which is devastating. Look, that M4 fires 5.56, right?"

I looked down at my rifle and shrugged like an idiot. "If you say so."

"It does," he nodded. "Also, you need to start memorizing this kind of stuff. It does you no good to carry a rifle if you don't know how to feed it. Anyway, 5.56 millimeter, which is equivalent to .223 caliber..." He looked at me pointedly.

"Okay?" I prompted.

He made a face. "Are you any good with math?"

I found this question a little insulting, but I let it go. "I've been known to *math* from time to time," I told him sarcastically.

"Okay, then stop thinking about what the bullets look like and start thinking more about what those numbers mean. .223 is the diameter in inches of the bullet and 5.56 is just the metric equivalent of that measurement. And, when you think about it, .223 is really just .22."

I stopped in my tracks. I wasn't a gun guy, but I was never opposed to them either. I knew enough to know what a .22 round looked like. I popped the magazine out of my rifle and looked at the round exposed in the top. "*That's* a .22 round?"

"Yap. I know what you're thinking. It's certainly a lot longer than a .22 long rifle bullet, and the shell and powder load is a lot bigger, so it has way, way more force and inertia behind it and better range but essentially, that's a .22 round."

I was shocked. I almost wished I had a .22 rifle there so I could poke a bullet into the barrel to see if it fit.

"Now look at this," he said as I inserted the magazine back into my rifle. He reached into one of the pockets on the front of his jacket and pulled out a shotgun shell. He handed it over to me. Feeling the weight of it, I realized how heavy it would feel to carry many of them at once.

"That's a number one buckshot load," he said. "It contains fifteen pellets, all of which are about .30 caliber. They certainly don't travel at the speed of your 5.56 round, and they don't have the range, but at a hundred yards or so, they dominate your rifle for muzzle energy. Your rifle makes, I don't know, maybe six-or-seven-hundred-foot-pounds of energy at the muzzle. It depends on the round; 5.56 has a little more ass behind it than .223, but call it around seven-hundred-foot-pounds just for shits. This shotgun produces anywhere between two and three thousand foot pounds of energy; that's how much wallop is transmitted into the target on impact."

An appreciative grunt was the only response I could come up with. I handed the shell back over to him. I must have been making a face because he chuckled when he looked over at me to take it.

"That's right," Billy agreed. "Now, that energy dissipates pretty quickly over distance, which is why the effectiveness of buckshot drops off a lot after about fifty yards. Again, your carbine has my shotgun easily beat for distance. But up close, you're still shooting high powered, high speed, tiny little .22 rounds. What I'm packing will turn you into a god damned canoe."

"Okay, okay, hang on," I interrupted. "You've still got to get to me. If we're coming at each other down a long stretch of street—say two-hundred-fifty to three hundred yards or so—you actually *have to get to me* in order to get me. That's a pretty long distance you have to make up while I get to take free shots at you."

"Well, yes, if I'm not seeking cover and just running straight at you like a dumbass, I suppose you get to light me up at your convenience. The thing about cities, though, is that there's a lot of shit to get behind. Also, there's this..." He held up another shell, extracted from yet another pocket. "This is a slug—essentially a big-ass bullet. This is something like .69 or .70 caliber. It's basically artillery. Now, you really have to know what you're doing if you just have a bead sight, but you can hit targets reliably at two hundred yards with this thing. I don't think I could make that kind of range with a bead (not while the target is moving, anyway) but with some kind of a scope or a decent optic on this thing set for that distance, it would be very doable."

He handed me the slug, and I looked down at the front of it. A huge, lead dome stared back up at me in place of the usual plastic starfish of a normal shotgun shell.

"The other good thing about a slug," he continued, "is that I can use it to get through a door that doesn't want to unlock."

I looked over at his shotgun with new respect. I knew they were nasty, but that last bit sounded excellent. There had been plenty of doors that I had to pass by because they were locked and I just had no way to get in.

"The only real drawback besides the range thing is the shitty capacity." He held the 870 out in front of him. "I had to modify the magazine on this just to hold eight rounds. These guns are pigs. You always have to feed them ammo. You are always, always reloading them in a fight. It's why most defense shotguns have these side saddles," he noted, pointing to a line of seven shells mounted on the side of the gun. "No matter what's happening, you're going to be reloading very soon. You might as well have your extras right by the receiver."

"It still sounds pretty good," I mused. "I'll make sure to keep my eye out for one."

"Well, as to that…" Billy gave me a sly grin out of the side of his mouth. "I'll just say it's damned convenient that your folks live on Decatur. It turns our route into a straight line, more or less. There's this place I want to check out along the way. It's not a storefront so much as it is a shipping warehouse. I have this theory: most of the outdoor places like Big 5 and Turners are going to be stripped bare. Hell, you can see the firepower on the racks right through the front windows plus people would be turning the place over for camping gear and other stuff like that. A warehouse, though, well…it's still possible that the place is picked over, but it won't be obvious what it is, I hope. There's a chance we find many good things."

"Make strong like bull, huh?" I asked.

"Hey, there you go, Whitey!" he said with approval. "I'll be teaching you the secret handshake before you know it."

As we entered the main drag of the city, we took an abrupt left and started making our way towards Decatur. It amazed me how much congestion dropped off as we moved away from that main drag. The 15 is really the dominant artery into and out of that city, so it makes sense that traffic would be absolutely jammed along this channel, but I had a hard time imagining what the owners of all those cars were actually up to sitting in all that mess. If they had just moved a little off the beaten path, they would have found a multitude of options for getting around in the city. Perhaps they found themselves locked in and immobilized in the press of the traffic; I certainly saw plenty of cars and trucks with no bodies in them—just abandoned on the roadway. Some of them had doors that were left open, completely and utterly discounted by their owners.

We spent the whole morning and midafternoon first locating and then fueling two vehicles. The first became Billy's vehicle; a blue Ford Transit van. The second, a white Dodge 1500, became my ride. I had argued for smaller vehicles, perhaps even motorcycles, to help us navigate the really bad areas, but Billy eventually sold me on the idea of the larger trucks. They both had the ability to go off-road (the truck more so than the van) in the really nasty areas; as long as we kept out of major choke points and took our time circumnavigating cities and major congestion areas, our mobility would be maintained. The main point was the ability to haul gear, he said. You couldn't beat what we had found. Fueling them became the main problem.

There had been a run on gas in the final days, so we weren't going to find any fuel at actual gas stations. Moreover, there was no power to pump it up to our tanks. Even so, we did go to gas stations and auto shops to get our hands on any gas cans we could find. In this regard, we did well. They were empty, but we managed to load a respectable collection of various sizes into the truck bed. We would be able to keep ourselves topped off reasonably well assuming we could keep the cans filled.

Finding actual gas was much easier than I originally suspected. There was about a half a tank in the van and less in the truck when we found them, so we were initially able to move them around and get them to those places we needed to be. We found a Pep Boys just off of Jones Blvd and invited ourselves in. Surprisingly, there were quite a few useful things in the tool category left in the shop. We grabbed a socket set, some jumper cables (I berated myself silently for leaving the set of cables in the old sedan I abandoned), and an extra tire for the van and truck each, even though I was pretty sure that they both had full sized spares. When I stated that I had no clue how we would get the tires on a rim, Billy noted while picking out a can of spray sealant that he'd show me how to do it with a crowbar if the situation presented itself.

The whole collection was rounded out with some rather large drip pans, funnels, a mallet, and ¼" taper punch (what amounted to a big, metal spike). When I asked him if he'd like to include floor jacks, stands, and spare water pumps he stopped to consider it, and I really couldn't tell if he was toying with me or not. He asked me to take the first round of goodies out to the truck, which we had backed right up to the door along with the van, while he continued to look around. He went to a corner of the store and righted an overturned shopping cart, much to my chagrin.

As I was loading the tires into the pickup bed, I noted to myself that we would need some way to pressurize them. I just turned to poke my head back into the store and tell Billy when I saw movement across the street out of the corner of my eye. I immediately dropped to a crouch behind the bed of the truck and started cursing at myself for leaving the rifle against the window inside of the shop. I pulled the Glock from my waistband (a weapon I was totally unfamiliar with and had yet to fire) and crept around the side of the bed to look across the street. There was nothing. I must have sat there for a good five minutes, barely willing to breathe and looking for any hint of movement whatsoever. Presently, my knees started to ache horribly, and I was just beginning to consider relaxing when Billy's voice issued from directly behind me, unexpected.

"What're you doing, there, Whitey?"

I jumped in place. My outraged knees collapsed as a final "screw you" to my unreasonable demands and I plopped down directly on my tailbone.

"See something out there?" he asked. He had his shotgun up to his shoulder and was scanning all around.

"I can't be sure. I thought I saw some movement, but it was just peripheral. I might just be jumpy. Seeing a completely deserted city takes getting used to."

"I get yah," he said, offering his hand. I took it, and he levered me up to a standing position. He pulled rather effortlessly, I thought, and my feet may have left the ground a little at the top of the motion.

"Strong for an old man," I mentioned.

He chuckled modestly. "Yeah, training for general strength is a thing you do at my age if you want to be able to wipe your own ass past a certain point. A thing you do at any age, really."

"Why do I get the impression that you've been practicing for everything to fall apart?"

"Oh, well…" he muttered, going back to the shopping cart inside, "I don't know that I was practicing for all of this, but I've always been a bit of what you might call 'a prepper.' It was one of the things I always focused on in my tribal council days…when I still had a tribe. Self-reliance in *all* things. Being in a position where you don't have to rely on anyone else makes you stronger. From the perspective of our tribe, that meant achieving self-reliance in our sovereignty from the U.S. government. That was where all the gaming came from—we wanted a genuine and powerful mode of income on whatever scraps of land we had left that didn't rely on the sufferance of outside forces or governing bodies. Gaming casinos were an outstanding way to realize that dream—a self-contained, little ecosystem of revenue generation that relied very little on outside sources or suppliers. No manufacturing, no supply chains to consider. It was beautiful."

I noted that Billy spoke with genuine pride when he discussed these concepts. I wasn't sure how high up he was in his tribal government, but it was fairly obvious that he had some significant skin in the game.

"Anyway," he continued as he reached out to toss various odds and ends into the cart, "as I continued to push these values in council, I became more interested in ways that I could pursue self-reliance in my own personal life. Because of that, I picked up a thing or two that ended up being useful when the world went to hell."

"Seems I have some catching up to do."

"No worries," he said, offering a light slap to the shoulder. "I have one or two things I can share."

We went through the store getting more items that made sense. Some of it was picked over but not as bad as I had feared it might be.

Common sense stuff like roadside emergency kits were completely pillaged; there wasn't a flare to be found anywhere in the shop. Other things like tools and replacement parts could be found if they were items not commonly replaced. I probably could have turned that whole place upside down looking for replacement belts for our vehicles and never found a thing, but items like alternators and torque wrenches were still available.

We threw a few more tools into the cart (more wrenches, pliers, channel locks, vice grips and the like as well as a replacement battery each for the trucks. Billy finally found an emergency air compressor in the back of the shop that could be plugged into a cigarette lighter port, and we finished out the plunder with as many tire patch kits as we could find. Things like batteries, flashlights, and so on were simply no go.

Satisfied that we had established a successful balance in need versus capacity, we gave each other a nod and rolled the cart toward the front door of the shop. I picked up the M4, slung it over my shoulder (Billy hadn't laid his shotgun aside at any point since we'd been in there; he literally slept with its sling over him), and exited out the glass double door.

Directly across from the front entrance was the Dodge truck, backed in with the gate about five feet from the door. To the left of the truck was the van, also backed in. To the right of the truck were two men of entirely questionable nature. They looked rough and ragged, but then we all looked rough and ragged after the fall, so I wasn't exactly holding that against them. What I didn't like, what set me on edge immediately, was that they had positioned themselves such that the sun was to their backs and in our faces and they were spread out far enough that they made two discrete targets about thirty degrees apart. Their demeanor suggested a friendly conversation, but everything about their placement screamed ambush.

Billy must have seen it immediately and processed it much faster than I did. When I stepped outside, he had already moved out to the left and positioned the truck bed between himself and our two new visitors. He had his shotgun held loosely in his hand and resting lightly over his left forearm. It looked comfortable, but it would take an idiot to miss the fact that he could have it up and ready in an instant.

For my part, I froze for a beat, grunted, and swiveled my rifle up under my arm and aimed it at their general direction. If they had actually had a firearm ready to go, there would have been ample time to kill me several times over. Thankfully, they had a plan slightly more complicated than simply shooting us full of holes. The one on the right was armed, as far as I could see, with a pistol jammed into his waistband like some sort of gangster. They both raised empty hands when my barrel came up.

"Whoa, whoa, stranger! No harm meant. We're just passing through, is all," said the one on the right. I didn't like his look, and his voice settled the deal for me. He had a weasly, greasy look with an unctuous, assuming little voice that set my teeth to grinding the minute words came out of his mouth. His friend was harder to get a read on; he just stood there silently.

I swiveled my eyes over to Billy, who was in my peripheral view and who, to my shock and horror, put his back to the whole thing and began to focus his attention in the opposite direction. I wanted to ask him what he thought he was doing, but I didn't want to do so out in the open in front of Weasel and Mum.

"Passing through," I repeated. "Fair enough. What can we do for you?"

Weasel put on what I supposed he thought was his most winning smile; it was grotesque and unnatural. Mum divided his attention between me and Billy, who had seemed to lose interest in the whole thing. "Nice of you to ask, there, friend. Quite nice. Larry and I couldn't help but notice that you and your partner had these two outstanding fucking rides here. You look like fellas who have straightened your shit right out. We were thinking maybe you'd be interested in joining forces or maybe just trading?"

Weasel and Larry, then. Fine.

"Joining forces, huh? Just what kind of force are we talking about?"

"Oh, it's just me and Larry here. Not much of a force, really, but four is better than two, after all, wouldn't you say?" He chuckled at this, seemingly pleased with his ability to do simple math. He and Larry were both stealing glances over at Billy now, who continued to look down the street in the direction opposite of where I would really have rather he devoted his time, shotgun now in low ready with butt in shoulder and muzzle down.

"Hey, uh, what's yer buddy looking at, there?" Weasel asked, then louder and directed at Billy, "Conversation's over this way, bro. We boring you over here?"

"Fucking rude, is what it is," rumbled Larry. His eyes were dark and nervous and now bouncing back between Billy and me like he was watching an Olympic Table Tennis match.

Getting fed up with the whole stupid scenario rather quickly, I wanted to ask Billy just what he thought he was doing as well. Forcing back my frustration, I kept my eyes locked on the two men with my rifle muzzle up and spaced at the midway point between the two of them and said, "Bill?" I always called him Billy because that was how he'd introduced himself so I strongly hoped my calling him Bill would knock loose whatever it was that had gotten stuck in his brain.

He had apparently noticed, either by my tone or my usage of his name, because he said, "It's okay, Jake. These two just really want me to turn around. They don't want me to see…"

I'm going to do my best to describe what happened next without getting it all confused. I remember everything happening at the same time, and I'm not sure I can explain this coherently.

In the middle of Billy's sentence, the sound of gut shaking explosions thundered off to my left—one blast followed by two additional blasts in rapid succession. After the first explosion but before the second two, Larry raised his hand in the direction of Billy and shouted, "Danny!!" At the same time as that, Weasel reached into his waistband and started hauling on the pistol.

I immediately began to drop into a crouch, swinging the barrel at Weasel and yanking on the trigger. The trigger itself didn't move and nothing happened—I suddenly remembered that I had the safety on in response to Billy's instruction from the night before. I cursed (or at least I tried to; it came out sounding like "Fyurk!!!") and slammed the safety as far in the other direction as it would go. In the meantime, two more explosions detonated off to my left for a total of five.

Weasel had gotten the pistol out of his shorts by now and was lifting it towards me while Larry appeared to be digging furiously in his butt (I supposed at the time that he was going for his own weapon). I instinctively kicked out with both feet in an attempt to get away, like a kind of jump reflex. This propelled me backward two or three feet and landed me on my back with my feet pointed towards the attackers. This most likely saved my life as the first shot from Weasel's gun passed over me and through the glass double doors of Pep Boys. On my back, I spread my legs to avoid shooting my own feet off and pulled the trigger.

I nearly soiled myself as the M4 came alive in full automatic fury, stitching a line up and down Weasel, with little dusty penetrations appearing all over his torso and thighs. In the movies when you see someone shot, you always see copious amounts of blood splatter flying all around the screen. Well, the movies are full of it. I saw puffs of dust rise off the impact points, and his clothes rippled about as holes appeared. If there was any blood, it was in a fine mist, and it was too fast for me to see. The guy didn't start bleeding until after he hit the ground.

I whirled my muzzle over to Larry, who was still in the process of losing a tug of war battle with his keister and pulled the trigger. I recall very clearly how hard he flinched as the first few rounds hit him. He pulled his head way back, squinted his eyes nearly shut, opened his mouth, and stuck out his tongue while putting his hands out in front of him. He looked like nothing so much as an awkward schoolyard bully trying unsuccessfully to fend off a haymaker.

As Larry went down, I heard a snap very close by (I would have to place it just above my head, were I forced to guess) and something sharp and hot stung my cheek. I rolled over onto my left shoulder to look in the direction of whatever chaos was breaking loose down the street. As I did, I just noticed some mass peaking around the side of the building at the corner while, at the same instant, two more ear-shattering explosions detonated a few feet away, now to my right with my new position. The mass at the building corner disappeared and was replaced by a kicked out foot.

I rolled to my back again and looked at both Weasel and Larry, confirming that they were no longer moving. When I rolled left to look up the street again, Billy was out from between the van and truck. He was walking quickly to the outstretched leg. He was bent over, and I felt a moment of sick panic when I thought he had been shot. When he reached the end of the building, he swiveled left, and I realized he was just bent into his shotgun. He discharged it at the ground behind the building where I couldn't see. It was at this point that I finally realized the explosions I heard were Billy's 870. I was completely shocked; I had not realized a pump action shotgun could be fired as quickly as Billy had managed. He was walking back towards me, thumbing new shells into the magazine. As he neared me, he stopped abruptly and said, "Hey, are you okay? Did you get hit?"

I looked myself over, patted the length of my torso. "I don't think so," I replied.

"Your face…"

I reached my hand up to my face and felt wetness. It came away streaked with blood. "Awe, Jesus…" I said and levered up to my knees to look at my reflection in the shop window. There appeared to be a nasty cut under my left eye, and it was running red all down my cheek. Billy came over and turned me by the shoulders to get a look at it.

"That's not a graze or a hit of any kind. You just got nicked by something." He stuffed a hand into one of his pockets and pulled out a green handkerchief. "Here, dab that up. It's fine," he said, "I don't blow into that. Just use it to wipe off sweat."

"Lovely…" I said and began to wipe at my cheek. The cut wasn't too bad; it was already clotting up.

"You got damned lucky," said Billy. "I don't know what it was that cut you, but that could have been your eye."

I nodded and handed the kerchief back. He crammed it back into its pocket absentmindedly.

I looked back towards the end of the building where that ominous leg was sticking out. "Just how the hell did you know he'd be back there?"

"Didn't," Billy stated. "Was afraid he might be. I figured you had the two assholes covered well enough. That was really the only direction someone could have used to sneak up behind us. Seems like that was their idea, too."

He came around the truck bed and had a look at what remained of our assailants. Whatever blood that was in them was oozing out freely by this point—two fat rivers of the stuff were running out from under both of the dead men, joining together and disappearing under the vehicles.

He said: "Jesus, that's messy. Did you really have to go full Rambo on the Mario Brothers?"

"It wasn't my intent. I had an issue with the safety lever."

"You mean *they* had an issue with the safety lever. Damn!"

"Have it your way," I sighed. "Can we get out of here now before any more of them show up?"

"Sure, sure, keep your shirt on, Kemosabe. I just want to go over them and see if they have anything worth having."

"Oh, Christ's sake," I moaned, looking up and down the street. "That's really morbid, man." I conveniently left out that I had acquired my Glock in the same fashion. I wanted to get out of there at that point and was arguing over anything.

"They're not using it anymore," he said, totally unashamed. He had a look at Weasel's gun, held it up, and sighted down the length of the barrel. "Hi-Point," he muttered. "Eh, screw it..." he decided and slipped it in his back pocket. He moved over to Larry and rolled him over onto his stomach. What we saw stopped both of us in our tracks.

The front of each man that I killed was relatively undisturbed, with little pin-prick bullet holes dotting the surface area at various points. When Larry was rolled over, we could see that the whole back of his shirt and most of his jeans were soaked through with dark red blood. The surfaces of both articles of clothing were torn and perforated. Billy squatted down and pinched the tail of Larry's shirt between two fingers and lifted. Some forty percent of his back had been reduced to a mutilated crater, as though an explosive had been set off just under his spine. The whole area looked like nothing more than raw, ground up hamburger with bits of spine and ribs exposed. Smaller racket-ball sized craters surrounded the main focal point of damage.

"God damn," said Billy, letting go of the shirt.

"I thought you said they were just .22 rounds?" I asked him. "I've never heard of a .22 round doing that to anything." I felt queasy from what I had seen.

"Evidently, I was wrong." He sat there on his haunches for several seconds simply shaking his head. Finally, he said, "I've never seen anyone shot by a 5.56 round before…or maybe it has more to do with him being shot by an M4 on full auto or something. I don't know. I'm going to have to rethink this whole carbine versus shotgun thing."

I must admit I was a little taken aback by Billy's attitude to the whole situation. Having learned that his assumptions were incorrect, he became curious and inquisitive. He levered the body back up on its side so he could get another look at the entry wounds, set the body back down, and attempted to lift and separate the leg of his jeans to get a look at the damage done to the rear thigh.

I looked away. My initial viewing of the mass crater in the man's back had been a shock to my system; I felt the same sensation in my stomach that you undergo when you suddenly feel the bottom drop out from under you (similar to a roller coaster ride). Subsequent looks just made me feel sick. This was the first time I had examined anyone up close after shooting them with the M4; the first time at Whiskey Pete's had been in near total dark. I walked to the truck and leaned against the bed with my forearms draped over the top of the tailgate, breathing deeply. My attention was drawn back to Billy only a few moments later.

"Hey, shit, this one shot himself in the ass. He literally shot himself a new asshole, Jake."

"You seem to be enjoying yourself, considering we just killed these men."

He stopped probing around Larry and looked up at me. He then stood and walked over to me. His face was serious then, all joking gone.

"These dubious motherfuckers were set up to ambush us, Jake. They were going to kill you and me both for our trucks and whatever we had in them."

I didn't have any response for this, so he kept speaking.

"I can see your point of view; I'm not a total bastard. It's just that I don't really care. If you spend your time in this new world agonizing over everyone you have to kill when they force you to kill them, you're just not going to last that long. For those people you meet that are worth preserving, you hold onto them and give all to keep them safe. And," he turned and pointed at the dead, "for such as those, they're worth less than your contempt. They're not evil. They're not big game or good sport. They're an obstacle. They're another challenge that the world throws at you; something you have to best. They aren't worth any more consideration than that."

He walked back over to Larry while I stood there trying to absorb what he had just told me. He picked up the pistol (another semi-automatic) and read the side. "Taurus," he scoffed. "*Fuuuuuck* you," he said and left it on the ground.

————

It turned out that Billy had a plan for the taper punch and drip pans. In modern cars, all entry points into the gas tank have anti-rollover valves to prevent fuel from pouring out everywhere in the event of a vehicle roll. These valves also have the unfortunate side effect of blocking siphon hoses. You can get around this by using a really thin, stiff tube cut at an angle; you have to twist it into the tank just so, and you can typically get past the valve.

Billy had neither the tube nor the patience for that, so he fell back to plan B; a method he said he read about in a book. Basically, we were going to get gas through the cunning means of punching holes in gas tanks and catching the spill in drip pans. We had a couple of pans, so as one filled up, we could swap in the empty and let it fill up while pouring the first pan into one of the gas cans.

Neither of us were excited about hanging around the area in which we had just engaged in a firefight, so we drove south towards the 215 and then swung out due East in search of cars with gas tanks we could access easily. We didn't have to go very far to find likely vehicles, but we pushed out a few miles anyway just to put some distance between ourselves and Pep Boys. The closer we got to the 215 and the 15, the worse the pile up became and we eventually had to call off the advance. We got out of the trucks with tools and equipment in hand and made our way over to a red Toyota.

I handed my rifle over to Billy. "Here, take that. Keep an eye out."

"You sure?" he asked as he reached out to take it. "It sucks to get a face full of gas if you're not careful."

I smiled and gave him a pointed look. "You see yourself getting under a Toyota any time soon, big guy?"

"Yeah, okay. I'll keep an eye out."

I could hardly fit under the car myself. I could see the tank, and I could even reach out and touch it, but I simply could not get far enough under to drive a hole with the punch. "Well... shucks," I muttered and got back up.

"Okay," Billy said. "Next one, then."

"Nope." I was walking back to the truck.

"Hey, where're you going?"

"If we limit this to only the cars we can easily crawl under, we'll be out here all week," I called back as I rummaged around in the back of the crew cab. I finally found the jack and lever and brought it back over to the Toyota. After I had the car up on three wheels, I swung around to lie on my back.

"God damn it, we should have grabbed some jack stands. This isn't safe, Jake."

I looked over at the jack and struck it with the meat of my hand; two solid shots. "Seems okay. We're probably not going to be written up by OSHA."

"Wiseass..."

"Oh, yeah!" I said, sliding under. "There's all kinds of room under here now!" I lined up the pan beneath the tank, set the punch directly over it, and gave it a whack with the mallet. The punch dimpled the tank and partially broke through, at which point fuel started dribbling out and ran all over my hands. "Gaaah, damn it," I grunted and gave it another quick hit. Having punched through fully, I yanked it out, producing a dribble of a stream that pulsed at regular intervals.

"Huh," I said.

"What's up?" Billy asked from somewhere off to the right by my legs.

"Well, I could have sworn there was more in this tank from the sound it made when I started tapping it, but the gas is just dribbling out."

"Oh, right. I'm an idiot. Hang on…"

I heard the sound of his boots rattling away as he ran back to the truck. A short time later, he ran back. I heard a metallic slam followed by a wrenching squeal. A few seconds later, the fuel stream started running fast and even into the pan.

"What did you do?" I asked.

"There was no way for air to get into the tank to replace the fuel coming out. We were fighting suction. I just busted open the gas cap and stuck a crowbar in there to wedge the valve open to let the air in. How's it going?"

"Better slide that other pan in here…" was my answer.

We spent the rest of the afternoon going up and down the street punching tanks. The first few took some time, but after we got the hang of it, we fell into a sustainable rhythm. It wasn't long before we had both the van and the truck topped off and all the spare gas cans filled.

"This is pretty good," I said, lifting the last can into the truck. "This never would have occurred to me. I bet we could keep a vehicle moving for years doing this as long as we don't run out of cities and no one else gets wise."

"Three to six months," Billy said.

"Huh?"

"This will work for about three to six months. After that, the gas will have gone to shit. It expires a lot faster than you'd think. You can maybe extend the life of regular gas out to two years if you load it with additives and store it in some high-quality stainless steel tanks, but we don't have any of that. So: three to six months."

"Well…shoot," I said. "There's nothing we can do about that?"

"Well, there's always something you can do." Billy leaned on the truck bed and wiped his forehead. "You just have to decide if the result is worth the effort. There're more important things to deal with. Shelter, sustainable food, sustainable water. By the time you have all that figured out, all the gas will have gone bingo. The only viable option after that point will be diesel."

"It lasts longer?"

"Oh, yeah," Billy nodded. "Diesel is just a fantastic technology. The engines are really forgiving and run on just about anything, and diesel fuel will last a good ten years even if you don't baby it. The only problem there is finding diesel vehicles, which were less popular for some damned unknown reason."

"Should we not just be tracking down diesel right now?" It sounded like we might as well just pull the Band-Aid off fast instead of slow.

"Naw." He kicked himself off the truck and started wandering towards the van. "Regular unleaded is plentiful right now. It makes sense to use it while we have it. We'll know when it's time to trade up. The gas engines will start running rough." He pulled the van door open; levered himself up into the cab. "Come on, Whitey. We got another stop I been thinking about all day. Time to test out my theory."

5

# TRAFFICKING

## Amanda

We were already with Dwight and his group by the time Jake and Billy found us. I had no idea what to think at the time. I didn't know if they would be any better or any worse than Dwight. They looked just like Dwight's people. They were men, they were stronger than us; had more guns than us. Certainly, they knew how to use those guns better than us. Obviously, we were saved when Jake and Billy came along, but I didn't know that at the time. As far as I knew, Lizzy and I were just being passed along to someone stronger.

Dwight was running a caravan when we found him. It was him along with three other men driving two motorhomes: Dwight, Hugo, Richard, and James. I never got their last names—don't really care. Dwight appeared to run the whole thing, though. The other three just seemed to be the sheep following along.

It was actually me that found them and flagged them down, if you can believe that. Lizzy and I were out foraging among some busted up shops looking for anything the looters might have left behind when I saw the motorhomes rolling by at a crawl, weaving around the wrecks and other trash in the road.

I said, "Oh my God! Come on, Lizzy!" or something close to that and started running (or at least tried to run) in their direction with all the crap I was carrying slamming off my sides. I started screaming for them to stop; I screamed so loud I was hoarse for two days after. We were almost out of food and completely out of water. I was desperate.

I remember both laughing and sobbing when I saw brake lights. Doors opened on both of the motorhomes, and four men came out, every one of them wearing the same shocked expression. They were too far away for me to hear them say anything, but Dwight turned to look at the rest of them, said something, and made a gentle, pushing "stay calm" gesture with his hands. He turned and ran over to meet us.

"Hey, are you two okay?" he asked. "What the hell are you doing out here?"

"We're looking for food and water," I nearly sobbed. "Please, can you help us? Do you have any water? Please... my daughter..."

You would think that I would have been able to see that something was off with him but I swear to God, there was nothing. He gave absolutely no indication of who he was or what he planned. I think it's possible that even he didn't know at the time.

"Yeah, come with me. We have plenty. Other stuff, too, if you need it. Hugo! Grab some waters, man!" He started leading us back toward the others. He didn't so much as lay hands on us. I was so relieved that my legs were weak.

In the lead motorhome, he sat us down at the little dining table while all the rest of the men stood around us, hands in their pockets and looking very out of place. He put bottled waters down in front of us, which we both grabbed and started sucking down as fast as we could.

"Whoa, whoa, easy!" he said. "How long has it been since you had water?"

"Two days," I gasped and started drinking again.

"Okay, okay, slow it down a little. *Sloooow*... good. Don't shotgun it, lady. You'll make yourself sick. Are you both hungry?" I nodded. Lizzy said, "Yes, please," which shocked me. The most I had gotten out of her in a while were grunts.

"Richard, would you set them up, please?" The one named Richard rummaged in a pantry and pulled out a can of beef stew. He retrieved a pot from another cabinet and turned on the gas stove. I stared at the stove. I couldn't remember the last time we had eaten hot food.

"Let's start with splitting this up between you," Richard suggested. "If you keep it down, I'll warm up another can."

"Thank you," I said.

"I'm Dwight. This is James and Hugo. The chef is Richard." He pointed at each of them as he spoke.

"I'm Amanda. This is my daughter Elizabeth."

"Lizzy," she said. I squeezed her hand. It was so good to hear her speak.

James, who had been completely silent until now, finally spoke up in a rough, cracking voice. "Amanda, I'm going to reach out and take your rifle, okay? I don't want you to be alarmed or nuthin'. We've run into some crazies out here, is all. We'd prefer to be careful until we all know each other a little better, see?"

I agreed and gave the son of a bitch my own weapon.

Lizzy and I ate the soup when it was ready, which was delicious, and they made us another can after.

They were all on their best behavior for the next few days. Every other day, two of them would head out together to go scavenging among the deserted houses and shops, which was nasty work. You always want to prefer the shops because they're mostly just boarded up and empty, but they're also almost always picked over for all the best stuff. That means that your chances of finding useful items are actually better if you go house to house. The problem there is that you'll find dead bodies in most of the houses; people who died in the Plague. We all learned to stop being squeamish a long time ago, but the average sane person still wants to avoid a rotting corpse if possible.

I became restless before too long (I had always been an active person) and started asking Dwight for ways to contribute. "Give me a rifle," I said. I'd go with them into the city looking for supplies. Just sitting around with Lizzy and eating their food made me feel anxious. I didn't want to wear out our welcome. I even offered to do their cooking and cleaning. All of my offers were refused politely.

"You and your daughter just need to rest easy for now," he said. "You've both had a rough run of days, and you're still recovering; we can all see it. When you're better, when you've gotten a bit of your strength and color back, we can all sit down and talk about what you can do to pitch in."

As it turned out, that discussion came late one night after we had all gone to bed. Lizzy, Dwight, and I were sleeping in one of the motorhomes while James, Richard, and Hugo slept in the other. They gave me the queen bed in the back bedroom while Lizzy took the bed over the cab because she was excited about having a bunk bed. Dwight was on the fold-out between us.

I was woken out of a dead sleep by Dwight shaking my shoulder gently. I was startled at first because I could only see a dark shape hovering over me, but I realized who it was and relaxed immediately.

"Dwight? What's up?" I whispered.

"Shh, it's okay," he whispered back. "Nothing to be alarmed about. Don't wake Lizzy. We just need to talk outside. The, uh, the group needs to get your input on something." He turned and walked back to the door. He looked back at me, held his index finger up to his mouth in a shushing gesture, and quietly let himself out.

Wondering what was so important that had to be dealt with this instant; I sat up and pulled my jeans and shoes on. They were all waiting for me in a solemn half circle when I stepped off the doorstep. It was the middle of the night and dark; there was no moon to see by, and all I had was starlight.

"Hey, what's going on, guys?" I asked, hugging my arms.

"Well, the boys and I have been talking," said Dwight. "We all agree that it's time for you to start helping out around here."

"Okay... sure," I said. I was confused why the discussion had to take place in the middle of the night, but I was still foggy from having just come awake. "I can head out with someone tomorrow to..."

"No, no," Dwight interrupted. "Deserted as things are, there's still plenty of danger out there to be found. Hell, we had to put some marauders down just before you two found us, even. I think you're a lot safer right here."

"Okay, we can come back to that later," I said, not wanting to let it go. "We talked about me taking on some of the chores. Where can I help?"

I could hear Dwight smiling as he spoke. "No, look, that's very gracious of you, but what we were thinking of is that there are things you can do... things you can *provide*... that the rest of us are incapable of."

"Provide? I..."

"Comfort, Amanda. Companionship. It's been a while since we've all seen a woman. There are certain... appetites. Drive a man crazy."

I took a step back. "What the hell is this?"

"Easy, easy," Dwight said. He was putting on his best reasonable politician voice. "Look, we're not unreasonable. Aren't we providing you and Lizzy with food, safety, and shelter? We don't like it rough or anything; we all want this to be friendly. We certainly don't want to all tag team you in a single night..." he shuddered. "Unsanitary..."

I couldn't believe what I was hearing. With the exception of James, who was always quiet, they had all seemed so normal up to this point. I did notice the occasional lingering stare on my body every so often, but that wasn't any different from before when things weren't completely crazy. As they said, there weren't a lot of women around. I just put it down to men being men.

I started to back further away, and they all spread out and encircled me, keeping close and putting my back up against the camper.

The window on the door slid open, and I heard Lizzy's tired, slurred voice up over my shoulder. "Mom? What's going on out there? Why is everyone awake?"

"Just go back to sleep, okay Lizzy?" Hugo called out. "Your mom and us are just talking. Nothing to be worried about, babe."

"Lizzy doesn't have to know about any of this," Dwight continued. "We'll keep it from her and only do this at night. I mean, shit, is it really that bad? All you need to do is roll over, let one of us have a turn, and this'll all be nice and easy."

Despite how disgusted I was, I actually began to consider what he was saying. What he was describing didn't actually sound like the worst thing that could happen. Our culture has it all built up like rape is the absolute worst thing that could happen to a woman, but it's really not. It's especially not if you're a mother.

James, who was always so quiet and sullen, spoke up as if to emphasize my thoughts. "This is easy as long as you make it easy. I'm tired of all the talking…"

"Now, uh, James, we all agreed there was a better chance of this working out if we all just…"

"Shut the fuck up, Dwight. I'm tired of hearing you."

Dwight clamped his mouth shut immediately and took a physical step back, head down. I had always assumed he was in charge, but that one exchange demonstrated how badly I was mistaken.

"Now," James said, a cross between a purr and a growl, "your kid is up there in that camper. One of us is going in there with her. Dwight wasn't shitting you; none of us is interested in a fuckin' kid. When she gets older we'll talk, but for now, no thanks. So, if you play along, she'll be fine. Fuck this up; she won't."

James turned and looked at the rest of them. "Dwight, since you're feeling so fucking chummy this evening, you can go babysit. And…" he leveled a finger at each man in turn, "…any… one… of… you cunts comes in her cunt…" he pointed at me as he said this, "I swear to the blessed baby Jesus himself I will personally thumb fuck your eye sockets. Not one more mouth to feed—I mean it. If one of you idiots gets her pregnant, I'll fucking kill one of you off at random to make up the god damned difference."

All of them were staring down at the ground by now. I was shaking in disbelief. I can't tell you what I was thinking at that point. It was as though some part of my brain, the important part that makes me "me," had switched off.

James walked over to me and put his face close enough to mine that I could smell his breath, which had the scent of Certs on it for whatever fucking reason. It can't have been to make a good impression.

"I'm first," he rumbled. "Don't keep me waiting."

He turned and walked to the empty motorhome, opened the door, and climbed in giving every indication that he expected to be followed. There was nothing I could do. I went. Completely numb, I went.

Things went as promised for the next few days and fell into a predictable routine. During the daytime, they all behaved as if nothing had changed. Dwight was still chatty (which now took on the added characteristic of feeling completely scummy; I wanted to wash myself whenever he so much as said "hello"), Richard and Hugo kept to themselves as they were the younger of the four and rather stupid, and James was quiet, sullen, and terrifying. Everyone carried themselves lightly around James, reminding me of Jack trying to sneak by the sleeping Giant. I eventually learned why from Dwight.

"You just want to go easy and don't argue when you're dealing with James," he told me in a low voice one afternoon. "There used to be five of us."

"Why the hell are you sticking with him, then?" I asked, barely able to keep the venom out of my voice. I don't think I succeeded, actually. Dwight shrank back into himself at the question. Whoever he was from before, it seemed he had enough self-awareness to be ashamed of himself. Not that it stopped him from taking his turn on his nights.

Presently, he perked up and gestured over to Hugo, who was sitting next to Richard (they were both in folding camping chairs; Dwight and I were sitting at a fold-up picnic table that was set up inside the half-ring of the motorhomes, which were themselves parked nose to tail).

"Hey, Hugo. Your night to cook, ain't it? I'm starving from being out all day with Rich. Fucker has enough energy for three of us, always running every damned place."

"A brisk walk ain't the same thing as running, you old bitch," Rich offered without looking back over his shoulder. He took a drink of warm beer and belched while Dwight chuckled at him.

Hugo groaned softly and hung his head back. "Ah, man. I'm so fucking sick of canned food I almost don't want to eat at this point. I definitely don't want to build up a fire right now. Are there any bags of jerky left? Can't we just have some of that?"

"You can't have just jerky for dinner, you knob," Rich said. "It's, like, all unbalanced and shit."

"I'd kill for a slice of fresh bread," Hugo complained.

"Okay, okay, okay," Dwight spoke up. "Why don't we just crack out a couple of the MREs Amanda brought with her? That okay with you, Amanda?"

The look of friendly hope on his face when he asked me that was so out of place that he surprised a, "Are you fucking serious?" out of me. His smile fell instantly, as though he had just learned that some jerk had eaten the last of his favorite ice cream.

"That's a plan, right there," Hugo said, levering himself up out of his chair. "I swear to Shiva, if I have to eat one more of those cans of vegetable beef, I'm going to shit out my pancreas."

"Who the hell is Shiva?" Richard asked.

"It was that one god from Indiana Jones." Hugo disappeared for a moment into the rear motorhome and came back out a moment later with three bags under his arms.

"These things are something like fifteen thousand calories," he said. "We probably want to go easy on these, in case we don't like them, huh?"

"Good idea," said Dwight. "I understand you can cook these without a fire, so it's probably best to save them for special occasions, such as if you suspect another night of soup will throw you into colorectal distress."

"Without a fire, huh?" Richard said, coming over to the table where Hugo had thrown the brown packages. "How d'you manage that?"

"Well, there're instructions on the side. Read 'em," said Dwight.

Hugo picked up a bag and began to read to himself, his lips moving silently. After a few minutes, he said, "Okay, we gotta find a rock or something."

"Huh?" Richard grunted. "The fuck does a rock have to do with this?"

"Well, I guess it doesn't have to be a rock. We could get something like a rock. It just says 'rock or something'".

"Wait a minute," Dwight said, reaching out to take the package. "The instructions actually say 'rock or something'??"

Hugo handed it over and pointed at a spot on the bag with an I-told-you-so look on his face.

Dwight stared at the bag where Hugo gestured. "Who the fuck wrote this? Beavis and Butthead?"

It was obviously a mistake to say this, as Hugo and Richard instantly started imitating the two characters, grunting and chuckling like a couple of morons.

"Hey, Beavis. Go find a rock or something. Uh, huh-huh."

Dwight was in the process of rolling his eyes heavenward when James' voice erupted from the back of the leading motorhome loud enough to make the slide windows shake.

"Shut the fuck up you inbred, goat-fucking bastards!"

Everyone shut up immediately. I didn't want to be outside among the idiots any longer, so I got up and went to the rear camper to check on Lizzy. She was no fool; I don't think she knew exactly what was going on, but she did understand that we were not with nice people, so she spent most of her time shut up in the rear of the camper keeping to herself.

"Hey, how you doing, Mija?" I asked as I sat down by her on the bed. She was sitting with her back against the wall, so I scooted on next to her.

"I want to leave, mom. I don't want to stay with these people anymore. They're not right. None of this is right."

I had no idea how to explain the situation to her in a way she could understand, and that wouldn't horrify her. She was still just a little girl, yet to have her first period. I wasn't even close to having the talk with her yet. My stomach churned with nausea as I searched for something to say that would make any sense. Finally, I just told her, "I know. We can't go yet. Maybe soon but not now."

"How soon?"

"I don't know. We have to be very careful. Very quiet. Don't talk about this with any of the others."

"I don't want to talk with them at all," she muttered.

"That's good," I said. "Only don't give them any reason to be mad at you, okay? If they ask you a question, you answer, okay?"

She stared out the window and said nothing. She reached a hand up and wiped at an eye.

"Elizabeth, look at me. I need you to say okay."

"Okay," she finally said, and I put my arms around her.

The door to the other motorhome slammed open, making us both jump. Through the cracked window, I heard James growling at the other three.

"Well, you fucking idiots have done it. There's no..."—There was a loud slap, followed immediately by a grunt and the sound of someone falling over chairs—"...chance of me getting back to sleep now. God damned, brainless fucktards, every one..."

The sound of his footsteps approached the door of our camper. My spine began to coil up on itself, and I felt a cold wire wrap around my insides and tighten. The door opened, and James lumbered into the kitchenette area.

"Elizabeth," he growled. "Go play outside a while."

Elizabeth did the exact opposite of that. She dug her hands into my arms and buried her face in my shoulder. I began to panic.

"You said only at night..." I babbled at him.

His eyes went wide while his face reddened in anger. "I? I said no such fuckin' thing." He came at us both like a charging rhino. I struggled to untangle myself from Lizzy and put myself between them, but he reached out with a single hand, wrapped his fingers in my hair, and threw me aside. With the other, he grabbed Elizabeth by the arm and hauled her out of the bed. She was shrieking in terror.

He began dragging her toward the door. I don't recall coming to my feet at this point; I only remember being across the camper suddenly and hitting him in the back as hard as I could with fists and elbows. He turned and gave me a single shove, which sent me all the way back through the dining area, past the bathroom, and onto the bed. As I sat back up from being flat on my back, I saw him shove the door open and throw my daughter out into open space bodily by the back of her shorts and the collar of her shirt. Her panicked screaming and crying was interrupted by the sound of her little body hitting the ground, after which I heard her groaning and making frantic choking noises. I realized she'd had the wind knocked out of her. James slammed the door shut and locked it.

I lost all control of myself at that point. I came across the camper at him at full speed, shrieking and cursing, telling him I'd kill him, promising to rip his motherfucking balls off. He reached out, caught me by my throat, and slammed me into the wall. My mouth slammed shut on my tongue, and I tasted blood. I lost consciousness for the shortest of moments when the back of my head bounced off the wall. When things cleared up again, I realized he had probably slammed me into the wall two or three more times.

He didn't say anything after that—nothing menacing... didn't ask me if I'd had enough. He waited a few seconds to see if I would do anything else, then nodded. He walked me over to the table, bent me over it, and ripped my pants off of me. I felt him spread me open and he spit between my legs. He took what he wanted. I could still hear Lizzy crying outside.

---

Jake and Billy arrived on the following day in the midafternoon. James and Dwight had left to go scavenging in town, leaving Hugo and Richard to keep an eye on things. During this time, one of them would usually sit up on top of one of the motorhomes in a folding chair with a rifle (my rifle, I noted) while the other kept to the ground. They weren't exactly vigilant. I'm sure someone could have snuck up on them without too much effort. I don't think Jake figured out for sure what was going on until after he arrived, though, so he wasn't really trying to sneak up on anything.

I was in the camper with Lizzy, trying to come up with a way to kill four men at once without any weapons and without endangering my daughter when I heard voices outside, as well as Richard's coming from above my head periodically. With the camper windows all closed, it sounded like listening to people talk while being underwater. I could tell that English was being used, but it was all muffled and distorted; just beyond any comprehension.

I got up from my spot on the couch (Lizzy was to my right at the table, coloring) and moved over to the window just above the little sink. I cracked the blinds to look outside.

Hugo was to my left and had his back to me. He was talking to someone about ten feet in front of him, who was facing me. It was Jake, obviously, but I didn't know that at the time. All I knew then was that there was suddenly a fifth man that I'd have to deal with.

Jake was thinner in those days, well… we were all thinner. I was never overweight at any point, but I did have a healthy little sheen of mom fat left over from when I gave birth. Then the apocalypse happened. The day to day grind of survival, of always having to scrounge our food or go hungry—that burned whatever fat we might have had right off. Before everything fell apart, I knew all these moms who spent tons of money on all kinds of stuff to get the perfect body. They were doing yoga, Crossfit, Pilates, P90-whatever…

I'll tell you what: you ever want to see your ab muscles in the mirror? Try a little Apocalypse. Does wonders.

So, here's this fifth guy who doesn't look particularly impressive. He's not really tall, not fat but also not rail thin—but still much thinner than he is now. He also had hair back then—brown, a little too long. It was almost a Beatle haircut. I'm sure it looked well-tended back in the day, but a lack of barbers or pressing need to maintain it made him look like he was fresh out of the '70s. Don't tell him I said that…

He was wearing jeans, some sort of thick and clunky hiking boots, and what was some kind of long sleeved over shirt buttoned all the way up to his neck, despite the day's growing heat. His hands were empty. Hugo held a rifle pointed not at the newcomer but just at the ground between them. They appeared to just be talking.

I cracked open the kitchen window and their voices suddenly clarified.

"...look like you have much to trade," Hugo was just finishing.

"Well, I don't have it with me, obviously. I don't know what kind of people you are. I have my stuff stashed a ways off. I can tell you what I have. If any of it interests you, maybe you have some stuff that interests me, see?"

"Yeah, okay. Makes sense, I guess. So what do you have?"

"Have bullets..." offered the new guy.

"Hey, no shit? How much?"

"Enough to feed that rifle of yours. I'm light on food and water and could use whatever you'll spare."

This deflated Hugo visibly. "Oh, yeah. I don't think I can give you any of that... not without the others here to say if it's cool."

"I understand."

"Is there anything else you want?" Richard asked from overhead. "We got other stuff."

"Honestly, not really. Food or water are really the only things I could use more of."

"Fuck," Hugo mumbled, looking down. Presently, his head snapped up. "Hey, I got something, maybe." He walked to the left out of site. Almost as soon as he disappeared, his knock came on the motorhome door. "Hey, Amanda. Come out here a second."

I had seen this coming. When it came to commodities, I had a resource that none of the other men could provide, assuming a condition of general heterosexuality. I took a deep breath and tried to figure out what I'd do if this new guy preferred children. I was going to kill him if he even so much as looked at Lizzy, or at least do my best to kill him. I was banking on the hope that the others wanted to keep me alive more than the newcomer and that they would save me if things went very bad. Pussy's pussy, as they say.

"Elizabeth," I whispered, "go into the bathroom and lock the door. Don't make any sound." She whimpered but got up from the table and did as I asked.

My hands were shaking as I stepped out the door.

"Eh??" Hugo said, returning to his position as I came out. The newcomer was very still now. He wasn't resting his weight on one leg as he had been when I first saw him. He was poised. He looked very alert. I shuddered; he reminded me of some predator you see on nature shows just before it jumps out of the bushes to kill some poor, unsuspecting creature.

"Here's something you don't have, I'll bet," Hugo proudly stated.

"Hugo," Richard said from behind and above us all, "I'm really not sure this is…"

"Chill, man. This is what's called 'taking initiative.' I'm problem-solving, here, dude."

"What is this?" Stranger asked. His voice was flat, and his face was unreadable, doing the best Terminator impression I'd ever seen.

"How much are those bullets worth to you, friend? How about some alone time with Amanda, here?"

The newcomer stared at me. I can't remember for how long, but it felt uncomfortably long. His gaze did not rove over me. He stared straight into my face. Right into my eyes.

"Would that be alright with you, Amanda?" he asked.

I was surprised and didn't know how to answer. "No" was the obvious choice but I was terrified of making anyone mad at this point. I didn't want to say "yes" because, well, I couldn't bring myself to say it. I physically could not bring myself to ask to be raped. Finally, I said the only thing I could think of.

"Please…"

The newcomer nodded. He raised his right hand up next to his head; made a peace sign with his index and middle fingers.

"'Two'? Two *what*, man?" Hugo asked.

At the instant Hugo spoke, I heard a gunshot from far away and the sound of Richard grunting and falling down from behind me. The gunshot and Richard's grunt occurred simultaneously.

The newcomer had snaked his hand behind himself by this time. Hugo growled, "Buttfucker…" and pulled his rifle up. It had only been pointed at the ground, so he had it centered on the stranger's chest well before the stranger had whatever it was he was going for at the ready.

Hugo's rifle sputtered three or four times (I swear to God, it literally made a "pew, pew" sound—Billy later told me it was a .22

rimfire). I couldn't tell if he hit the stranger or not; I thought I saw his shirt jump, but I couldn't tell.

The stranger seemed to care about this not at all. He completed his draw, and he suddenly had a pistol in his hand pointed right at Hugo. He fired once, hitting Hugo in the head, but I heard two gunshots. I realized that whoever was shooting from far away must have put another round into Richard. Richard did not make any noise on either shot.

The new guy was up close to me by now. I hadn't seen him coming. It was like he just appeared next to me.

"Are there only the four of them?" he asked.

I was speechless, unable to think of anything to say. I just nodded.

He pointed out in the direction that the lead camper was facing and said, "There's a friend out in that direction about three hundred yards or so." He waved wildly over his head with both arms and then pointed in that direction again, indicating with his eyes that I should look. Way out in the distance, I could just make out the shape of a man waving back at us with one hand.

"You need to run out there to meet him."

At this moment, I didn't know what to think. I didn't know if we were being saved or if there was just someone stronger and even more evil assuming ownership of Lizzy and me. The only thing I did know was that I couldn't let myself be separated from her. "My daughter! Please!" I said, gesturing at the motorhome.

The change these words brought was subtle and immediate. The expression on his face (or his face's state of expressionlessness, rather) never changed, but his back stiffened noticeably. "Get her. Can she run?"

"Yes."

"Then get her and hurry. The others will have heard."

This got me moving. I ripped open the door and tore down the length of the vehicle to the bathroom and slapped on the door with both hands.

"Elizabeth!" I said, frantic. "Come out of there, right now!"

The door unlocked and swung out, revealing a shaking, tear-soaked little girl. I grabbed her hand and began to tug.

"What's happening?" she asked as she came along.

"We have to run right now."

As we came out of the motorhome, the stranger was outside hoisting Hugo off the ground with both hands, one under the belt and one at the collar of his shirt. He was holding Hugo like James had held Elizabeth when he threw her. I felt a black wave of rage wash over me. "Get going," he said and jerked his head toward where his friend was, now concealed again, out in the Utah desert.

Lizzy and I ran. I don't remember how far we ran or how long. It seemed like it wasn't very long at all before we saw the top half of an older man raise up from the ground and wave at us. He was wearing a blue chino work shirt; the kind my father used to wear.

"C'mon, Little Sis!" he said, waving his hands at us in a "let's go!" motion. "C'mere and belly down on the ground here!"

He got back down on his stomach, and I saw him put his cheek down on the black stock of a bolt action rifle. He looked through a scope and adjusted his grip on the weapon as Lizzy and I laid down beside him and looked back at the motorhomes, now far away. I couldn't see anything outside. The form of Richard was just barely visible on the top of the camper. His chair stood empty and undisturbed.

"Are either of you hurt?" the man asked.

"No, we're okay. A little shaky," I said.

"Good. That's good. My name's Billy," he said and offered me some binoculars. Slightly surprised, I took them and said, "Amanda."

"Pleasure. How about the little girl?"

"You go anywhere near her, and I'll fucking kill you, do you understand?"

He pulled his face off the rifle to look at me. "God damn," he said in dismay. "We were afraid you might have had it rough. I'm sorry, Amanda. And don't worry. Nobody's going near your girl."

He took his right hand off the trigger long enough to reach around behind himself. When his hand came back, it held a small revolver. He handed this to me as well, grip first.

"Here," he said. "You just hold onto that for me, okay?"

I reached out slowly and took it, afraid I was being tricked in some way that I couldn't imagine. My hand closed around the grip. His didn't let go.

"Do me a favor, Little Sis. Don't shoot me."

He let go and put his face back to the rifle.

I fumbled with the revolver, trying to figure out how to open it. "Push the tab on the left side forward," he offered. "Drops the cylinder right out."

I did as he suggested and saw six rounds. They all said, ".38 SPL" on the back of the cartridge.

"Anyone gets too close to you or the girl, you unload that thing in their face," Billy said.

I put the pistol in front of me and lifted the binoculars to look at the motorhomes. Richard suddenly jumped into focus. He was sprawled out on top with his feet toward us. I looked all about the rest of the site and saw no one. There was no sign of the other man.

"Where is he?" I asked, not bothering to clarify who I meant.

"Jake," Billy said. "He's inside one of those RV's. He'll be waiting for the rest to come back."

Something occurred to me suddenly. "He knew there were four men?"

"Yap. We been watching you all a couple of days. Wasn't sure what to make of it. We knew that one of the men was a bit of an asshole, but we had kind of a hard time figuring out if they were abrasive, danger-ous, or just evil. We knew you were there with 'em; didn't know about your little girl."

He was quiet for a moment.

"I... uh, well I wanted to move on," he said apologetically. "Jake insisted on finding out for sure."

"Finding what out for sure?"

"Erm... finding out if everyone actually wanted to be there," he answered. He seemed to become uncomfortable at this simple statement.

"Oh. Here they come," he said as he looked through the scope again. He sounded relieved.

"Are you going to shoot them?" Lizzy asked?

"Should I shoot them?" Billy replied.

"Yes," I confirmed. "Shoot the large one several times."

"Okay, if I can get a clear shot and a definite kill, I'll do it. I'm terrible at hitting moving targets, though, so they'll have to…"

Out in the distance, Dwight and James ran full-tilt at the campers, yelling out for Richard and Hugo as they came. Without slowing down, they yanked the door of the rear RV open and piled in. The sound of gunfire followed immediately after, sounding small and muffled in the distance.

"D'ah, shit…" Billy groaned and was up running before I knew what was happening. He could move pretty fast for his size, even in those cowboy boots he always wore. Even so, he was very big, and I judged I could catch up to him easily if I wanted to. I decided to stay put with Elizabeth. I thought momentarily about leaving but decided not to. Something about Billy's manner put me at ease in a way that I never was when I was with Dwight, Richard, Hugo, and James—even before they turned out to be a bunch of fucking bastards. There was also the fact that he handed me a loaded gun. The others had made a point of disarming me. Billy didn't know who I was—certainly didn't know if I was safe or not. He just handed me a gun because he thought it would make me feel better. That counted for a lot as far as I was concerned.

The sound of gunfire stopped almost as quickly as it started. That seemed to increase the urgency for Billy, who actually sped up as he went rather than slowing down, his head and arms pumping maniacally as he ran. When he arrived at the RV, I looked through the binoculars and saw him take a deep breath, shoulders heaving. He then set the rifle into his shoulder, pulled open the door, and slowly climbed in. Following this, the scene remained quiet for several minutes. I was starting to fidget and wondering if I should make my way over there or take Lizzy and run when the RV door opened up again. At first, all I saw was a hand, and I literally felt my bowels go soft as I waited to see who it would be.

Billy stepped out and waved in my direction. I didn't realize I was holding my breath, but it escaped me that moment in a gasp. He made a sweeping "come on over" gesture with his arm.

I patted Lizzy on the shoulder, grabbed the revolver in front of me, and began to walk over. I had misgivings about bringing Lizzy back to that place with me, but there was no way I was leaving her alone out there.

When we made it back, Billy was still outside waiting for us. "The girl stays outside. Jake would like to see you inside."

I drew up short at this. I felt whatever trust he had managed to establish begin to evaporate. He seemed to sense this. He held up his hands and said, "You don't want her to see. Trust me."

Giving him a look that said "don't try me, asshole," I stepped into the RV. Dwight's body was in a pile and bleeding directly on the other side of the door, obviously dead. Deeper into the living area, James was on the floor, also bleeding from the leg. He was on his stomach with his hands bound behind him. It looked like heavy-duty zip ties around his wrists. Dust and debris hung in the air, giving the interior a cloudy, dream-like quality. There were bullet holes all throughout the cabinetry, and some of the windows were shot out as well.

Jake was sitting behind him on the couch. His nose was mashed in, and there was blood all down his face and his front. His shirt was unbuttoned, and I could see a black vest underneath. There were scuffs and tears on it from bullet impacts.

"I ran out of bullets," said Jake, making it sound like an excuse or an apology for not finishing James off. His voice was clogged and nasal like he had the world's worst cold. His nose was clearly broken. "So, now that I'm not actively trying to keep them from killing me," he continued, "it seemed right to me to give you some say in what happens to this one here."

"Fuck you. Fuck this bitch. Keep that bitch away from me, you hear?" James was practically growling and spitting from his position on the floor. He kept trying to crane his head up to look at us. I could see that his lips and part of his face had swollen up considerably.

"What?" I said, stupidly.

"Look," he said and groaned as he got up off the couch. "I have an idea of what's been going on here. Billy and I have been watching the site the last couple of days, and we're aware that it wasn't all friendly games with these guys. I think I understand what this has been for you."

He picked up a roll of duct tape off the table and moved to the back of the RV, toward the bedroom. He started rummaging in drawers as he continued speaking. "My plan initially was just to kill them all clean and avoid having to deal with this kind of...dilemma. I'm not terribly excited about execution as a rule."

He pulled out a pair of socks, nodded, and made his way back toward James.

James began to twist and struggle. "The fuck you mean 'execution,' motherfucker? You just want to think about what you're do-UNGH!!!" Jake stuffed the socks into James' mouth quick and rough to avoid being bitten and started wrapping duct tape around his whole head, making several complete circuits. I could see that the knuckles on both of his hands were bleeding as he did this. By the time he was done, the only things exposed on James's head were his eyes, nose, ears, and the top of his head. He was still grunting and jerking around, but he could make very little noise at all now. Strings of snot flared from his nostrils at each frantic breath.

He stood up and looked back at me. "It occurred to me," he continued in a reasonable, professor's voice, "that you should have a say in what happens next. Strictly speaking, you're probably the most aggrieved person involved in this whole situation. I'm content to make this your call."

He stepped over James to come closer to me. The process of him stepping over James felt as though it carried weight. He did it slowly and deliberately, as though he had to make a conscious decision of will to take that step. "Billy gave you a gun, yes?"

I nodded, frozen in place by a gaze completely lacking in all expression—a reptile's gaze. Jake reached behind his back and pulled out a large, black knife—what I would eventually learn is called a Ka-Bar. He offered it to me, handle first.

As my hand closed around the grip, he said to me, "Make sure whatever you do is something you can live with, whether it's quick or not. If you can't live with either, come and get me and I'll put him down fast."

He moved past me toward the door and stopped to look back. "Whatever you end up doing: fast, slow, or not at all—no one's going to hold it against you. Do what you have to do. I'll give you ten minutes."

He stepped out of the RV and shut the door while James bucked and kicked behind me, grunting and screaming through his nose wordlessly.

I walked toward him and kneeled down. He instantly went still and became deathly quiet. I held up the gun on one side of his face and the knife on the other, both pointed at the ceiling. I looked between the two weapons and back to his face. His gaze was doing the exact same thing.

I thought of him with his hands tangled up in my hair in the middle of the night. I thought of him bending me over the table and spitting between my legs.

I thought of him throwing Elizabeth through the door of the motorhome out into space; the sound she made as she struggled to recover her breath. I felt a wave of heat start in the pit of my stomach, washing up my body and over my face.

I put the gun down on the dining table overhead and switched the knife to my right hand.

I took all from him that I wanted.

# 6

# COMPANIONS

## Amanda

"I have some land up in Wyoming," Billy said as we loaded the last of the supplies into the truck. "Jake and I were heading up that way. There's more than enough room for two more."

"Oh?" I said. "How much land are we talking about?" I reached my right hand down to feel the butt of my recovered rifle, which Billy had informed me was an M16A4. It was becoming a real habit; I had to keep convincing myself it was still there even though I could clearly feel the weight of it on my shoulder.

"Around one-hundred-and-fifty acres," he said, "but that doesn't matter so much anymore, I guess. Land just goes for as long as you need it to, these days."

"Uh huh. And if I say 'no'?"

Billy looked at me out of the side of his eyes, sighed, and lifted a plastic crate full of water jugs into the bed of Jake's truck, the available space of which was rapidly diminishing. "Look," he began, turning to face me as he leaned against the truck, "no one is going to force you to go anywhere. I certainly don't want you around if you don't want to be around. Be too much like having my ex-wife back." He shuddered and lumbered off to grab something else to load.

Despite my urge to smile at his antics, I called behind him with a steady voice, "So if I decide to take Lizzy and just go, that's it, huh?"

"No," Jake's voice materialized from behind me. I jumped about a foot and spun around, heart hammering in my chest. I know there are some things that I've done that aren't so pretty and some of them I'm not exactly proud of, but Jake used to scare the hell out of me in those early days. It seems like he's loosened up a little by now, but when I first met him, it was like nothing was going on behind his eyes. I felt like I was dealing with some kind of robot instead of a person. He rarely talked and spent a lot of time inside his own head. He'd sneak up on you without trying to sneak up on you. His natural, unconscious state was that of someone who appeared where you didn't expect him. He was even grimmer at this instant, with blood still seeping from his nose and both eyes beginning to blacken angrily. Billy had done his best to set Jake's bridge back in place a while ago, which had produced an outraged howl. Even so, it always had a flattened, mashed in appearance. He's often indicated troubles breathing for as long as I've known him.

"Sorry," he said as I took a step back and muttered something like "It's fine."

"Anyway, no, that's not 'it' if you decide to go. We'll stay long enough to get you set up with a vehicle and outfitted with supplies. Or we'll leave if you don't want our help. It's up to you."

"I really advise against that, Little Sis," Billy said from behind me. "Maybe you and your girl find a space where you can carve a spot out for yourselves, maybe not. Maybe you find some other people. But maybe the wrong people find you. Again."

I hadn't told them that it was actually me who had flagged down James and his crew; I couldn't bring myself to admit that at the time.

"But there's strength in numbers, Amanda. We can watch each other's backs. We can accomplish different tasks, practice complementary skill sets."

What he was saying made good sense, of course. We weren't doing very well at all when we were on our own before. We had run completely dry on water, and I wasn't finding any more in all of the places I knew. I began to wonder just how deep in we were, how much there was that we needed to learn to survive. Ancient cultures used to live off the land and thrive but as our knowledge had become more specialized and focused in the modern age, we had lost that entire accumulated general competency. I could figure out how to launch my own web blog in about an hour or set up a brand new TV, but I didn't know the first thing about growing a tomato or how water could be made safe to drink.

I began to think about how much we'd lost and how much there was to do; how far we had to go to make up the ground that had been lost in just a few short months. I was beginning to realize that there really was no going back. The government wasn't going to come in and save us, there were no work crews banging away on the grid to get the power turned back on, there was simply nothing left. As far as I could tell, nearly everyone had died off, and those who had managed to survive through dumb luck didn't know enough about how everything worked to turn the lights back on. If you had someone who knew how to write software, for example, you didn't have anyone who knew how to build the circuit boards and components to run the software. If you had someone who could build those components, you didn't have the people who knew how to run the facilities to make those components. Even if you could find those people, you certainly weren't going to find anyone who knew how to process the raw materials found in nature to make things like silicon boards, conductors, resistors, or any of the rest of it.

Our whole society had evolved to a point where it couldn't possibly function or produce *literally anything* unless all of the workers involved in the entire supply chain, from digging material out of the Earth to putting wrapped packages on shelves, specialized in a microscopic portion of that entire process. Our world was such that manufacturing a single shoelace required an infrastructure and support network of thousands of people and interlocking parts all playing together nicely, all knowing their unique little piece of the puzzle and ignoring the details in any process not related directly to their own. We thrived through the process of extreme micro delegation.

And then the Plague came along and wiped out nearly all of the people who played a part in every process imaginable. As a species, we were back to digging insects out of the dirt with sticks.

Or, at least, we would be just as soon as all the "stuff" ran out. Everything we had—every item we scavenged; that was the last of that item that would ever be manufactured. Once exhausted, there was one less of that widget in the universe, never to be replaced. Any kind of comfort we could derive had an expiration date, and that date was imminent.

Contemplating this, I felt utterly defeated. Finally, I said, "To what end? What would be the point, honestly?"

As an answer, Billy pointed over at Elizabeth, who was sitting quietly in a chair by herself and sipping from a bottle of water. "Life," he said, simply. "To rebuild. To thrive." He took a long drink of water himself. "Look, I get that the universe doesn't exactly give a damn about what happens and that this year has proven to be one elaborate illustration of that fact, but honestly? We're still here. This was supposed to be our mass extinction event just like the dinosaurs had all those millions of years ago. We should all be dead and gone now, but some of us aren't. I believe that means something. I know I'm certainly not ready to go yet. There's more life to be had for those of us with the resolve to just… *try*."

I looked at Lizzy and knew he was right. Even so, I thought of what lay ahead in the coming years and felt exhausted just to contemplate it all. "There's so much to do," I said.

"Don't think about it all at once," Billy said. "If you do that, you'll never get anything done; you'll just freeze in place. Just think about the next thing you have to do. There's always one more thing that needs to be fixed. One more problem to be solved. I can think of a few right now."

"Such as?" I asked.

"Well, we gotta solve getting that damned truck loaded up," he said, waving in the general direction of the Dodge. The poor guy was looking pretty well spent. I walked up next to him and grabbed a duffel bag that we had stuffed full of dried goods, canned food, and the few remaining MREs. I grabbed it, hauled it over to the truck bed, and stashed it among the plastic bins and other items.

I turned and looked back at him. "What next?"

He was smiling at me. "Load up the rest of this here, I guess, and I'll go through the site and see if we forgot anything."

"Stay out of the rear camper," I advised. I had left things badly in there.

He had frozen halfway to standing up. "Hadn't planned on looking there. Nothing in there anyone needs." He straightened up with a groan and walked off.

I turned back and saw Jake, who was also watching Billy make his way toward the leading RV. He stood there thinking his own hidden thoughts.

"What about you?" I asked. "You're going to Wyoming to start over, too?"

"Billy helped me to get somewhere. Stayed with me when he didn't have to. When he maybe shouldn't have. I'm going to help him get to Wyoming."

"You're not staying once we get there?"

"We?" he asked. He gave me what passed for a Jake smile: slightly raised eyebrows. "You've decided you'll join us, then?"

"Don't deflect. You won't stay?"

He became very quiet and still. Just when I thought he wouldn't say anything at all, he finally answered. "Hadn't thought about it. I'm only thinking as far ahead as the next problem, see?"

We finished loading up the truck and made ready to depart right around sunset. We weren't planning on going very far, but we all agreed that spending the night by the motorhomes was out of the question; we didn't even have to discuss it.

"Why don't you guys ride in the truck with Jake, huh?" Billy said. "There're only the two seats in the van, and I can't imagine you want to be apart from your daughter. Truck has a quad cab. Nice and roomy."

"Umm, okay…" I said, not excited about riding with Jake. Rather than saying anything, Jake just nodded and walked to the driver side of the truck. He got in, shut the door, and then sat there facing forward. Waiting.

"You sure you don't feel like driving the truck?" I asked, looking over at the back of Jake's head.

"Well… uh, you see, the truck has a manual tranny," Billy grinned sheepishly. "Never learned." He shrugged and made his way to the van.

"Of course," I sighed. "C'mon, Mija. Let's hit it." Lizzy jumped into the back of the truck, and I climbed into the front passenger's side. As I was situating myself and arranging the seat belt, Jake reached up and turned on the dome light.

"Elizabeth, if you look around back there you should see a back-pack. Look around in it; you may find some books that you like."

There came the sound of rummaging in the back. I looked back at her and saw her pulling several small books out of a bag. Craning my neck further, I saw titles like Junie B. Jones, Olivia, Charlotte's Web, and the like. "Some of those are pretty good," he said. "You may enjoy them."

Lizzy reached forward into the front seat and actually patted him on the shoulder, which floored me. "Thank you, Jake," she said in a tiny voice.

"Welcome," he replied. He turned off the front dome light and then reached back and turned hers on for her. "You go ahead and leave the light on. Doesn't bother me."

"Where…" I struggled to find words. "Where did you get a bunch of kid's books?"

"Picked them up a few towns back." He glanced in my direction; looked back out the front windshield. He started up the engine, put it into first, and gave a short rap on the horn to let Billy know he was ready to go.

"Jake."

"Yeah?"

"Thank you, Jake."

He shifted into second as we got onto the road.

"Welcome."

---

When we finally stopped for the night, it was only a little further up the 15. Billy found a spot that he liked the look of and pulled off the road. He led us away for a good distance; less than a mile but far enough that anyone passing by would miss us in the dark. The men both had their own tents that they set up outside. When Jake was finished with his, he came back to the truck and offered to let us take it. Sleeping out in a tent felt a little too exposed for me so I thanked him but said we'd stay in the truck. I would get over this inhibition later on, certainly, but at this point, I wasn't very long out of civilization.

The next morning when I woke up, it took me several moments to remember that we weren't with James or his gang anymore. I'm struggling to find the words to describe what this was like; when you're in a situation like that, you don't awake every morning in a terrified state. No matter what kind of situation you're in, you only have so much energy. Being terrified takes a lot of energy, so you don't stay in that state indefinitely. Eventually, you wear out. You simply get too exhausted to be scared. The state that you go to after you wear yourself out being scared is the state that I woke up in every morning. Exhausted, numb, impending sense of doom, hopelessness. You walk around on eggshells all day feeling this way. If someone close by moves too quickly, the deadened feelings flare up inside you instantly into a kind of electric panic but then subside back to the low thrum quickly if nothing actually happens.

Waking up in that truck was like a shock of cold water. The absence of danger was as shocking and electrifying to me that morning as any present danger I'd encountered previously.

I lifted the back of my seat out of a reclined position, stretched my neck a bit, and looked in the back seat.

I came up off the seat and must have rotated in midair because I came back down on my knees facing the rear of the cab. Elizabeth was gone. I grabbed my rifle and slammed into the passenger side door trying to open it. I had to fumble with the handle before I could operate it properly. I finally got the door opened and jumped out of the truck. I was barefoot. I remember the rocks on the ground hurt and that I didn't care.

I ran around the front of the truck and stopped immediately when I saw Elizabeth, Billy, and Jake sitting around a smoking campfire. All three of them turned to look at me, all wearing the same wide-eyed, confused expression.

"Mom?" Lizzy asked.

I felt a sharp throbbing pain in my right hand along the ring finger. I lifted it up to look at it and saw an angry, white crease along the back of the nail. I must have folded it back when I was fighting with the door handle.

Billy came over with a wool-lined denim jacket and offered it to me. "Put some shoes on," he suggested. "It's chilly out this morning."

I was distracted then by an incredibly savory smell coming from the fire. "Oh... oh my God," I said. "What do I smell? What is that?" The smell was making me salivate; it was so good that I had forgotten to be pissed at Lizzy for scaring me half to death.

"Sausage!" Billy said in his best homemaker voice.

"Sausage? Where did you find sausage??"

"Freeze-dried sausage!!"

I only stood there, alternating my gaze between him and the fire. I think he actually shocked me stupid.

His shoulders slumped a little, and he finally said, "Look, go put some shoes on. You're going to hurt yourself." He returned to his spot at the fire. "I have some coffee brewed up. We'll save some for you when you get back."

"You have... coffee?"

"Well, we have it for now," he said. "We'll run out at some point, of course. That doesn't mean we have to live like a bunch of savages right now, though, does it?"

I didn't even bother to tie my shoes. I just pulled them on and rushed back to the fire. Lizzy was opening up a chair for me to sit in, humming to herself and chewing at the same time. I had just finished pulling on the jacket when a metal plate was thrust in front of me with a little pile of crumbled sausage and some crackers. "I've got a fork or something here in the Kitchen bin," Billy muttered, digging in a plastic container. He turned back to me to hold out a fork and saw that my plate was empty. He stared at the empty plate and then looked up at me. "More?"

"Yes, please," I said through a mouthful. I wiped my eyes, which were watering because my tongue was stinging from where I had bit it when James attacked me.

He took the plate and offered me a cup filled with black coffee. "Sorry," he said, "I don't have any creamer or sugar."

"I don't care, this is amazing," I said and meant it. I never would have done black coffee once upon a time, but the smell of this stuff alone perked me up. I felt a panicked urge to gulp it down and had to restrain myself from burning my mouth. Thinking of this, I felt an unhappy twinge in my bladder. I handed the cup back to Billy. "I have to go take care of some business," I said.

"Yes, ma'am," Billy said, taking the cup back. "Bushes and such over there," he gestured to a thick patch on the other side of the trucks.

When I came back to my spot by the fire there was another plate of food and my coffee, now cooled down a bit. I dug in, going slower now and taking the time to savor it.

"Be a nice day today," said Billy happily. "Clear sky. Beautiful weather."

"What's the plan?" I asked.

"We were discussing that before you woke up," Jake said.

"We're going shopping for a new car, Mom," Lizzy interrupted.

"New car?"

"Yeah, it's probably a good idea to find you a vehicle," Billy said. "We need to get you started on gear and supplies and the truck and van are just about filled to capacity carrying all of Jake's and my crap to begin with. If we find something really good, we might could hook up some kind of trailer to whatever we get you. There was no ball hitch on either of ours."

"What about gas?" I asked.

"No worries. We have ways."

I thought about all that for a minute. Something about taking the extra time to locate a suitable vehicle, fuel it (however that was done), and load it full of supplies that had yet to be acquired seemed off to me.

"How far is your place from here, Billy? How long will it take to get there?"

"Well, the town I'm closest to is Jackson. From here I'm guessing that's about a ten-hour drive? Maybe less—but that was how long it took before. Who knows what road conditions are on the way? I suppose we'll either get there tomorrow or the next day."

"And how are we set for food and water?"

Billy nodded. He was probably beginning to understand my train of thought. "Before when it was just Jake and I, we could have probably stretched out what we had for a week, assuming we minimized physical activity. Now that you've joined us, we're down to maybe half of that, depending. I'm not sure how much Elizabeth eats—maybe not too much at all—but you just murdered enough canned pork to put your face on The Little Pig's community watch list, so…"

I burst out laughing, surprising myself and everyone else around the fire. It was a peaceful morning, interrupted suddenly by my cackling. I couldn't help myself. I had gone so, so long without laughing and it just felt so good to do it. All of the tension and the fear, the anger, resentment, the despair, and hate; every bit of poison that had been building inside of me ever since that first day when the lights went out broke loose and poured out from me like a flood. It was a vomiting forth of raw, pent-up emotion. I tried to tamp it all back down and control myself, but the mental image of my face on a "Have you seen this woman?" poster got me going again in fresh peels of chortling.

It was worse when I tried to look up at the rest of them. Lizzy was laughing along with me, not understanding what was funny but infected by my behavior even so. Billy had a ridiculously goofy grin on his face (which is about as close as I ever saw him come to laughing;

he would joke with us constantly, but his delivery was always straight and deadpan). I then looked over to Jake and lost any remaining reserve of control that was left to me. His look of mild confusion sent me right over the edge.

Before I understood what was happening, I felt a hand on my back rubbing gently along the length of my spine, and there was another, much larger hand resting on my shoulder. I realized Lizzy was standing next to me saying, "Mom? Mom, what is it?" and Billy was soothing her, telling her, "It's okay, Girly. This was gonna happen at some point. It just had to shake loose and work its way out. This is normal. She'll be okay."

I realized I was sobbing uncontrollably and rocking in my chair. Billy was down on one knee next to me with his arm around my shoulder. He stayed like that with me until the worst of it was passed, reaching out every so often to squeeze Elizabeth's hand.

"What the hell?" I said after things had calmed down a bit. "I wasn't even feeling sad. I don't know where that came from."

"It's fine," said Billy. "It turns out the part of you that makes you laugh lives right next to the part of you that makes you cry. All that stuff is controlled by the same buttons. You just went through a hell of a thing. You gotta give yourself some time; this will happen every so often. You'll have to let it work its way out of your system."

I looked up; saw an empty chair in front of me across the fire. "What happened to Jake?" I asked. Billy was heaving himself up off the ground to settle back into his seat.

Some paper towels materialized just to the right of my face from behind me, and I jumped. "Jesus-FUCK, hijole!" I yelped.

"Mom!"

"Sorry, Mija. Sorry."

"Pardon..." Jake said as he walked back to his chair.

"So getting back to the point," I continued as I wiped my eyes and blew my nose, "call it three days' worth of food from this point and three days' worth of driving. Would it not make sense to just push through with what we have right now and get where we're going?"

"You have a valid point," Billy said. "I've been thinking about this myself. I guess it's not a bad idea if we all just discuss it right now and agree on it. What I was thinking was this…" He held up his hand and started extending fingers as he talked, beginning with the thumb and working his way down, as he listed off points. "This is the Spring/Summer period right now. It's been, what, three months? Four months? Since everything really went south? So that means Northern Utah and the great state of Wyoming has just been through a winter period. We don't know what the state of the roads is or even if any road crews had begun repair work before it all went to hell. California and Nevada were more or less okay because they don't get a lot of rain to begin with but, the further North we go from here, the nastier it's going to get, I think."

"That's a good point," Jake agreed. "Roads fall apart a lot faster than anyone realizes. You have to constantly be repairing them."

"Yap. Give it a year. You won't be able to get anywhere far without four-wheel drive. This brings me to the point. The Dodge can handle some mild off-roading if it comes to it." He pointed over at the van. "I don't know about that Transit. It's long, looks kind of top heavy, and is close to the ground. I don't think the path can get very rough before we have to abandon it."

I saw Jake give Billy a pointed look in response to his statement. Billy nodded and sent a calming "it's cool" gesture back his way.

"If that happens, we won't be able to haul everything we have plus ourselves. The truck bed is already overloaded as it is."

He eased back into his chair and took a sip of coffee. "We prepper types have a saying that we ripped off from the military: Two is one, and one is none. So, applying that math to our situation, we really only have one vehicle. I'd like to have two—what you would call three. I don't want to leave anything behind and I sure as hell don't want to find myself hoofing it again."

"On top of that, we have time, guys. My place isn't going anywhere. It'll be waiting for us whether we get there three days from now or one week from now. It won't hurt to take it a little slow and collect things as we go." He took another sip. He had given up on tracking points with extended fingers by now; I think he preferred to keep them wrapped around the warm coffee cup in the cold morning air instead of extended out in space.

"The more supplies we have when we get there, the better we'll be as well. We'll be able to take a few days to settle in before we have to head out again."

"Head out why?" Jake asked. I was curious as well.

"We're going to have to go out and get everything we can get our hands on," Billy said. "Everything. None of the things we rely on to live are being manufactured anymore. At some period, all of this stuff that we need is going to run out. Maybe not for a year or two but it is coming. We need to get as much of it as we can to our home base like apocalyptic squirrels. This will buy us the time we need to develop a more permanent situation. The main thing will be food; living on a subsistence basis. There's definitely enough land to support us, even if we start cultivating livestock. The main thing is that we have to get it planted and producing enough so that we can wean ourselves off all the manufactured shit. Oh... excuse me, Girly."

"That's alright," Lizzy said. "Mostly, I just don't like the F-word."

"What? Flapjacks?"

Lizzy giggled.

"So, yeah," Billy continued without missing a beat, "it's like the man said: 'the best time to plant a tree was twenty years ago and the second best time is right now.'"

There was a bit more chit-chat after that, but we had all come over to Billy's way of thinking. Wyoming wasn't going anywhere within the next few days. Additionally, I have to admit I was a little excited about getting a new vehicle. I guess that, by definition, whatever we found would end up being "used," but any car I had ever owned in my life up to that point had been at least an eight-year-old beater. This was probably going to be my one chance to own a relatively new car or truck (or whatever) and drive it before all the fuel expired. Who knew when humanity would figure out how to start refining gasoline again?

I leaned back in my chair and sipped on my own coffee while Billy and Jake planned out the first place we would stop over an old, dog-eared Thomas Guide. Sunrise over Utah was just at an end; that in-between point where the clouds stop being dark-blue and pink and start being dark-blue and white. The sun was up over the East looking out at a red desert shot through with vast expanses of muted green sagebrush and the more vibrant green of the defiant juniper trees holding themselves overall. The clouds in the sky were stretched into the distance for miles in long, fat ropes made hazy at the edges, as though they had been pulled across from one horizon to the other by God. I will remember the look of that morning for the rest of my life. It was a morning on which I was free after a time when I thought I would never be free again. Elizabeth sat next to me and held my hand (she would still hold my hand at that age), and I thought of how much I loved and missed my husband. The only thing that could have made that morning any more sacred to me is if he had been there to share it with us.

———

The main guideline we set for ourselves was to never go backward or deviate too far from the main path. It was north of St. George that we had met up, so the next big location on the map along the 15 was Cedar City (the real one this time, not the tent city). I was relatively familiar with the area so our idea was that no matter who was going out looking for a third vehicle, I would be going along with that person filling in as a local guide/navigator. There was no way that I was allowing Elizabeth to come into the city with me (just based on past experience alone) so we would swing out left on the outskirts of the city itself and take the Cross Hollow Road up and around the densest area; we assumed that the 15 would be slammed with traffic once we got to the city's edge and all but impassable as it made its way through the center of Cedar City. At or about the point that we hit the airport, we would set up a staging area as a base.

When it was clear that Elizabeth was staying with the vehicles on my order (something she grumbled about quite a bit), it became apparent that someone would have to stay behind with her. Jake volunteered for this, which made me nervous at first. He did not strike me as a bad or evil person, not like the others I'd run into, but he still scared me. He struck me as a dangerous person. It was him, after all, who had put the knife and gun into my hand and effectively absolved me of any social guilt within the group for what I might do to James. Then again, it occurred to me that I had taken Jake up on his offer; opting for the knife in the end and using it slowly (thankful that Jake had so effectively gagged him—I learned later that he had taken Lizzy several yards away as soon as he left the trailer to ensure she couldn't hear). Thinking about this, I realized that I was actually confirmed to be every bit as dangerous, if not more dangerous, than Jake. It was this knowledge plus the fact that he hadn't known of Elizabeth's existence when he came to help me that informed my decision to agree with the arrangement. To my surprise, Lizzy was totally fine with it as well.

As we approached the edge of Cedar City, we saw that the 15 was not as bad as we had imagined. We very well could have navigated our way in for at least a few miles and then gone off the main road if we found ourselves blocked. Even so, we held to our original plan and swung up Cross Hollow. Rolling down the middle of the city felt too exposed to all of us—as though we were just asking for trouble.

We pulled off the road just before the 56 and parked in the shade of a factory on the southeast corner, putting ourselves between the factory and the main area of the city. Jake said, "Let's get you outfitted," and got out of the truck. He started walking over to the rear of the van, where Billy already had the doors open.

"Wait here," I told Lizzy and got out to follow.

As I was just approaching the rear of the van, Billy was already slamming the doors shut and locking them. Jake came around with what appeared to be a very heavy black duffel bag slung over his shoulder. He settled it onto the ground between us, and I could see that it was large enough to hold a full-grown man. On his other arm, he had a couple of black vests. He held one of them up to me, tsked, and shook his head.

"This might still be too big for you. This is really a shame. It never occurred to us to look for feminine-sized armor."

"We'll keep an eye out in the future," Billy said. "I think we can make that work on her. We may just have to duct tape it instead of using the Velcro."

"What is this?" I asked.

"Ballistic armor!" Billy said, happily. "Good stuff. Probably not good for high-powered rifle rounds but it'll stop handguns and knives."

"It's the same stuff I was wearing when what's-his-name shot me," Jake said as he squatted down and unzipped the duffel. He reached inside and pulled out a rifle the likes of which I had never seen before. It looked like a space gun from a science fiction movie; I felt as though I had seen Sigourney Weaver use one to blow the face off an alien at some point. Impressive didn't convey half of what I felt when looking at this thing. What first struck me when I saw it (the thing I appreciated the most, really) was how small it was. The rifle from before that I had been lugging around always felt big for me. I had never shot a rifle in my life before all of this started, and a long rifle like that M16 just felt clumsy in my hands. The kick wasn't that bad; I just couldn't keep it steady.

This new thing that Jake was holding out to me was easily half the length of the M16.

"What on Earth is this?" I asked as I took it from him.

Billy answered. "That is an Israeli-made IWI Tavor X95 bullpup rifle. The Israelis were using the earlier variant of this in their military; the X95 was just starting to get some real popularity here in the states when everything fell apart. You didn't see a lot of them around because they were so damned expensive and a lot of people hate on bullpups. Even so, these things are great for tighter control and close quarters."

I looked over the top of the gun. There was a little window mounted on top. When I looked through it, I could just see a red dot that moved around on the screen as I shifted my gaze around from side to side.

"That's a red dot optic," Jake offered. "I don't really know how to set them up, but Billy managed to get it zeroed at about a hundred yards. We played around with this thing for a few hours after we picked it up. This was shortly before we found you."

"They're really cool," Billy added. "You don't have to get the gun lined up with your target the way you would if you had regular iron sights. If you can see the dot through that window and it's on your target, you'll hit your target. Even if the dot is way over to the edge of the window—if you can see it, that's where the bullet is going."

"Where in the actual hell did you find all this stuff?" I asked. They both became quiet at this question, going from excited twelve-year-olds to circumspect poker players instantaneously.

"Here and there," Billy finally said. "We got a bit lucky in Vegas."

Jake scoffed to himself and nodded.

Changing the subject, Billy said, "Look, I want you to put that vest on under your clothes, okay? Just go over there around the side of the building or something and pull it on. When you come back, I'll tighten it up with the tape if it needs it... your waist is pretty small, I'll just go get the tape now. Should probably put a flannel on you, too, to help hide the edges."

Handing the dangerous looking little rifle back to Jake and slinging the vest over my shoulder, I asked, "Why under the clothes? What does that matter?"

"Two reasons," Jake said. "First, Billy read about some shit-hit-the-fan situations in other third world countries once upon a time. It seems that people outfitted with the best gear tended to get ambushed by marauders far more often than guys just roaming around in jeans and sneakers with beat up backpacks. This included soldiers loaded up in tactical gear. The less savory of the world see all that fancy looking military stuff, and it doesn't deter them at all; it paints a big target for them that says, 'this person right here has way better equipment than you, and you should come take it.' It's counterintuitive, but the truly bad people of the world tend not to be intimidated by the sight of GI Joe, especially when those bad people are moving in numbers."

"What's the other reason?" I asked.

Jake cleared his throat. "Yeah. Well, if you have to get shot, we want them to shoot you in the vest where you're protected. If they see you wearing a vest, they'll shoot you somewhere else, like the head. So, just hide the vest."

His words had a sobering effect. I walked off to find a relatively private place to put the gear on.

It turned out that it was a little loose after all. Billy got down on his knees in front of me while I lifted my shirt up to my ribs; high enough for him to wrap the sides down tight with duct tape. I felt the shoulders bunching up slightly around my neck when he finished, but the fit was still much better now than when I first put the vest on. I was amazed at how light it was. I was assured that the heavy duty stuff was not as comfortable.

The Tavor was handed back to me, this time with a sling attached to a little swivel at the back, which Billy helped me to pull over my head and adjust the length. He had me shoulder the rifle a few times to ensure that it was all comfortable and that I could get a good view through the optic. He left to rummage around in his baggage for a flannel shirt.

As he did that, Jake moved in front of me and undid my belt without warning. I felt my heart slam in my chest, and my sudden rush of indrawn breath stopped him.

His hands instantly dropped to his sides, leaving each end of my belt to dangle, and he said, "I'm sorry. I wasn't thinking."

I took a deep breath and got my heart under control. "That's okay, I'm sorry too. I know you didn't mean anything. What were you doing?"

He dug through the duffel bag and pulled out a hard plastic pouch about as big as my two fists held together. "For your magazines. This will hold four twenty-rounders. We'll hang this off your belt on your left hip. It should be natural for you to reach down with your left hand for a magazine change if it becomes necessary."

"Got it," I said. "Look, again, I'm really sorry about freaking out. Will you help me to get it on?"

He nodded, not meeting my eye. His face was bright red. His hand reached out and pulled the belt out of the first two loops of my jeans. He threaded the belt through the pouch and then ran the belt back to its original position, taking great care not to come into contact with my body.

"You can cinch that back up," he said.

"Hey, you're okay," I said. "We're good."

"Yeah," he grunted. He went back to the truck to peek at Lizzy and make sure she was alright. He opened the door and started talking quietly to her.

"Here we go," Billy said as he came back. He was holding out what looked like the world's oldest and most comfortable flannel by the shoulders for me to slide into. "That looks pretty good," he said as he circled around me. "Just let that rifle dangle on the sling. Yeah, perfect." He pulled out four magazines and jammed them into the pouches on my hip.

"Okay, reach back there and grab one of those."

I did as he asked, noting how hard I had to pull to get it loose. They wouldn't come bouncing out if I had to run, at least.

"Okay, shoulder the rifle... good. When you reload, you're going to continue holding the grip with your right hand just like you are now. You'll insert the magazine with your left hand like so..." He guided my hand into position and showed me what it felt like to set the magazine home. "Good. Now you'll use your left hand to charge the weapon by pulling that operating lever there on the side."

I reached up and did so.

"Okay, good deal," he said, "but now you're set to pop. You need to be aware of what's happening with your muzzle at all times, okay? Wherever you have that thing pointed, what's on the other end will have a really bad day. Pointing down at the ground isn't enough. If I'm standing in front of you and the rifle goes off, the ricochet from the ground will still bounce into me and kill me, got it? Always point in a safe direction."

"Got it."

"In fact," he continued, appraising me, "you just stay in front of me when we're out on foot, got it? I want to watch you a bit before I let you get behind me."

"That's probably the right idea," I agreed. I didn't want to shoot him in the back any more than he wanted to get shot in the back.

"The safety operates just like the one on your M16… you do know how that works, right?"

"I do," I told him and showed him with my thumb.

"Well, that's at least one-up you have on Jake," he mumbled. "Okay, moving on—you eject your magazine with your index finger; just press this button on the side of the guard. Go ahead and do it now."

I did, and the magazine dropped all the way out of the gun and bounced in the dirt.

"That's how you do it," he said. "Don't reach up to grab it when it comes out. Don't bend over to pick it up if you're in a firefight. Just let it fall out on the ground, slap another one in there, and press this little button back here under the stock with your left thumb, understand? We can always come back and collect magazines after any fighting is over."

"Wait," I interrupted, "so I pull the lever when I put a magazine in, or I press this button back here?"

Billy nodded. "I get you. It depends on the position of the bolt when you put the magazine in. He rolled the gun over while I held it so I could look at its side. "See that window there? You see how you can't really look inside there?"

I nodded.

"Okay, watch…" he said and pulled the charging handle back. When he did, a bullet dropped out onto the ground. "See how it's open now? If you've shot the gun dry, that little window will be wedged open. This thing here," he indicated a hunk of metal deep inside the opening, "is basically the bolt, which blocks another bullet's entry to the chamber when it's closed. If the bolt is closed when you load in a new magazine, the top of that magazine slams into it and there's no way for a bullet to get chambered, so you have to pull that handle to open the bolt and get a bullet into the pipe."

It started to make sense. "I see. So if the bolt is open when I've finished a magazine, I don't have to open it again."

"That's right," Billy said. He put the dropped bullet back into the magazine and stuck the magazine back in my gun. "Okay, run it."

"Huh?"

"Point at some spot out in the distance and shoot that mag empty."

"Aren't you worried about attracting attention?" I asked.

"Not as worried as I am about getting jumped with a partner who has never fired her weapon. Honestly, we're pushing the bounds of sensibility as it is. You'd be spending several hours getting comfortable with that thing if this was a perfect world. Now go ahead. Run it."

I pulled the handle and aimed. I pulled the trigger. Nothing happened.

"Safety…"

"Yep, sorry," I said. I flipped the safety lever down, aimed, and pulled the trigger. I want to say that the gun didn't fire so much as it sneezed; a short little jerk up against my shoulder. From the looks of it and the thickness of its stock, I was expecting it to slam into me, but that wasn't the case at all. A light, refined little jerk was all it gave me. The sound, on the other hand…

"That's really loud," I said, massaging my ear.

"I know, we'll see if we can find you ear plugs somewhere," Billy agreed. "As for the kick, it was the first one of its kind I had encountered when I shot it too. 5.56 isn't exactly a hard kicking round, to begin with, but I was amazed at how manageable it is with this gun. It's why I'm giving it to you: small, easy to lug, easy to fire—it all makes up for how awkward it is to load. Okay, go ahead and keep shooting and when you do, I want you to focus on squeezing the trigger down until it starts to resist your finger and then take the shot."

I did as he advised and shot the magazine empty. As soon as I was finished, Billy was beginning to tell me what I should do next. Instead of waiting for him, I released the magazine, yanked another one off my hip, slapped it in place, and reached back to hit the release button. It all felt relatively smooth until I had to find that button; I searched around for it a little with my thumb before I got it.

"Not bad, Little Sis," he said. "Now put the safety on that thing before you end up shooting my favorite Indian," he said as he bent over to get the dropped magazine. While he was down there, he pulled another full magazine out of the duffel and handed it up to me. I stuck it into my hip pouch.

"What else is in that bag?" I asked, squatting next to him.

"A few extra goodies, just in case," Billy said and spread it open for me. It was loaded full of gear—I could see at least three rifles, several magazines of various size and shape running around loose, and what appeared to be enough boxes of shotgun rounds to choke an elephant.

"Wow," I whispered. "You're carrying an arsenal around."

"This is just a small piece of it," he said. "There's more in the van. I told you, we did really well in Vegas."

"What, did you guys raid a police station?"

"Naw, those were the first places to get picked over. There was a low-key shipping warehouse that I knew of out there; I used to buy a lot of goodies from the company online and noticed that the stuff was always coming to me from Vegas. When the world went to hell, I started looking for supplies in the obvious places like your Walmarts, outdoor stores, and the like. Those places were all picked clean because everyone knew that stuff was there. I figured very few people would know about a nondescript shipping warehouse. Turns out I was right." He smiled, eyes twinkling.

"I'm going to get geared up," Billy said. "Go grab yourself a backpack; throw some food and some waters in it."

I walked over to the truck, experimenting with the rifle as I went. I noticed that I could just let it hang from the sling, which was fairly comfortable, but the barrel still bounced off my legs as I walked. I grabbed the grip with my right hand to steady it and point the barrel off at an angle to my left, and the problem went away. I suddenly understood why the soldiers I had seen in the footage from the Middle East all seemed to have the exact same stance and posture with their rifles. I feel silly saying this (I never went through one-tenth the training that those people did, not even now with the benefit of Gibs's drills) but I felt a connection to them at that moment. It occurred to me that this new world was something to which people like me would quickly have to adapt or die. For those men and women who had done tours in Iraq and Afghanistan, this would just be like any other day. If they had survived the plague, I imagined they would be doing just fine right now.

As I began to move items around in the truck bed, Lizzy got out of the cab. She walked by shooting me an angry look as she went, and approached Billy. She spoke to him, her voice sometimes rising, and he nodded to her the whole time.

I hung my head into the truck to look across the seat at Jake. "What was that?"

"She's mad at you for going into town. She thinks you should stay here where it's safe. I imagine she's explaining to Billy that there will be hell to pay if he doesn't keep both eyes on you."

I looked back over to her and Billy, who was now squatted down in front of her and talking quietly. "Crap," I said. "I'd better go deal with that."

"This is really none of my business," he said, "but she's probably too angry to hear you right now. Might as well wait until you come back, so you have the proof of your results to back your position."

"You're right, it is none of your business," I said. He nodded and looked off toward the city. "But you're also right about her, as well. I'll follow your advice on this one."

He nodded again, without looking back at me.

Billy approached as I finished loading my backpack. He had his own backpack as well as a couple of belts full of different colored shotgun shells crisscrossed over his chest and under his survival jacket. His shotgun hung from a sling on his shoulder. A pistol was strapped to his belt on a holster.

"You look like less-thin Poncho Villa," I told him, smiling.

"Watch it, Little Sis. You're talking about the man I love."

He heaved the heavy duffel bag up into the truck bed and then walked around to the driver's side of the truck and got in. "You ready?"

I stood there for a moment, trying to process what I was seeing. "Never learned," he had said. I stared at him, unmoving.

"Amanda?" he prompted.

I shook my head and climbed in beside him. Before I could say anything, Jake came to the driver's side window and said, "Billy, keep your eyes open for a chess set, okay?"

"A… chess—what the hell for?" asked Billy.

"I told Elizabeth I'd teach her to play if we could find one. She's read most of the books I found, it turns out."

# 7

# CAR SHOPPING

## Amanda

Billy drove away from our staging area due east toward a gentle rise of hills about a hundred yards away, over which the roofs of a housing tract were just visible. The ground was fairly gentle, and we could see a dirt road out in front of us that angled straight for the homes but Billy took his time, creeping along at an easy pace. I watched as he worked the stick and clutch effortlessly.

"So..." I said.

"So?"

"So, you never learned to drive a manual?"

He grimaced, and his left hand momentarily squeezed the top of the wheel where it had been resting loosely a moment before.

"Forgot about that," he said.

"You want to explain why you were bullshitting me? You get one chance to do this right."

He pulled a sigh all the way up from his stomach. "Let me ask you: what do you think of Jake?"

I was so surprised by his question that my eyebrows rose all the way up my forehead. "You're playing Apocalypse Match Maker, now?"

"No, no. Don't look at it like that. I'm being serious here. Just as one person to another, what's your impression of Jake?"

I gave the question due thought because it was obvious to me now that this was bothering Billy. I had the impression that not much bothered him. "He scares me. Or, he scared me at first. Not so much now—I mean, I trust him alone with Lizzy, right? He does make me nervous, though. I can't get a read on him. It's like he doesn't feel a particular way about anything at all."

Billy nodded. "Exactly. Now I'll tell *you* something about Jake. I haven't really known him that long, and we'll just say that he's always been the private type, but he was different when I found him, all the same."

"Different how?"

"Easier going. He was never what I would describe as chatty, but he spoke with me more than he does now. We weren't trading jokes back and forth or cracking each other up. Actually, I don't know that I've ever heard the guy laugh. But he was communicative. Responsive."

"Jake??" I asked. I couldn't picture it.

"Yap," he confirmed. "Listen, we all *lost* when the world fell apart, right? I know I lost people I cared about, you did too. I don't know anything really about the kind of life Jake had before; who he knew, if there was anyone special or the like. I do know that whatever loss he suffered, it hit him hard. If I had to put money on it, I'd bet on you being the emotionally stronger of the two."

"How can that be?" I asked. "It's like he doesn't have any emotion at all."

"He does. I was with him when he found some of his people from before…what was left of them."

"What happened?"

"Not my place to say," he sighed. "What I think I *can* tell you is that Jake is trying very hard to be someone who doesn't need people around him. The problem with that is no matter how hard a fish tries, it simply can't be a bird, as the man says."

"You think Jake needs people to be happy?"

"I think Jake needs people to *function*," Billy emphasized. "As far as I can tell, he doesn't give much thought to his own welfare or safety. It's like he has to have someone to live for or he just...drifts. Perfect example: after—well, just after, the best I could get him to agree to was to just come with me to Wyoming and see the place. I got the impression the only reason he agreed to come was to see that I arrived safe. I told him to stay with me but who knows what the hell he's planning on doing when we get there? I'm fairly sure he plans on getting me to the front door and then just disappearing somewhere."

"Okay, I get it," I finally said. "You're putting me and Lizzy out in front of him as a kind of anchor... or something. You could have told me."

Billy glanced over at me with a "who the hell are you kidding?" look in his eyes. "You weren't exactly in a state where I felt like that was an option when we met."

This shut me up.

"Don't get me wrong. I can only imagine what you and the Girly went through at the hands of those sons-a-bitches—I don't want to know!" he exclaimed when I drew breath. "I didn't know what to expect out of either of you. I know I didn't expect you to be as functional as you both are so soon after you got out of there. I think you're tougher than Jake and I put together."

We drove on silently for a while, Billy weaving his way around the odd derelict car in the middle of the road, which had transitioned from dirt to pavement not long ago.

"Okay, so what now?" I asked. "Try to draw him out of his shell?"

"Nope. I think just let him keep hanging out with Lizzy. He's talked more with her in the last eighteen hours than he has with me in days. I don't know if there's anything else you or I could do."

I thought of how hard Jake had blushed when he fumbled at my belt and wondered.

We drove in silence for a while. The general idea was to cruise through residential areas in search of anything that looked like it could handle rough terrain and, if we turned up nothing useful, to move in closer to the 15 a little bit at a time and find more knots of traffic to try again. Billy was constantly rechecking our position against the Thomas Guide to ensure we maintained a good escape route, stopping in the middle of the street to do so. I had been through Cedar City in the past plenty of times but had stuck to the main drag for the most part; my local knowledge and usefulness as a guide increased as we came closer to the 15. Unfortunately, the 15 freeway was the major landmark Billy was doing his best to stay away from.

When we weren't threading our way around cars, we had to work our way through barricades and various abandoned checkpoints—those relics left behind by the now absent military. We attempted to get out and clear a way through the first time we came to one that was blocking our path but soon gave up. Outside of piles of sandbags, boxes, and mounds of garbage that had blown into the area and lodged on the various parts and pieces that made up the structure of the barricades, there was razor wire wrapped around everything. Between the two of us, the effort required to make one of these obstacles passable would have taken the majority of the day.

Cedar City itself appeared to be in much better shape than some of the other places I had seen both in person and on TV. It was almost a quaint vacation getaway when compared to parts of Salt Lake City, for example, which had seen wide-scale rioting toward the end before the inhabitants became too sick to engage in such activity.

There was the occasional burned out hulk of a building; however the fires themselves appeared to have been extinguished fairly quickly —only the immediate surrounding buildings were affected. It became obvious that, wherever property damage had occurred, the people who were still capable of doing something about it had rallied together to keep things from getting out of control. I can vividly recall looking down residential area streets as we crawled by that, in isolation, appeared to depict any normal American afternoon minus the people or activity. I experienced the unsettling illusion that I was looking at a staged model or a movie set. Witnessing those pockets of sane normalcy bookended by evidence of a dying people and the Army's best efforts to maintain control and public safety was profoundly depressing. To this day, two years later, such sights still impact me emotionally. The roads now are all cracked and overgrown with the fauna of the locale and those buildings that saw the most damage are just beginning to crumble under their own weight as nature takes back control of the land, but sometimes I'll see a lone barbeque sitting on a porch or a rusted tricycle left in the middle of the street. Such things can still make me cry.

We eventually turned onto 265th street off Casa Loma and reset our search, driving up and down the street looking at houses as we passed. The homes in this area were nice; not large palaces of the rich like you could sometimes run into without warning, but it was clear that these people lived the comfortable lives of the upper middle class. The construction of the homes themselves lacked any kind of pattern or sense of uniformity—it became clear to me that they were most likely all custom-built, following various styles and designs. With the exception of some of the trees, which tended to be evergreen, the landscaping was universally brown and dead throughout.

"This... looks pretty good," Billy said absently as we drove along. "Keep your eyes peeled. Some of these SUVs we're passing are okay but let's take our time and look for something special. We can always come back if we turn up nothing."

I would guess that we spent an hour or so weaving our way past houses and cul-de-sacs when something finally jumped out at me.

"Stop!" I said, patting the dashboard rapidly and craning my neck to look out my window. He complied, and I said, "Back up a bit, please. I think we're in business."

He rolled the Dodge back forty feet or so before I signaled him to set the parking brake. "Go ahead and turn it off," I said.

"I don't get it," he said. "What are you seeing?"

"That car."

"The Toyota? You *do* get what we're looking for out here, right?"

I turned back to him with my 'don't be a smartass' face. "Look at the plate," I told him.

"I 'heart' Moab," he read. "What the hell's a Moab?"

"It's a city. It's a major destination for off-roaders in Utah. They even used to host a yearly event where all the big time enthusiasts would get together and drive some of the nastiest trails. I've seen some of those guys take their Jeeps up near vertical inclines." Billy's eyes widened at this as he stretched his neck out to look past me again at the Toyota.

"Whoever lived here wasn't doing any of that in a Camry," I said, "but I'm thinking we crack open his garage and see what he's hiding in there."

"Ho-ho, shit," Billy giggled. "Wouldn't that be something?" He grabbed his shotgun and hopped out of the truck; walked around to the bed to dig around. Finding the crowbar he was looking for, he began to stroll up the driveway.

I opened the passenger side door and struggled briefly with my new rifle as I swung my legs out (Billy had so far neglected to show me how to detach the sling's swivel studs, so I had just left it hanging off my chest the whole time). Finally situated on the ground while managing not to shoot myself, I closed the door to the truck and followed.

Billy made a straight line for the roll-up garage door, planted his feet, and positioned the crowbar just past his hips like it was a shovel that he was going to use to take a scoop out of the driveway. Before he could swing, I said, "Wait."

He was actually mid-swing by the time I spoke, so he had to arrest the downward motion of the very heavy steel bar, grunting out a "Christ!" as he did. He straightened, placed the tip of the bar gently on the concrete, and crossed his arms over the top to lean on it. Thus composing himself, he said, "Yeeess?"

"What if someone's in the house? What if someone still lives here?"

"What...seriously?"

"We're here, right? We survived."

He pursed his lips and nodded. "Yeah, fair point. It may be the end of the world, but good manners never go out of style." He shouldered the crowbar, turned, and walked to the front door.

At the door, he leaned the bar against the wall. He then placed his shotgun next to it. He looked over his shoulder at me. "That gun's safe is on?"

"Yes," I said.

"Take it off." He knocked on the door.

We stood there a few moments, after which he knocked on the door again. Glancing down at the wall, he pushed the doorbell button. There was no discernable sound from inside the house and Billy muttered the word "dumbass" under his breath.

We waited another few minutes. Billy finally looked back at me with his eyebrows raised in question. I nodded that we were good and backed up to give him some room. He hefted the crowbar.

I expected him to slam it into the door or perform some other act of violent destruction, but he did the exact opposite. He placed the flat tip of the bar into the crack of the doorframe where the bolt would be, gave it a shove, and began to pry at the crack almost daintily. I was shocked. I had no idea how much noise he had been preparing to make with the thing over by the garage door, but the only sound he produced here at the entryway as he tickled the door was a mild grinding. I half expected him to raise his pinky off the bar as he levered it around. After about five minutes' worth of work, he had destroyed enough of the jam, the door, and the deadbolt that the whole thing swung open easily.

"Hello?" Billy called into the home. The lack of response carried a psychological weight with it, as though the air in the house was pushing back against us. He set the crowbar aside and shouldered the shotgun. Not looking back, he said, "Muzzle, Little Sis. Don't point that at anything you're not ready to kill." He lifted his own muzzle and passed the threshold.

The inside of the home was unexpectedly tidy. Having been conditioned to find disarray in all things, the cleanliness of the front room was off-putting. I had to force back the urge to look back out the front door and confirm that it was still the same fallen world outside. We made our way from room to room, Billy always in the lead. We stayed in each location long enough for him to clear the area and look in all the closets before moving on. At one point, Billy reached out and tapped my right elbow lightly with his hand and whispered, "Not so high, Little Sis. Makes it hard to maneuver. Pull 'em in tight to your ribs." I did as he suggested, noting immediately how the new position felt easier for my shoulders to maintain.

As we moved toward the back of the house where the master bedroom was, a foul, rotten smell became apparent, becoming more oppressive as we went deeper. I don't really know that I can do the experience justice through description; it was the smell of rotting meat and sweet, cheap perfume. As we approached the final door at the end of the hallway, I was holding my rifle one-handed by the grip and, with my left hand, holding a tail of the flannel shirt up over my mouth and nose. I had to breathe slowly and shallowly to avoid gagging.

Billy worked the knob on the door and swung it open. Inside, there were two bodies lying in the king-sized bed. Vast expanses of bone were visible among soupy ropes of red, meaty tissue. They were both glued to the mattress by brown pools of congealed liquid and surrounded by a tornado of flies. I just had enough time to make out that something white was moving along their surface before Billy bellowed, "Gah, sonofawhore!!!" and slammed the door. He and I both stumbled back down the hallway, coughing and gagging.

We made it back to the front room, turned right, and exited straight out the front door. Outside on the doorstep, Billy leaned over and placed his hands on his knees while coughing violently. I leaned against the wall of the house and tried to teach myself how to breathe normally again.

A few minutes later, still bent over and panting, Billy said, "That was pretty much the worst thing ever. Can we just leave now?"

"I'd love to," I said, "but we haven't seen inside the garage yet."

"Ah, God damn," he coughed and spit into the bushes. "Excuse me," he said, wiping his mouth with the back of his hand.

"Ready?"

"No," he grumped and walked through the front door.

We both engaged the safeties on our weapons and let them hang as we walked in. Billy indicated off to the left, and I followed. I could smell that rotting odor as soon as we stepped in this time; subtle but still there. I don't know how we missed it the first time around.

Once in the hallway, Billy tried the handle on a door on our immediate left—what we were both sure was the garage access. It opened into a dark garage with the bumper of something large and grey just visible. There was a spool on the front of the bumper with a coil of steel cable.

Billy pulled a flashlight out of his back pocket, turned it on, and shined it at the vehicle. It lit up what may have been the most gorgeous Jeep I've ever seen. Along the side of the hood in black and red letters was the word "RUBICON."

"Holy shit," Billy whispered. "Jackpot. Nice wor—Hey, where are you going?"

"Keys!" I called back as I went back inside the house. I had a panicked image of having to go back to the master bedroom to fish in someone's pants to get the keys—I didn't think either of us could do it. Luckily, I found a set of keys hanging from a wall hook in the kitchen. Confirming that the largest one on the ring said "Jeep" on the side, I grabbed it and returned to the garage.

Billy was just rolling up the exterior door as I came back out. When he took his arms away, it began to roll back down, so he pushed it back up into place. "Good, you're back," he said as I approached. "Would you look around and see if you can find anything to wedge this open? There isn't enough tension on the springs to hold it in place."

I started digging around, conscious of the fact that he was standing there exposed to the outside world with his hands extended high in the air. After what seemed like way too long, I said, "I'm not finding anything."

"It's okay, take your time. This thing isn't heavy; the springs take up most of the weight of the door. I can hold it here with a finger. Look for something like a long piece of wood, or maybe even some rope."

A few more minutes and I finally found an orange extension cord. "I found this," I said, holding it up for him to see. "Does that help?"

"That'll do." He pointed up at the top corner of the door where it connected to the track. "You see how the top of the door has a wheel that rides inside the track?"

"Yeah."

"Okay, now do you see how the track is suspended from the ceiling by that support bar?"

"Okay, I see what you mean," I said. I put the cord aside and found a step stool. I positioned the stool under the top corner of the door, grabbed the cord, and climbed to the top step. I was just able to reach the door. I threaded the extension cord up over and around the wheel that road in the door track and tied it off. I then took the other end of the cord and wrapped it a few times around the track's supporting frame and tied that end off as well. "Okay, let it go."

He did, and the door stayed open. "Nice one," Billy said and approached the driver side door. I went to meet him.

At the door, Billy held the key up in the air between us. "Let's keep it under a hundred, okay?" he smiled and handed me the key. I couldn't help but grin back as I took it from him and opened the door.

I slid into the leather seat, which was much more comfortable than I expected, and inserted the key into the ignition. I turned it to the right without actually trying to start the engine. The dome light and instrument panel lit up. It had a touch screen integrated navigation and radio system in the center of the dashboard that was set to the radio tuner. I could hear light static over the speakers.

"That's a good sign," I said and turned the key all the way forward. The engine started right up, smooth as silk, and ran much more quietly than I expected a badass, ruggedized Jeep to be. The fuel gauge needle indicated three-quarters of a tank.

"Jesus, we caught a break," Billy said as he looked the whole situation over. "It won't be much for hauling weight, but I don't think I care. Go ahead and back it out and we'll go get you topped off." He began to chuckle. "I'll be damned—just like that! I guess we were just due for some good luck."

8

# CARJACKED

**Jake**

We had been sitting in the van for a while now, chatting about various things—mostly the kind of things that your average seven-year-old finds to be intensely interesting. A lot of this involved me explaining to her how characters like Big Bird and Kermit were actually the main stars of Sesame Street instead of the supporting cast when I was a kid. It seemed that this had changed and the producers of the show were highlighting characters that skewed more infantile like Elmo, Abby, and Baby Bear.

Our conversation began with her asking me to explain how Chess worked, which ended up being much more difficult than I had imagined. In the end, we decided we needed an actual board in front of us before I could start teaching her the rules to the game—it was just too abstract otherwise.

The conversation had hit a lull, and I was just contemplating getting out of the van to fix us something to eat. I looked over at her and said, "You hungry?"

She looked back toward me and froze. I noticed she was actually looking past me. I turned to look out the side window and saw the barrel of a revolver pointed at my face.

My right hand was resting on my knee about a mile away from the Glock, which was propped up behind my back against the seat. I began the process of moving my hand back toward my hip when I heard a squeak from Lizzy and looked back her way. There was another gun being pointed in through her window as well. I moved my hand back to my knee.

A head began to manifest from the side of the window past Lizzy's face, so slow that I may have laughed under other circumstances. First an ear, then an eye, half of a nose and mouth. The eye locked onto mine, widened, and the rest of the face came into view quickly after. The face was all beard, greasy dirt smears, and a ratty brown beanie.

"Jake…"

"Calm down," I said. "Panic will make the outcome certain."

There was a hard clicking sound on my window. I turned back to see the other man, not all that distinct from the first with the exception of flat, matted down hair in place of a beanie. His other hand came up and beckoned at me. "Out of the van—both of you," he said, his voice muted through the window.

I had half a moment where I thought of just grabbing the pistol to start shooting, but Elizabeth was halfway out of the van with a gun on her. I reached back and pinched the grip of my gun between thumb and forefinger. I held it up in the window so the man could see it, then opened the door and got out.

"Put it on the ground and back away."

I complied. He bent over to grab it, craning his head hard to keep me in view while holding the gun in a bizarre position above his head. The more natural way to do it would have been to just squat down over the gun, keeping the torso vertical and thereby keeping me (the target) in sight from a much more natural angle. The guy either had joint issues in the hips or knees or he was just an idiot.

As he straightened up with my gun, I saw Lizzy and the first man moving around the front of the van and back toward the southeast corner of the warehouse building. She was looking at me as she was dragged along by the arm, eyes wide and frightened. I watched her until she disappeared around the building.

I looked back to the man holding the gun on me. "Where is she being taken?"

"Don't worry about that now. No one will hurt her."

"What is this about?" A third person was coming out to us now, having emerged from the spot at which Lizzy and Brown Beanie had disappeared a moment ago.

"Keys in the van?" Number three asked. It was a woman.

"I don't fuckin' know!" said the man. "Have a look in there. I'm a little busy."

She opened the door and looked inside. "Bingo," she said and swung herself up into the seat. She slammed the door, turned the key to start the engine, and rolled the window down.

"I'll take this back, unload it, and then come back to pick the rest of you up."

"Yeah, don't be long, Molly."

"What are you gonna do with this one?"

He looked at me. "Don't know yet."

She gave it a beat and then nodded. "Anyways, I'll be back after sundown." She put the van in drive, did a U-turn, and drove it back onto Cross Hollow road. She turned due south and was soon lost to view. All of the artillery from Vegas left with her.

"Is this just about the van; that's all you want?" I asked.

The guy clenched his teeth. "Yeah, something like that."

"Well, fine," I said. "Just let me have the girl back, and you guys can be on your way. Take the van."

"Nope. Holding onto her ensures you play nice."

I'm somewhat embarrassed to admit that I felt something like rage at his blithe response. Struggling to keep my voice steady, I said, "Give her back. Either that or plan on killing me."

"Hey, exactly who the fuck do you think you're talking to here?" he said. He began to physically expand like a balloon. He took a step closer to me. The gun was a foot away. "The only one making threats around here is the guy with the gun. Me. The fuck is she to you anyway? Daughter?"

I didn't say anything. I just kept my eyes locked on his.

"Listen, fuckstick," he shouted, "the way it works is I ask questions and you… fucking… answer them." As he said the last part, he closed the remaining distance between us and put the barrel up to my forehead.

This felt like as good a time as any. I mentally said 'screw it' and went for it. I jerked my head to the right out of the path of the gun. At the same instant, I clapped both hands on his wrist and pushed the gun out to the left. The gun went off well after I had it safely away.

"You fuckin…" he grunted. I didn't give him any time to fight for control. I pulled him toward me to get him off balance and then swung the gun and his hands in a massive arc over my head, ending with the revolver down by my right knee. His lack of balance plus the speed of my pull meant that he ended up on his back. I planted a foot on his chest and began to bend the revolver backward, rotating it around in his hand to point at him. His finger was bound up in the trigger guard, and he began to growl in pain as I forced it back. I resolved either to break his finger or rip it off and yanked the gun away from him hard.

The gun went off, (which I had not actually intended) the bullet driving into the man's jaw and blowing out the top of his head. There was a sudden intense and throbbing pain in my right hand (my smart hand); it felt as though someone had driven over it with a car or slammed it in between two massive books. I didn't understand what the cause was at the time—I guessed it was just the kick of the revolver. Later I would learn how a percentage of the explosive forces of a fired bullet escape out the sides of a revolver in the gap between the cylinder and the barrel; the place around which my right hand was firmly grasping when it discharged. Not having the benefit of this knowledge at the time, I knew only that it hurt terribly and my hand had gone numb shortly after.

I retrieved my Glock and patted the man down, finding nothing useful outside of a nearly empty cigarette pack and lighter. I kept the lighter.

I ran to the wall of the warehouse, stuffing the hand murdering revolver into my back pocket. I fumbled the Glock into my left hand. As I made my way along the wall to the corner, I shook my right hand vigorously and rubbed it on my leg, trying to get some feeling back into it. I looked down at my palm. There was no permanent damage that I could see, but there was a black line running along the padding of the inside knuckle joints peppered with numerous black specks. I flexed it several times. It moved the way I wanted it to. Feeling was coming back slowly but only pins and needles so far. I contemplated holding the pistol in my left but soon abandoned that idea. I trusted my right hand with reduced feeling better than my left with clumsy mobility.

I peeked around the corner of the wall and, seeing no one there; put my head out far enough to see that there was a door leading into the warehouse at the corner opposite mine. There was also another building extending further south that seemed to be attached to this one. I suffered a moment of indecision: take the door or continue searching along the outside of the building? If I was wrong, I could end up burning a lot of time on a fruitless search while Lizzy was taken further out of reach. I was also well aware that standing there would eventually result in the same outcome. I decided to flip a mental coin and take the door.

As I entered, I heard a voice close by say, "Had to shoot him, huh?" I put eyes on the speaker—it was Beanie guy. "Oh, shhh-!"

I shot him twice in the chest. He leaned back into some vertical storage racks, alternating between looking at me and looking at his chest with a very confused expression on his face. I shot him in the forehead and made my way deeper into the shop floor.

To my right were roll-up doors leading out to loading docks. Some of them were opened, allowing light into the area and making it possible to see rather well. There were a number of line machines arranged at regular intervals along a mirror smooth concrete floor covered in dust. Ringing the line machines were more storage racks loaded with various kinds of packaging material; rolls of plastic and cellophane, small black plastic containers and clear plastic lids. They all looked to me like little single-serving food containers.

I scanned the area, which appeared to lack any other people besides me and the man I had just shot. On the far side of the room, there was a dividing wall anchored to a huge glulam beam spanning the warehouse. From the columns I could see running vertically down the length of the wall, I assumed the wall was structural.

I went through the door without even slowing down. This new room was much darker; anything I could see was only shapes and shadows. I had the impression of more storage racks. I fumbled in my pocket for the lighter and started thumbing the wheel. I don't remember anything immediately after that moment.

———

The next thing I remember was an all-consuming, throbbing ache in the back of my head, demanding attention and lifting me up into consciousness. The more awake I was, the more it hurt. I groaned and tried to find my way back to sleep.

"There, see? He's coming around. I told you I didn't kill him."

Now in chorus with the ache in the back of my head, there came a familiar throb and pressure centered at my sinuses. I found it was impossible to breathe except through an open mouth. Tremendous. Someone had smashed my nose in again.

I levered my eyes open and was met with the low light of a gas lantern. We were in some kind of office, the walls on two sides (to my left and ahead of me) housing large picture windows looking out onto the shop floor. I was hunched over in a rolling chair with my hands bound behind me. I looked up and had to fight through a wave of nausea as the room tilted on its side. I ground my teeth while I waited for the feeling to subside.

"Jake!" I heard Lizzy call from somewhere ahead of me. I looked out and squinted. She looked shorter than she should have been and her body looked wrong; it was reflecting the light of the lantern in strange patterns. I was confused. Clothing is not typically reflective.

I looked around and just made out three other people; a woman and two men. I couldn't tell for sure if it was the same woman who drove away with our van but I thought this was a new person I hadn't seen before. About all I could tell from the low light and my swimming vision was female, neither young nor old. The two men were a mystery; I had killed all of the men I had encountered so far.

"Easy, there, fella. I hit you pretty hard," one of the men said.

I tried to speak, coughed, and then spit out angrily, "The fuck is going on here?"

"Whoa, whoa," the woman said indignantly. "You just killed two of ours, buddy. Maybe you want to rethink your tone."

"Killed two that were stealing my van! Drug the girl off to God knows where. What did you expect? High-fives and fist bumps?"

There was silence for a few beats. Finally, she said, "Donny, cut his hands loose."

"The fuck you say?" exclaimed someone (presumably Donny).

"Cut him loose, damn it. You have him covered with guns from two different directions. Look at him; he can barely breathe."

I had my head down again as it was taking a lot of energy to keep it up and the strain along the back of my neck was aggravating the migraine. I saw a pair of feet in sneakers come around from the side and move behind me. There was a sharp tug at my wrists, and then my hands were free. I was able to sit up fully.

I sat up too fast and was struck by another wave of vertigo. I closed my eyes and took deep breaths. When I opened my eyes again things were better. I looked around and noted that this was definitely a different woman than the one who had driven off with the Ford. I looked over at Lizzy and saw that she had been shrink-wrapped to a chair.

"Look, about your van? I'm truly sorry about that. Our people need what you're carrying. This was a simple case of you versus us."

"Again, if you want the van, take the van. You're welcome to it. Let me and the girl leave."

"Well, that's a problem, isn't it? Is she your daughter?"

"No."

"I see. Well, what are you doing with her?"

I started to see where this was going. Though I hated to admit it, I understood where she was coming from. I was in her same position only a few days ago when Billy and I were deciding what to do about Amanda and her situation. Was she dealing with someone who needed saving or someone who was where they wanted to be? Unfortunately, I could also tell by looking at her that she had already made up her mind. I don't know why she bothered to continue talking to me.

"She's my friend. I'm watching her until her mother gets back." It sounded lame, and I knew it.

"Your friend." Statement not question.

"That's right."

"You want me to believe someone your age is lugging around this little kid because you enjoy her company?"

"Ask her, why don't you?"

"Oh, yeah, I could. But how do I know you haven't coached her? How do I know you haven't frightened her into telling me whatever you want her to say?"

I couldn't help but roll my eyes, which also hurt miserably, by the way. "You're right, lady. When we woke up this morning, just after I finished doing unspeakable things with her, I told her, 'okay, here's your story just in case we get ambushed by a really suspicious broad and a crew of gun-wielding henchmen! Listen up now...' Are you insane? In what god damned universe does that sound even remotely plausible?"

I felt a barrel press into the side of my neck. "Easy, there, shit for brains. You don't get to talk to her like that."

"I haven't decided what happens to you... yet," the lady said to me, hanging on that last word. "I do know that I can care for this girl better than some caveman who runs around killing people he doesn't even know..."

"Yeah, again, people who were stealing our supplies!" I interrupted.

"We stole. You killed. Who's the real bad guy here?"

"Well, I would have been pleased as punch to let them live. All they had to do was not stick guns in our faces." Her superior, school-marm attitude was really starting to get under my skin. "Besides, where the hell do you come from talking about her wellbeing? One of us has saran-wrapped this girl to a chair, and it sure wasn't me."

"None of this conversation matters. The girl stays with us."

"Now listen, you…" I groaned as I started to get out of my chair. When I came to a standing position, the entire planet (never mind the room) tilted on its axis. My thigh slammed into a desk, and I had to brace my hand on it to keep from going over. I leaned forward again because that seemed to be the only position my inner ear was happy with. The pressure in my sinuses immediately built up to intolerable levels. It seemed that no matter what position I put myself into, there was some portion of my body waiting to tell me why my ideas were stupid. I reached my hand up to my nose and fingered around the wreckage gingerly. It felt all crooked and mashed in again. I gave a gentle squeeze, and pain blossomed from my nose and wrapped all the way around my head. The tear ducts in my eyes shot water like a couple of sprinklers.

"Which one of you schmucks broke my nose again?"

"S… sorry," a voice said from my left—who I guessed was the guy standing next to the door to the main warehouse floor. "You fell on your face when I clubbed you."

"Yeah, about that…" I began, "what did you club me with anyway, a Volks…" I had raised my head to look forward. The woman I had been talking to was standing behind Elizabeth. She was holding a knife pointed at the girl's eye.

I froze. The guy behind me said, "Hey, Brenda, come on…"

She silenced him with a look. Turning her attention to me, she said, "Not another step now."

"What happened to looking out for her wellbeing?"

"Well, it's clear you have no regard for your own safety. Something had to be done to get your attention." I scanned her face for any trace of shame or guilt for what she was doing. There was none. If I made a move on her, that knife was going in Elizabeth's eye, best as I could tell.

A great sense of calm and acceptance came over me then. It's the kind of feeling you get when you realize what comes next will be ugly but that there is also no other alternative.

I had resolved at that point that either I was going to be killed or I was going to kill everyone in the room not wrapped up on a chair. There was no reason for me to say anything else.

"What, that's it? Nothing clever to say?" she asked.

I didn't need to say anything else. The sound of vehicles approaching outside could be heard through a small window set in the concrete wall of the office. It immediately became clear to me what had happened. These people had been in this building when we arrived; probably doing the same thing we were…scavenging. They must have heard us pull up and watched us the whole time we were out there making plans, waiting to see what we'd do. Billy and Amanda drove off, and two people appeared much easier to handle than four.

But if that was the case, why the whole line of questioning about the girl just now? What was the point of that? I decided I didn't care. I looked down at the knife hovering by Lizzy's left eyeball. No matter what else happened, there was only one possible outcome for Brenda, assuming I lived.

"That'll be her mother," I said. "Here's your chance to straighten all this out."

She looked at the two men and said, "Go look. I'm fine here; he can barely stand up without holding the edge of the desk."

Both men went to the door and exited, disappearing into the shadows of the warehouse as soon as they left the lantern light in the office. In the distance, a door opened to admit two shadows and closed again.

"You'll be giving my friends the same warm welcome, I take it?"

"If they come waving a white flag I'm sure it will be fine." She removed the knife from Elizabeth and stepped away. She lifted her other hand to show me a revolver, which appeared to be the same one I had in my back pocket a moment ago.

"Nothing stupid, huh?" she said. She was interrupted by several loud reports of what I had learned to identify as Billy's shotgun, peppered with higher pitched bursts of gunfire.

Brenda jumped and turned to look out the office window. She didn't exactly have her back to me, but I decided it wasn't going to get any better. I rushed her. Halfway to her, the world made another one of those asinine tilts, and my vision started to swim with blackness. I could see her turning toward me, raising her gun in slow motion, her face drawn up in shock and anticipation of a body check.

I slammed into her head and shoulders first. From far, far away I heard screaming and the sound of my name. I fought to keep from passing out, certain I would lose consciousness at any second. I felt something writhing under me, and I realized it must be the woman I had just smeared across the floor. I brought my hands up in front of me and started grabbing blindly, trying to find anything to hold on to so I could rest a second and catch my breath. Maybe wait for my vision to come back if I was lucky.

Something stung me across the back of my hand, which immediately started to burn afterward. This concerned me, so I gave up holding on and instead began to punch in the direction I deemed most likely to contain her head. I connected a couple of times, and I felt the body under me jolt like it had been electrocuted with each hit.

I sat back and rested on my knees a moment. Having gone from prone to vertical, the vertigo wave returned, and I had to wait yet again for it to pass. I finally opened my eyes and was able to see in front of me without a bunch of black spots whirling around in my vision. Brenda was on her back on the floor holding her hands to her face and moaning. I noticed that her knife was close by. I lurched to my feet and kicked it away. I saw the revolver lying on the floor by the door. I went to it, braced myself for the nausea wave I knew was coming, and squatted to pick it up. Squatting seemed to help with the dizzy spell; it didn't seem so bad that time. I turned back to Brenda, thumbed the hammer back, and pointed it at her face.

"We weren't going to hurt her. I was going to take care of her." Her voice was pleading now.

"Maybe or maybe not," I said. "Regardless of intent, the one thing you never do is fuck with a kid." I pulled the trigger.

# 9

# REUNITED

**Amanda**

B illy and I returned to the meeting area by the warehouse not long before dusk. I was following him in the Jeep, and when we came over the hill and brought the area into view, he immediately sped up. It caught me by surprise, but I soon saw what he was doing. We were at least a hundred yards away, but that was still close enough to see that the van was gone and that there was a body in the dirt.

We both pulled up to the body and jumped out to examine it. I was so convinced that it was Jake when we came up that I became confused at the unfamiliar face. I stood there a few beats trying to reconcile what I was seeing. My brain kept telling me that he must have been beaten unrecognizable, but that didn't make any sense; there was no trauma to the face outside of the small hole just underneath his chin and the larger, baseball-sized hole in the top of his head.

Billy took his hand off the pump of his shotgun and pointed to the dirt next to the body. "Look," he said, "someone stumbled away from this."

A part of me giggled internally when he said that (Really? You're going to do the Indian Tracker thing?) but most of me just wanted to know where the hell Elizabeth was. Also, being fair, the tracks were hard to miss. No one had been this way for a while.

He followed the path of the footprints down the side of the building, hunched over slightly, shotgun shouldered, barrel down. I followed behind with the Tavor pointed out in front and to the right so the muzzle wouldn't be in his back. It seemed Billy had forgotten to be afraid of having me behind him with a loaded gun.

We rounded the corner and started to run the length of this new wall. At the end, we came to a door. Billy came to stand in front of it and then motioned for me to come around him and get on the other side. The door opened outside, right to left, so he wanted me positioned to get in behind him without having to navigate around the door. He grabbed the handle, turned it, and pulled the door open, plunging in with me trailing close after him.

Just as my eyes were adjusting to the lower light, I saw a door closing on the other side directly across from us with two men rushing into the room. I felt Billy's hand on my shoulder as he shoved me down in front of one of the line machines and he took a knee right next to me. As soon as his knee touched the ground, I heard gunshots from the other side of the warehouse.

He peeked his head over the top to look, and then pulled it down again as a few more shots rang out. He lifted his shotgun over the machine and sent a few blasts back their way, more on general principle than any real hope of hitting them.

"Assholes are placed behind their own line machine. We gotta get closer or something."

"Hey!" I called out. "What are you shooting at us for?"

"C'mon out and we'll tell yah!"

Billy looked at me. "I don't have to tell you, right?"

"You got my daughter back there?" I asked. They didn't answer for several seconds, and I felt my heart skip a beat. They knew who I was talking about.

"I'm telling you right now," I said. "If I find anything wrong with her I'm going to kill you motherfuckers a piece at a time, starting with your god damned kneecaps and work my way up!"

"Jesus, woman!" Billy grunted as he looked at me, shock painted across his face.

A few more shots came our way, but they were being stingy with them. Billy noticed this too. He said, "I don't think they have that many bullets."

I crab-walked down to the end of the line and peered through a break in the machinery. There was just enough of a gap through the steel framing, drums, and wheels of our machine that I could see the end of one of their asses hanging out from behind their own cover across the way. I waved at Billy, pointed in their direction and mouthed the words, "get... ready." He nodded, pulled a few shells from his belt, and started thumbing them into his weapon. When he was ready to go, he nodded to me over his shoulder.

I steadied myself as well as possible and rested the barrel of my rifle on a nook of the machinery frame. I positioned the dot of the rifle's optic on the backside of the man in the distance. I took a breath and squeezed the trigger. The gun jerked back against my shoulder, and I heard a scream from across the warehouse (strangely, I can't remember hearing a gunshot when I did this). The man's back end was replaced by a complete body sprawling along the floor. I repositioned the dot to the newly discovered head and pulled the trigger again. I didn't miss.

Billy was already running along the shop floor by the time I got off my first shot. The man who had not been hit was distracted by his buddy sprawling across the concrete just long enough for Billy to get in and blow a hole through his ribs.

I ran to meet him where he crouched over the two. "Done," he said and moved to the door through which they had emerged.

On the other side, the room was dark enough that we had to slow our pace down considerably. I heard screaming now in the distance ahead; the screaming of a little girl. I pushed past Billy and started running blindly down the aisles. He shouted for me to wait but I wasn't hearing it. I heard my baby screaming.

It wasn't long at all before I saw a dimly lit enclosed office in the distance. I could see Jake standing up in the window with a revolver pointed down at the floor. Just beyond him was Elizabeth's head.

I grabbed the handle and pulled the door open. I heard Jake say something that sounded like, "…eye kid." It was hard to make out because I was in the process of opening the door when he said it. Maybe he said "bye kid," because he shot her in the face right after that.

Billy pushed into the room behind me, looked around at the mess, and said, "What the hell, Jake?"

Jake collapsed into an office chair. He slumped there, panting. "I… could use… a drink… of water."

———

"We don't have a lot of time," said Jake. He was still sitting in the chair, leaned forward over the desk with his head in his hand. "The one who stole the van… she said she'd be back to pick the rest up."

I was just cutting the rest of the plastic wrap off Elizabeth. I was taking my time, afraid I would cut her if I moved too fast.

Speaking of cuts: "You have a nasty cut on the back of your hand," I said, looking over at Jake. "We might have to sew that one shut."

"Later," he mumbled, panting heavily. "Billy. Go around and search everyone. Get the guns. Bullets. Want my damned Glock back."

"What happened here?" I asked as Billy went out the door.

"Ambushed. They were in this building the whole time. Snuck up on us after you left. Someone hit me with a bus or something."

"And the van?"

He took a few breaths before continuing. I started getting really worried about him from the way he was acting. "So, one of them, a female, came out and drove off in the van. Said she was going to unload it and come back to pick everyone up after sundown." He took a few more breaths. "What happened to the other two? What'd you do with them?" He wouldn't look up when he spoke to me, and he slurred his words like a drunk.

"We ended up shooting them both. Look, are you okay?"

"Nope," he said promptly. "Knocked me out I don't know how long. Think I'm concussed."

Billy came back into the room just then with a couple of pistols in his jacket pockets and an additional rifle. "So how about my van?" he asked.

Jake pointed at me with his left hand and then made a throwing gesture at Billy. I updated Billy on what had happened as quickly as possible. Lizzy looked like she was torn between holding onto me and checking on Jake; she kept stealing glances in his direction. Finally, she went over to him and rested her hand on the back of his neck. "You're bleeding, Jake, from your head," she said.

"Just a day fer...good news!" Jake rumbled and gave her a pat on the knee.

"So, she's coming back with the van. I suppose we could wait for her."

"Billy, no," I said. "Look at Jake. He could have a concussion already. He's in no shape to fight; he can't even lift his head up."

"Can," Jake grunted. He lifted his head an inch and then put it back in his hand. "Uh... shit." He burped softly.

"We don't know if she's coming back alone or with friends. I don't want to have any more gunfights with my kid around, okay?"

"Think we killed enough people today already, Billy," Jake said. "You get her a car?"

"Yeah," Billy said. "Nice one."

"Well, good. Let's call this a draw and get out of here."

"Yeah, I guess you're right. It's just..." Billy fanned his hands in the air, "there was a lot of good hardware in that van, man! It just galls the hell out of me. It's galling."

"Forget it," Jake said. "We got the kid. Good enough. We get settled in Wyoming, I'll drive all the way back to Nevada and get another load myself. We didn't clean that whole place out by half."

Billy brightened up at that. "Yeah, I guess you're right."

"Course I am. Now help me out of here before what's-her-face comes back."

Billy and I each took an arm and lifted Jake onto his feet. He grunted and moaned—some very unsavory things came out of his mouth. I felt naked walking out of there like that, with Jake draped over both of us and our weapons hanging uselessly from their slings. Goosebumps ran up my back as we passed through the door into the loading area with the line machines. That would have been a perfect time for a hidden someone to come jumping out at us. Such a thing never happened, thankfully.

When we got outside, the sun was sitting on the horizon under a red sky. Billy said, "He'll ride with you. Put him up front and roll the window down. Don't let him recline. Don't let him fall asleep. Soon as we get a ways out of town, we'll pull off the road, and I'll see about cleaning him up."

We almost made it to the Jeep before Jake stopped us to vomit. He couldn't stand on his own, so we had to hold him up by his arms but let him bend over to have it all out. There wasn't a great deal for him to get rid of, I imagined he hadn't really eaten all day. While I was waiting for him to finish, I asked Lizzy to go grab a few bottles of water out of the pickup truck.

"What all was in that van?" I asked Billy as Jake was finishing.

"Mostly weapons, tools, ammunition and body armor, that kind of thing. It's nothing we can't live without, but it still hurts. That van constituted a major advantage for us in the way of gear and equipment. The loss of ammo truly hurts."

"We'll make do," Jake groaned below us. We straightened him up. "We'll find a way. Besides, we're not totally helpless. Still have the duffel bag."

"Sure, that's fine," Billy said as we started walking him slowly toward the passenger side of the Jeep. "We'll have to get you set up again, though. Your M4 was in the van."

"Ugh, damn it! I liked that rifle. Just had it figured out."

He groaned enough for all three of us as we got him settled in the Jeep. "There we go. How do you feel?" I asked like an idiot.

"Like I downed a bottle of whiskey and got horse-kicked in the face."

"Lizzy, you get up in the back seat and help your momma keep Jake awake, okay?" Billy said.

"Why can't Jake go to sleep?" asked Elizabeth.

"He took a nasty shot to the head," Billy answered. "I need to get him to a place where I can check him to see if it's safe to let him sleep. If I get this wrong, he may not wake up."

Elizabeth's eyes went very wide and solemn at that. She jumped into the Jeep behind Jake and put her hands on his shoulders, shaking gently. "Stay awake, up there," she commanded.

"I'm serious," Billy said to me specifically. "Don't let him sleep at all. I want to look him over before we allow that."

"How long will it be before we know he's safe?"

"We've just got to get to a safe area where I can get a good look at his eyes," he said. "I've never dealt with a concussion directly; only read about them. But the main thing is if his eyes aren't dilated, and he can talk coherently, he can sleep. He's talking fine right now, but I just want to get a look at his pupils. Assuming all is well, we want him to get *all the sleep*. It still might be as much as a week for him to be back to full speed. Mostly he should find it easier to solve complex problems and use his memory, but I think we'll know we're through the rough part when he stops talking like he's drunk."

"Do you mean the slurring or just talking way more than usual in general?"

Billy just shrugged at this and turned to make his way to the truck. "Keep close behind me, Little Sis," he called back. "Soon as we get away from all these towns we'll pull off the road and see about stitching him back up."

───────

Billy led us about twenty miles North of Cedar City up the 15 before pulling off the road and taking us to a good stand-off distance.

He jumped out of the truck and came our way, his always present shotgun slung over a shoulder and a flashlight in hand. He opened the passenger side door to gain access to Jake and said, "Okay, let's have a look at you. Amanda, can you start setting up the tents? They're in the back of the truck. Alright, look over this way, Jake…"

The flashlight turned on and off several times with intervals of five to ten seconds in between. Billy let out a sigh.

"Good news. Here, Jake. Let's get this seat reclined back. You go ahead and get some rest."

"Well, thank God for that," Jake groaned.

Billy eased the door shut and came over to where Lizzy and I struggled with the tents. He passed us by and went back to the truck to shift bags around in the bed. I resigned myself to decoding the riot of poles and canvas without help.

Now, I have since learned to erect all manner of tent, so I know how the things work by now. It's just that at the time, this kind of thing wasn't a regular activity for me. We had been camping all of twice since Lizzy was born and Eddie did most of the work putting the campsite together both times. I knew enough to understand how the poles worked, though, so I started straightening them out with Lizzy and laying them aside. The two biggest challenges we had to deal with were that this was during the night (we had to do everything while juggling our own flashlight), and the two tents with their constituent parts had all been jumbled together, so it wasn't obvious which poles went with which tent.

While we straightened out the poles, I heard Billy grunt off to my right followed by the rattling sound of a pill bottle. This was followed by the sound of ripping fabric. Billy called over to me, "Hey, remind me to put washcloths and towels on the shopping list, huh?"

"Uh, okay!" was all I could think to say in response.

This was all followed by the sound of water splashing onto the dirt for a few seconds. He straightened up, replaced some items into the truck, and walked back over to the jeep. I heard him speaking to Jake but his voice was low, so I couldn't make out what was said. Billy shut the door and came over to check on us.

We had finished straightening out all the support rods and had the two tents spread out next to each other. Billy bent, picked up one of the rods, and said, "The longer rods go with the blue tent," before threading his through the green one.

"Ah, thanks," I said and meant it. "I was worried about getting one set up halfway and finding out I made the wrong choice."

"Sure, no worries. I've mixed them up several times."

Things were up quickly after that. I was concerned that my tent looked sad and deflated compared to Billy's until he showed me some little plastic clips running along the length of the nylon that I had missed. I clipped them to the rods, and everything looked much more squared away.

"I think he's gonna be okay," Billy said when it was all done. "He just needs a lot of rest. I don't know how long he'll be goofed up, but we need to make sure he understands that he's not to push it. He seems to me like the kind that will just try to tough it out through this sort of thing. With a head trauma, that's only going to make things worse. I think if we explain to him that pushing it will make him a liability, it'll get the message delivered, yeah?"

"Right," I said. "Sounds good."

"Okay," he continued. "Jake and I'll double up in the blue tent; you and Lizzy take the green. We're a pretty good distance from Cedar City now, but on the other hand, they do have a really nice van now... assholes."

Despite everything we had just been through, I couldn't suppress a grin at this. Billy really liked his van.

"Anyway, no fire tonight and I think we'd better keep watch. Let's get some sleeping bags laid out. I'll help Jake get settled in, and then I'll take the first watch. I'm not feeling very restful, myself."

We went to the Jeep and opened up the door. Jake stirred and mumbled, "Time to get up?"

"Let's just start with sitting up, Whitey."

"The hell you always calling me Whitey for?"

"Because," Billy laughed, "You da White Man, sucka."

"Heavens," Jake mumbled. "Anyone ever tell you that you talk like a teenager?"

"Look, you gotta hang onto your youth however the hell you can."

Jake sat his seat up, grimacing in the low moonlight as he did. A wet, folded up scrap of cloth fell from his eyes, which Elizabeth reached out and caught. I noticed that his right hand was bound up in a clean, white bandage. "His nose is all wrong again," Lizzy said.

"Yeah," Jake said. "Guess I fell on it a little."

"How is it?" Billy asked. "You want to fix it or leave it?"

"Ohhhhh, man," Jake groaned. "We'd better deal with it. It's giving me a nasty headache."

Billy motioned for Lizzy and I to back up, then he raised his hands to Jake's face. I saw Jake's hands grip the frame of the Jeep's door and brace. The muscles in Billy's shoulders tensed and Jake's knuckles went white. Jake himself unloaded a growl that sounded like a hot poker had been shoved up a grizzly bear's behind.

"God damn it, we're not quite there, boss. Gotta do it again." I could see Jake's head nodding past Billy. Shoulder muscles tensed a second time, and Jake howled.

"Grrrrraaaarrrrghhhhh—shit!" Billy pulled back and pointed a flashlight in Jake's face as he sat there, panting. Presently, Jake looked at Lizzy and said, "Sorry for that, kiddo."

"Okay…" said Elizabeth in a small voice.

"Hey," he reached out and patted her shoulder. "I'm okay. I actually feel better. The worst part of my headache is gone. It feels like he pulled a knife out of my head."

Lizzy looked at him dubiously. This probably had to do with the fact that both his eyes looked like someone had been pounding on them with a hammer and that there was blood running freely from his nose, which he dabbed at absently with the wet cloth.

"I don't know how well that's going to heal up," said Billy. "There's not much of that bridge left but splinters and floating chunks at this point. I feel like a proper doctor would know how to support it all somehow so it heals properly, but I haven't the first clue how to go about it."

"It's fine," Jake said. "I wasn't winning any modeling contests to begin with. Just gimme an old t-shirt that I can rip up and pack up there, and I'll be okay."

"Yeah, good idea. I already have one started." Billy walked back over to the truck.

I leaned in close to Jake. "You're going to have to take it easy for the next few days, okay? You can't push yourself. You might make this worse." I left the implication unsaid. I didn't want to bring out the big guns unless he decided to be stubborn later.

He only nodded slowly. "I understand. Any idea how long it'll be?"

"Well, Billy seems to know something about this. He says you're probably okay when you start acting like yourself again."

"Like myself? What does that mean? What am I like?"

"Well... you know..." I stammered. "Quiet all the time. No expression? Cold and aloof? Block of wood?"

Jake was silent a moment as he absorbed that. Then he looked down and placed the cloth back under his nose. "Huh..." he said.

Billy came back with a white, mutilated t-shirt and cut some small squares off of it with his pocket knife. Jake accepted them, rolled them into little tubes, and jammed them up his nostrils. He growled like an old drunk as he mashed them into place.

"Alright, you guys," he sighed. "I think I've had enough of beating my face up for the night." He stood up, looking much steadier than he had earlier when we carried him out of the warehouse and made his way to the tent. Lizzy was there holding the flap back for him. He stopped to look at her, reached out, and cupped her cheek in his hand. "Thanks, kiddo," he said and hunched to crawl in. I thought about what Billy had said to me earlier that day about Jake and Elizabeth, deciding that Billy was probably much more intelligent than I gave him credit for.

"What about his head?" I asked Billy. "Don't we need to stitch it up?"

"I cleaned it out with some alcohol and had a look at it," said Billy. "The bleeding has stopped. There might be a small scar, but I don't think it needs stitches. His hand will definitely need some stitches, but that can wait until tomorrow. I've got him pumped full of Ibuprofen and Amoxicillin so it won't go all infected. We'll keep him on both for another week, and he should be good."

We got Jake situated in the tent and Billy gave me a new scrap of wet cloth from the remains of the t-shirt to place over Jake's eyes. As he lay there, I leaned in close and said, "I want to thank you for protecting my little girl."

"If I'd been thinking, we would have cleared that damned warehouse before doing anything else. This whole thing was my fault."

I boggled at this. I failed to understand how any of this could have been laid at Jake's feet. It was something we would all come to learn about him eventually. The way Jake sees things, it doesn't matter what the circumstances are—if something went wrong, it's his fault. His natural instinct is to assume the blame for what happened and find a way to avoid the same mistakes in the future. People around our little commune all have their own ideas why Jake ended up in charge (and some of them are less happy about it than others), but whatever they tell you, this is the main reason: Jake owns everything whether it's reasonable or not, seeks to improve everything. He's always looking for failures in himself and ways to correct them. It is easy to follow someone like that.

"Elizabeth is alive and unhurt," I told him finally. "That's good enough for me."

I kissed him lightly on the cheek and left the tent.

Billy was sitting in a folding camping chair outside and facing the 15 about a half mile distant with his shotgun propped on the top of his thigh. "Lizzy's already turned in," he said quietly.

I threw my arms around his neck from behind him and kissed him on the cheek. "The hell??" he gasped. He came halfway out of his seat.

"Just thank you," I said, not letting go. He rested his shotgun across his knees with his right hand; his left hand reached up and gave me a couple of pats on the back of my head.

"No worries. It's fine," he said. I let go and made my way to our tent.

"I… uh… I had a daughter," he said before I entered. I froze for a beat; looked back at him. "Mary. You would have liked her. I think her boy and Lizzy would have been friends." He replaced the shotgun on his knee and said nothing more.

I climbed into the tent and laid down next to Elizabeth, not taking my shoes off and not getting inside my bag. After a few moments, her hand reached out and found mine.

I breathed deeply and closed my eyes.

————

I laid there in the tent for what must have been at least a couple of hours waiting for sleep to find me before I gave up. Elizabeth's breathing had become slow and even soon after she rolled over. It amazed me how she could do that after everything she had been through.

Quietly, I got up, worked the zipper on the tent flap slowly until the opening was just big enough to let me out and then slipped through. I closed the zipper, stood up, and turned to see Billy looking back at me.

"Couldn't sleep?"

"Not really," I agreed and went to the truck. I pulled out another chair while making as little noise as I could and brought it over to open up beside Billy. The air was on the chilly side, but I still had the wool-lined denim jacket, which was incredibly warm and comfortable. I wedged into the chair, jammed my hands into the pockets, and sighed.

"Nightmares?"

"What? Oh, no. I never got to sleep at all. Too much on my mind."

"I'm not going anywhere if you need to unload."

I was silent for a while, trying to figure out how to frame my thoughts into words. To his credit, Billy waited patiently while I worked it out.

"Billy, what did you do before all this happened?"

"I was a senior member on our tribal council and also served as the chief administrator of our casinos and other related gaming interests," he said promptly. "Like I said: Indian gaming."

"You… ran the casinos?"

"Yap. Also brokered the deals with the US government that allowed us to operate. Me and some of the other old farts; we built the whole operation from the ground up."

"I… I didn't realize…"

"Don't worry about it," he said. "I'm usually vague about my involvement. It's an old leftover habit that's hard to break. I liked to stay as unknown as possible. People tend to be more genuine when they don't realize you're the guy in charge."

"Well—okay. So it's safe to say that you didn't really live a life of, uh, violence? Before?"

"Eh, define violence. I mean, growing up on the reservation wasn't exactly a cake walk. A lot of us were hotheads. I used to get in a lot of fights. Even used to win sometimes, too." He smiled at me.

"Nothing after that?" I prodded.

"Oh, nah. Not really. I did a standard four years in the Army but that was after Vietnam was over and before we went sticking our noses into anything else, so that was really just four years of being stationed in various places doing a lot of paperwork. Never saw any action."

"So…" I hesitated; took a breath, "never killed anyone?"

"Ah," he said. "No, ma'am. Not until after."

"I hadn't really killed anyone until today," I said.

"Until… today?" Billy said, confused.

"James wasn't a person," I said. "He was some kind of animal or monster or…something. He just needed to be put down. He was truly evil. I don't feel anything at all for what I did to him. I'd do it again if I had the chance."

"Okay. That's fair enough."

"The people we killed today? They weren't evil. They were just trying to get along for the most part, like us I think. I got Jake to tell me enough of what happened so I could make sense of it all while we drove over here. It was how we kept him awake."

"Well, they did tie your daughter down to a chair," Billy said.

"Oh, I know. I also know one of them held a knife to her. Trust me, if I had seen that I would have killed the bitch myself. But aside from her, those guys who came out shooting at us? That was after Jake had killed two of theirs. In fact, no one had been killed before Jake went to work. All that happened was they stole our van."

"Are you suggesting Jake was wrong?"

"No, I'm not. I'm saying we'll never know how it could have gone because everyone (on both sides) started off by pointing guns instead of talking. I get that we're living in an extreme survival situation right now and that there is true evil in the world. I just wonder how much we're giving up if we start each encounter under the assumption that it has to end in gunfire. I wonder if there was anything I could have said in that warehouse that would have made those guys stop shooting long enough to listen to us. It's bugging me."

I was quiet a moment while I worked up the courage to say the next thing. "I don't know how to say this, really. When I shot that man, I was excited. I felt this intense rush, like, 'Fuck you! I *own you*, bitch!' That feeling, more than anything else, is what scares the hell out of me."

Billy hefted his shotgun and held it out to me. "Hold onto this a second."

"What?"

"Just take it a minute for me."

I did. He went to the truck and dug around in one of the plastic bins. I heard the deep clink of a liquid filled bottle. He came back with two plastic cups and a bottle of some sort of hard liquor. "Jim Beam," he said, "the cheap kind, sorry. I have some better stuff where we're going. This'll have to do for now."

He sat back down and poured us both some cups. He offered me one and took back his shotgun. He saluted me with his cup and took a drink. I did the same, coughed, and shivered.

"Hijole, that's nasty," I gasped.

"You get used to it," he said. After a moment, he cleared his throat. "What you're dealing with, what's bothering you right now? It's a pretty natural thing. In fact, if it wasn't eating at you, I'd be a little worried. It doesn't make it any easier for you to deal with, of course, but it's still a normal reaction."

"Yeah?"

"Yeah. I've got this book in the library of the cabin…"

"You have a library?" I said, giggling.

"Yes, I have a damned library. It's nothing crazy; just an office with a bunch of books on the wall. May I continue?"

"Sorry. Go ahead."

"Thank you." He took another drink and snarled. "Oof. This is pretty horrible. So anyway, this book is called 'On Killing' by Lt. Col. Dave Grossman."

"Ugh, that sounds lovely," I said.

"Yeah, I know, but stay with me. He spends a lot of time examining the act of killing and how it impacts people; mostly from the perspective of the soldier on the battlefield. His point is that the vast majority of the population, ninety-eight percent or so, has this instinctive, hard-wired resistance to killing its own kind. By and large, unless their life is directly threatened, the act of killing another human is just something they wouldn't be able to do.

"Now, this makes sense from the perspective of evolution. The ability to easily murder your own kind without any sort of psychological trauma isn't all that conducive to the preservation of the species. Mother nature has made it so that it's just really hard to kill something that looks like you."

"Wait," I interrupted. "Ninety-eight percent? How can that be? Our prisons were overflowing with murderers."

"Well, yes," he agreed. "But a lot of those murderers came from a culture and society that had been systematically dehumanizing those around them from the time they were able to start watching TV. On top of that, the prisons may have been crowded, but the numbers were still well within the limits of Grossman's data. Look at this: the population of the United States was some three-hundred-twenty million when the Flare hit, right?"

"If you say so," I said.

"It was. So ninety-eight percent of that is… uh—three hundred thirteen million, six hundred thousand. Or in other words: six million, four hundred thousand people in the United States were capable of killing without any real remorse or psychological impact, according to Grossman."

"Well, okay. I'm going to assume all those numbers are correct," I mumbled and took a drink.

"Oh, they are. I'm good with numbers," he said, winked, and took a drink of his own. He opened the bottle up and poured some more for himself.

"I thought you said this stuff was horrible?" I asked.

"Yap, just making sure, though. Want some more?"

"Yes, please," I said while holding out my cup.

"Alright, now the last time I looked up the numbers on this was because I was giving a presentation to the council on this subject in relation to violent crime and some local initiatives to get our youth off the streets—early intervention…that kind of thing. In the whole of the United States, there were two-point-three million people in lock up. That's everyone: local, state, and federal prisons both convicted and not convicted. Keep in mind; those aren't all killers. A lot of them were drugs, burglary, assault, and so on."

"So that means that Grossman's two percent estimate is a little high versus what reality actually is. The bottom line is that most people have a hard time killing other people without walking away from it psychologically damaged."

"Are you saying I'm experiencing PTSD?" I asked.

"I'm nowhere near qualified to make that kind of diagnosis," Billy said seriously. "I am saying that we were in the process of learning that the symptoms of PTSD were much more normal and natural than anyone in history was previously willing to admit. I am also saying that this new world that we find ourselves in is a lot more like what our Neolithic ancestors experienced. Killing is going to become normal again and will become easy if we let it be so. I believe it's going to be important for all of us to understand that and to understand the psychological impacts that killing has on the killer, especially what happens to a person when they become numb to the act. We need to understand all that if there's to be any hope of holding onto what little society we have left and not devolving into a bunch of shitheads. Given enough exposure, a human can become used to anything. That's just basic brain chemistry."

We both took sips from our cups and exhibited various levels of distaste for the contents.

"So…" I began, looking into my cup at nothing in particular, "what does Mr. Grossman say about coping?"

"He said that mental processing of the killing happens in stages. The killing itself is typically an automatic response, as in something you don't even think about at the time. Following that is the elation or euphoria you described. Later there is a period of remorse to work through and, if you're lucky, this will be followed by rationalization and acceptance. Working through these issues, you'll come to realize that you have a natural, God-given right to defend yourself and the lives of your loved ones, which is what you did today."

"So I'm doing the remorse phase right now, huh?"

"More or less."

"How long do these stages last?"

"It's different for everyone. Some people don't even make it all the way through to acceptance." He turned to face me. "The important thing to remember is that you're not alone. We're all going through this; learning how to deal with it. We're here with you, and we're here for you."

I reached out to squeeze his forearm. It was thicker than I expected it to be. "Thanks," I said. "How about you? Are you working through all of this okay?"

"Am," he confirmed. "But, I regret to report that sleep patterns will most likely continue to be affected. Can't say for how long. I'm pretty new to the whole thing myself."

I became mildly curious as to how many people Billy had killed since he'd been on the road but didn't bother asking. It seemed like a pointless and idiotic question.

# 10

# ROAD TRIP

**Amanda**

"Ow..."

I woke up the next morning to (or maybe I was awakened by) the sound of Jake just outside our tent signaling his discomfort with a flat and emotionless "ow." I was disoriented at first. Billy had eventually turned in for a few hours the night before while I stayed outside working through my problems. Sometime later, I heard him moving around inside the tent. He came back out, smacking his lips, and told me to go get some sleep. I was finally able to by then (the whiskey had helped) and I don't remember very much past laying down that second time. I don't know what time it was when I did go to sleep, but it seemed to me that I had slept only an instant before the sound of Jake's voice had me up again.

Lying on my back, I reached out with my right hand, ran it over slippery, cold nylon, and felt an elbow. Elizabeth was still there with me asleep in her bag. I rolled onto my left side and saw the Tavor. Satisfied that all was as I had left it, I sat up, grabbed the rifle, checked the safety, and exited the tent.

Billy and Jake were just outside. They were both sitting in chairs facing each other, with Jake's hand resting on Billy's knee. In front of Billy on the ground was a small box with a blue bottle of disinfectant and some bloody cotton swabs. Billy was working on the back of Jake's hand with a hook needle, needle-nose pliers, and some black suture thread.

"Morning, boys," I said.

"Hey, Little Sis."

"Good mor-ning!" Jake said as a new stitch was begun.

"Anything for breakfast?" I asked.

"Sure," Billy said. "Have a look in the pantry."

I went to the truck bed, which was looking a lot emptier this morning. I realized Billy must have redistributed some items over to the Jeep, which surprised me because I hadn't heard anything; I must have really been out. I noticed the gun bag was gone, but many of the infamous plastic bins were still there. He must have picked these up sometime after he met Jake but he'd had them for as long as I knew him. They were large, plastic containers about two foot by three foot—the basic three-gallon bins that you could find at just about any home store. Billy had a few of these all labeled in black Sharpie as though they were areas in a house. There was one that said "kitchen," another that said "tool shed," and even one that said "bathroom," which is where he kept items like the toothbrushes, toothpaste, soap, and toilet paper. He'd even managed to pack away different brands of deodorant in this container.

Such things may seem trivial in a survival situation, but I'm here to tell you: we were all grateful Billy had the sense to grab these items when he saw them. We were all pretty close in together at various points of our day to day lives and the ability to not smell like animals was a real bonus. It made it a lot easier for us all to get along. You don't spend much time thinking about something as basic as a stick of deodorant, but just try going without it for a few days. When your pits start maintaining a base layer of greasy sweat (if they're not just dripping outright), a speed stick becomes the only thing you can think about.

I pulled the lid off the bin marked "pantry" and dug around in it.

The MRE rations were starting to get low, mostly because (I suspected) they were just so convenient. All we had to do was mix in a little water to get that chemical heater fired up, and in a few minutes, the food was ready to go. Even if some of the meals tasted like boiled cardboard, it was hard to argue with. I pulled out a bag of Maple Sausage breakfast.

"Can I get you two anything?" I asked over my shoulder.

"Nah. We both ate already. You go ahead, Little Sis."

There was a jug of water on the ground by the guys, probably used to clean Jake's wound. "Can I steal some of that?" I asked. Billy nodded; he was bent nearly double over Jake's hand while tying a knot. I got my food pack set up, leaned it against a rock, and claimed a chair (two additional chairs had been put out for when Lizzy and I finally woke up). I messed around with the positioning of the rifle in my lap; it dangled on its sling much more comfortably than it rested on my legs in a narrow chair.

"How you feeling, Jake?" I asked.

"Better," he said, sounding refreshed. "Standing up can get a little hairy; I get dizzy spells and sometimes a wave of nausea if I move too quickly, but the headache seems to be all gone. My head is still sore and bruised where the guy cracked it, but that's just surface area. It only hurts if I touch it."

"Any cognitive issues?" Billy asked without looking up.

Jake was quiet for a moment. Then, in answer, he began to recite the alphabet in reverse at slow but regular intervals. "Z... y... x... w... v... u... t... s... r... q—yeah, I think I'm good. I couldn't get past X when I tried last night."

"Nice," Billy said, and you could hear the smile in his voice. "Those dizzy spells say you still gotta take it easy, but the rest of it is good news."

I heard more movement from our tent. Elizabeth was stirring.

"So what are the plans for today?" I asked.

"Road trip," Billy said promptly. "If it's all the same to everyone else, I'm reversing my earlier position about taking our time. I'd like to avoid encounters with any more assholes if at all possible."

"We do know how to help protect against that, now..." Jake said.

Billy sighed and looked up from his work. "You're correct that we should have cleared the warehouse. You're wrong that it was your fault." The exchange had the sound of an argument that they had worn out before I woke up.

"Agree to disagree," Jake returned.

"Stubborn..." Billy muttered under his breath. He cut the thread with his pocket knife, put his tools aside, and disinfected the area. He began to wrap the hand up in a bandage and said, "You're pretty damned lucky this was just skin. There's plenty of tendons back there; she could have crippled your hand."

"Can I make a suggestion before we hit the road?" I asked.

"Sure," Jake said. "What's up?"

"I know this area. There's a Walmart just down the way, maybe five or ten minutes." I pointed south down the 15 to emphasize. "We have a long way to drive. We need some tunes."

Jake's mouth quirked in what I could have sworn was the shadow of a smile.

Billy grimaced: "Uh, well, I dunno. I don't want us to split up anymore, and I don't want to leave the vehicles alone outside. Anyone could just walk up to the truck and help themselves. It's risky. We don't know if there's anyone in the store..."

"Billy..." Jake said. Billy stopped talking and looked to Jake. "Music is necessary."

I realize now how correct that statement is. We came pretty close to being wiped out as a species—I guess we still could be. Vaccines don't exist anymore so something could come along and finish us off, I suppose. The winters up here are pretty touch-and-go sometimes, too.

Even so, after two years our little community has slowly grown and is beginning to thrive, which gives me hope and tells me that humans aren't done. The Plague wiped out whatever was left over after the Flare did its damage and only a very small percentage remains, which means that creative expression was effectively halted. The development of the arts (as in music, movies, writing, or visual work such as paintings) was at a full stop in those early days. Now obviously, these things aren't at an end—humans have been creating music, telling stories, and doodling on cave walls ever since we learned how to make fire. But at that time, as we all sat out in our campsite, the world might never see the composition of a new song, as far as we could tell. I think Jake and I both were a little homesick for our culture, not because we had been without it for so long but because we knew we would have to be without it for so long.

"Music...is necessary, yes," Billy finally agreed having been infected.

"It's not just the music," I added. When they both looked at me, I elaborated. "You've done a fine job covering all the essentials in your kit, Billy, but those essentials apply mostly to men. There are some... uh... gaps to fill." I grimaced and rolled my eyes at the unfortunate choice of wording.

Billy slapped his forehead. "Of course you need... I'm sorry. That never even occurred to me."

"That's okay," I said. "Aside from that, I was thinking we could grab some things for Lizzy to keep her entertained. Maybe some toys or coloring books if we can find them."

They both nodded, and Billy said, "Absolutely."

"This time," Jake said, "You'll go with Lizzy and Amanda into the store, and I'll stay with the trucks. I think we've seen that Amanda is more than capable of handling herself... more capable than me, really. I seem to get soundly beat up every time I get into a fight."

"You sure you can handle that?" Billy asked, pointing to his temple and gesturing over to Jake's head in the same motion.

It sounded a little condescending to my ears, but Jake didn't seem to take it that way at all. "Yes, I'm good. I'm actually doing better right now if I can stay in one place rather than walking around. I don't think my inner ear is quite right yet. We'll move all the critical items like food and water from the truck to the back of the Jeep where they can be locked inside. I'll keep my eyes open."

Lizzy picked that time to emerge from the tent. Her hair stuck out in wild directions. She slept hard as a general rule and yesterday had been rough. "Hey, everyone," she said and floated into the last empty chair.

"Good morning, Girly!" Billy said.

"Kiddo…" Jake added.

I got up and started doing what Elizabeth calls "Momming." I got some plates and forks out of the "kitchen" and a bottle of water to share between us. "Here, Mija, have some breakfast." I divided the meal equally between us (I have a hard time finishing off a whole MRE by myself; there's a lot more in them than you'd think).

While we ate, Billy hauled the duffel bag out of the back of the Jeep and set it on the ground in front of him.

"Losing the van was a bummer but we're not entirely bereft," he said as he unzipped it. He reached in a pulled out one of the rifles.

"What all is in there?" Jake asked, leaning forward to look in.

"There're four rifles: three AR types and an AK. We have more ammo for the ARs than we do the AK; I almost didn't grab the AK because I didn't want to lug an extra type of ammo on the road but the rifle is so damned reliable that I couldn't pass it up. Aside from that, we have a few assorted pistols in 9 mm and some essential accessories."

"More reliable than these other rifles, huh?" Jake said.

Billy sat back and pinned Jake with his best "I'm serious" look. "I could cover the thing in mud, dump it in a lake to rinse it off, and it would fire happily without a malfunction."

"Well, I'm for that," Jake said. "Which one is the AK?"

Billy reached into the bag to pull out a rifle that was all black and more solid looking than the other rifles I had seen so far. He pulled back the lever and peeked inside. Confirming it was empty, he handed it over to Jake.

"Okay," Jake said while he looked it over. "This one's all different. You'd better take me through it, so I don't miss anything important."

"It's not bad. It has all the same controls you're used to; they're just in different places. The fire selector is on the other side—it's that long bar above the trigger."

Jake rolled the gun over and looked. "Huh. Liked the thumb lever better."

"It's just different, is all," Billy said. "Okay, charging handle is pretty obvious—this one's on the right, so you'll have to take your hand off the grip. I'm not crazy about that myself, but some people don't seem to care. Magazine release is that button just on the front of the trigger guard. Outside of that, fire it similar to the M4, cheek weld and all."

"Magazine?" Jake asked with his left hand extended. Billy bent over and pulled a long, curved bar out of his bag.

"That's thirty rounds," Billy said. "There's another one in the bag just like it. The AK fires 7.62. We have about two hundred rounds between the mags and some boxes."

"How much of the 5.56 do we have?"

"Three hundred-thirty to three hundred-fifty, give or take."

"And then just the assorted 12 gauge and 9 mm, right?"

"Yes," Billy said. "Around two hundred of the one and maybe one hundred-fifty of the other. All of these are round numbers, you understand. I haven't counted them off one-by-one in a while."

"That's fine," Jake said. "So, all of that to get us all the way to Wyoming, huh?"

"I see what you mean. Yeah, I can only think of one place to get more along the way—I'm really only interested in that and stopping for refuels at this point. And music, of course!" he directed at me.

"What about when we get where we're going?" Jake asked.

"Oh, I've been stockpiling a while; all sorts. It should hold us over if we don't get any visitors. But we should make it a practice to always be scavenging for more. I have reloading equipment as well. The issue there will be running out of primers, jacketed slugs, and powder. We'll have to be good about retrieving our brass."

"Can I have a gun?"

Billy and Jake both froze at the sound of Lizzy's voice. Things got intensely quiet as they waited for me to decide how I wanted to deal with the inquiry.

"No," I said. "You're too young for that."

I saw her put her "but, mom" face on.

"Too young," I emphasized.

She looked down at her lap. Billy cleared his throat, leaned forward, and started going through the duffel. Jake looked contentedly off toward the 15.

"Mom? Just listen to me."

Something in that little voice glued my mouth shut. The adult tone that she adopted combined with the timbre of its sound was unsettling. I found myself unable to do anything but comply, as though I had been hypnotized by a viper.

"Things haven't been going so well since we've been out here. There was James and them. Then Jake and I got picked up by those people. I'm always waiting for you or Billy or Jake to save me. If I had a gun, I could protect myself. I could protect you."

I was struck then by how she must have felt. Elizabeth is my daughter, and I will always love her no matter what but in those early days when we were on the run, I'm ashamed to admit that I didn't factor her in as much more than baggage with a mouth. She was a responsibility that had to be juggled along with all the other needs. If we had to scout an area, she was a problem that had to be solved first; a bit of logistics. I hadn't spent a lot of time thinking about her perspective up until that point. People want to feel useful, and they want to feel as though they have some sort of control over their own destiny—even seven-year-old people. This poor girl kept getting shucked from situation to situation without any real say in what was happening to her and she was just looking for some sliver of self-determination. Once upon a time, I would have become frustrated and angry at her continuing to argue with me after I had made a position final, especially on such a hot topic. Now, I was just tired and heartbroken.

"You're right, Mija. You're right. But seven is still too young. I know you'll be eight very soon, but no. I'm sorry. Just a little longer."

"Mom..."

"*No.*"

Now Elizabeth became frustrated. Years of conditioning at the result of being raised by a Hispanic mother meant that she didn't pound her fist, raise her voice, or exhibit any of the other temper tantrum behaviors that had become so common in our youth. Lizzy was old school (because I was old school) and she knew that didn't fly.

COMMUNE | 163

Her mouth only tightened to a line as she calmly but slowly stood from her chair, walked carefully back to the tent, pulled back the flap, and went inside. It was about as close as she came to storming off in a fury.

The boys both remained uncomfortably quiet after Lizzy had gone, studiously focusing on their own immediate areas. When I'd finally had enough, I asked, "Was I wrong?"

Billy shrugged. "You're the mom. Even when you're wrong, you're right."

There must have been some frustration left in my look when I glanced in his direction. He put his hand out gently in a holding-off gesture. "Take it easy. You were right in this case. I agree with you: seven is too young. There's still too much development that needs to happen at that age...too many fine motor control issues. She's old enough that we could start teaching her how to shoot a gun, if you're okay with that, but that's only under constant supervision with one of us over her shoulder at all times. You wouldn't want to just hand her a firearm and forget about it at her age."

This, of course, begged the question: "What age do you think is appropriate?"

"I don't want to put a number on it," Billy said while scratching under his chin and jaw. It was clear the white scruff of his beard was bothering him. "Depends on the individual. I make it a range from about ten to fifteen, if that helps."

"It does," I said. "It gives me about two more years before I have to start worrying about daily heart attacks."

Jake snorted abruptly from his chair, the sound made sharp and angry by his currently useless nose. It startled us both and Billy grinned sheepishly.

"Hand me your rifle a minute please, Amanda," Billy said.

I looked down and popped the swivel from my sling's attachment point on the stock (a trick Billy had demonstrated the night before during our drinking session) and handed the rifle across to Jake, who passed it along to Billy. I watched as Billy pulled the magazine out of the receiver and worked the operating handle to eject the bullet from the chamber. Sliding the bolt back to double check the chamber ("being triple and quadruple sure is always the right thing to do," he always told us), he took the safety off, pulled the trigger, and put the safety back on.

He laid the rifle down in his lap, bent over it, and reached into the duffel bag at his feet. He pulled out a small and irregular shaped flashlight from the bag—it was black, swelling from a cylindrical to a square, blocky profile. He stuffed this into the left breast pocket of his Chino shirt, working his wrist in a few circles to get the light around and under the pocket flap.

Reaching down to the rifle, he manipulated a panel on the front end just to the left of the muzzle. He slid it forward, and it came completely off the weapon, exposing a line of bumpy ribs that looked just like the spine along the top of the gun where the optic was mounted. He put the panel in the duffel bag.

He produced an Allen wrench, pulled the bizarre little flashlight from his shirt pocket, put it on the exposed portion of the rifle, and started fiddling with the wrench. He began talking as he turned it.

"They used to make about a jillion different rail accessories for these rifles back in the world but the only ones I ever thought made any sense were optics and lights."

"Those things are called rails, huh," Jake asked, saving me the trouble.

"Yap. Picatinny rails or Weaver rails. All the same thing: a place to bolt on a bunch of heavy shit and accessorize your weapon like it's a god damned bedazzled handbag."

He handed the rifle back to me by way of Jake. "In this case, it will most likely be dark in the Walmart. You don't want to be goofing around with a rifle and a flashlight. Best to put the flashlight on the rifle. Don't look into that light, now. The package I pulled it from said '1000 lumens.' That's enough to suck."

I found the little button on the back of the unit and pressed it. Even in the early morning light, I could see its beam in the dirt in front of me. I pressed the button to turn it off, but it started flashing at intervals. I pressed it again, and it went back to being solidly on.

"Hold it down," Billy offered. I did, and it turned off. I shouldered the rifle and put my left thumb on the button without activating it. I liked that I could reach the button without having to move my whole hand. I was distracted by Jake, who was holding the magazine out to me.

Taking it, I said, "What about you? No light for the shotgun?"

In answer, Billy grabbed it by the stock and held it straight out in front of him, rotating it slowly so I could see it on all sides. "No rails," he said contentedly and placed it back on the ground. "There are special kits and adaptors that you can get to modify the hell out of an 870... in fact you can even bullpup it, just like your Tavor there. But I could never bring myself to screw with perfection."

We finished out the morning by brushing our teeth, cleaning our hands and faces with wet wipes (Billy packed the essentials as good as any professional mother), and striking camp when all of this was finished. Billy began shifting critical survival items like food, water, and tools from the truck to the back of the Jeep where it could be locked up in an enclosed shell. The gun bag went in the back of the Jeep as well. I rolled up the sleeping bags and worked on taking down the tents with Lizzy. Jake tried to help in this activity, but he was forced to move slowly and deliberately to avoid dizzy spells, which meant that we ended up accomplishing three or four tasks for every one of his. We had our tent completely bundled and stowed while he was still busy breaking his down, even accounting for a false start in which the tent wouldn't fit in its carrying bag because we had folded it incorrectly. We went to him to offer help hesitantly, wondering if he would be irritable and insist on doing all the work himself. Instead of being annoyed, he gratefully accepted.

All things being put away, we went to the back of the Jeep and prepared ourselves. We only had the two vests; one went back on me with the help of a little fresh duct tape. The other went on Lizzy at Jake's insistence. It took a bit of work on Billy's part to get it to fit properly as it initially hung so low on her that too much of her upper chest was exposed for the vest to be of any use. Billy adjusted the shoulder straps down as tight as they would go and then doubled what was left of the straps back over on themselves, wrapping them in several rounds of duct tape each.

The midsection was taped down in a fashion similar to my own vest. We pulled a large sweater over the result and, though the shoulders stuck up like a woman's power blazer out of the 1980s, the solution was workable enough that she was protected adequately and could still move well.

In my case, I opted to put the vest on over my shirt this time and then just buttoned the flannel up over it. Jake and Billy's reasoning about keeping the vest hidden to keep opposing weapons aimed at my torso, which would be the most protected part of me, made good sense. I was beginning to wonder about the other point that had been made.

"Hey, Jake," I said. "Remember how you told me about that article Billy read—about how guys tricked out in military gear were targeted more than the average looking folks in those society breakdown situations?"

"I do," Jake said.

"Grey Men. That was a good article," Billy said as he slipped a bandolier over his head.

"Well, I don't think that applies anymore."

"Oh yeah?"

"Yes. As a society or a species, we've never actually been this bad off. Everyone is a target now, whether we look like soldiers or not. Someone pushing a shopping cart down the street used to be a hobo. Now that same person is a target because that cart probably has goodies, maybe even water. The fact that we're driving around in a convoy makes us more of a target than any fancy gear we're wearing. If that kind of gear really is useful or gives us any kind of edge, we should use it when we can."

"Yeah. Hell, she's right," Billy said. "Dammit…"

"What is it?" Jake asked.

"When you look at it that way, I should have grabbed all them tac-vests and MOLLE gear back in Vegas. Damn it!"

"It's fine," Jake said. "It all would have been stolen with the van, anyway."

"Don't bring that up again. I'm still pissed about that van."

We finished gearing up. I got in the Jeep with Jake, but Lizzy opted to ride with Billy up in the truck (I think she was still angry with me). I let her have it. She needed the time to cool off.

———

Billy followed us in the truck since I knew the way to the store, but once we got there, he extended his arm out the window and motioned for us to follow him. He drove us around to the back of the building where the loading docks were located. We reversed both of our vehicles down one of the ramps leading to a roll-up door, and I saw that we were easily below ground level once we had backed up all the way to the bottom of the trough. Even if someone happened by the back of the building, they wouldn't notice anything until they were right on top of us.

"Do you have any requests once I'm in there?" I asked Jake.

"I'd like to avoid Bro Country and Bieber, if at all possible."

"I can live with that," I chuckled. "How about what you might actually want? Makes it easier on me."

Jake's eyes squinted as he looked out over the dashboard. "See if you can find any Johnny Cash."

"Cash, huh?" I said, mildly surprised.

"You don't care for the Man in Black?"

"Oh, no, he's fine. I just didn't think of you as a Cash fan."

We were interrupted by Billy outside. "C'mon, let's get moving." I smiled at Jake, grabbed the keys, and hopped out of the Jeep. Billy was already moving toward the steps leading up to the door that was next to our ramp. He was carrying the crowbar with him.

Jake was out of the Jeep and walking up the ramp in the opposite direction to a point where he could just see over the edge of the walls in both directions, his eyes level with the ground. "How long do you think you'll be?" he called back to us. He was shifting his new rifle around and adjusting the spare magazine in his hip pocket.

"I think give us about thirty minutes," Billy said; trying the handle of the door and finding it locked. "After that, come check on us." He lifted the crowbar and started prying daintily at the lock just as he had done at the house the day before.

"I can give you what *feels* like thirty minutes," he offered back. "No watch."

Billy put down the bar and looked back at him. "What kind of man doesn't have a watch?"

Jake shrugged. "I just used a cell phone before."

Billy shook his head and threw the truck keys over to Jake, who caught them deftly out of the air. It was a throw of perhaps fifty feet and rather impressive for how casual it was. "Use the truck radio," Billy said and turned back to the door. He finished mangling it open (it took much longer than the house—there was a metal plate protecting the bolt that had to be pried back first) and returned the crowbar to the truck. "Well, come on you two. Let's get it."

It was dark and cold on the other side of the door; the only light was coming in from outside. Billy pulled a flashlight out of his pocket and handed it to Lizzy. "I can't deal with this and the shotgun," he told her. "I need you to manage it for me. Just pay attention to me and try to keep it pointed wherever I'm looking. If you hear a noise, shine that light on it for me, and I'll look into it. Whatever you do, don't shine that in your mama's or my eyes."

"Okay," she said and took the flashlight. She turned it on and pointed it out in front of her. I reached up with my thumb and activated the light on my rifle, which threw way more illumination than I expected for such a little device. Billy propped the door open with a box he found nearby.

We were in the back warehouse section of the store. It was a smaller area than I had expected it to be (I guess they wanted to get as much floor space for shoppers as possible when they were still operating) but it was still of decent size, with lines of storage racks running throughout the area. Most of these were empty, but some still had pallets sparsely populated with items. The whole area was ghostly and oppressively quiet, all things standing out in the no-color of our flashlights in flat shades of grey. Little motes of dust reflected the beams back at us, further limiting our visibility. The size of the storage area seemed to expand and contract by turns; if I set my light level with the floor, it spanned easily across the room and to the opposing wall, which was fifteen or twenty feet away at most. When I lowered the muzzle back to the floor, all shrank back in around us. Sounds became stuck as they traveled through the air and it was psychologically hard to breathe.

"I somehow pictured this all to be a lot brighter," I said. "I'm starting to feel as though this is a stupid idea."

"It'll be okay," said Billy from behind me. "There will be skylights on the main floor. He made his way around me and walked toward a set of double doors across the room. "We'll make one complete circuit around the store. One full track around the outer perimeter and then a few passes through the center to make sure it's just us in here. Following that, we'll grab a cart or two and go shopping."

He pulled the door open, and we all stepped through, heads turning in an attempt to look everywhere at once.

"Uh... damn..." said Billy.

The interior of the store was just short of obliterated. There was still merchandise in the store, but it appeared that an army of rear-ranging ninja elves had swarmed through the store with the sole purpose of taking everything off the shelves and placing it all on the floor. The merchandise itself was in various stages of repair, from entirely intact to completely pulverized.

I straightened up and squared my shoulders. "C'mon. There's stuff in here. It's just not easy to find and conveniently located."

"There's actually more than I thought there was going to be," Billy said.

We started moving out among the aisles, picking our way carefully among the debris. I left the rifle light on, and Lizzy continued to use her flashlight—the skylights helped, but without the electrical lighting to back them up it was still too dim to see in any detail. I tried to take note of items that might be useful as we went but soon gave up as the total chaos of it all defeated the attempt. I struggled to reconcile the carnage as we went.

"I get why a band of looters would have passed on the Cuisinart

Waffle Maker," I said, nudging the unit over with my toe, "but what the hell? Why would anyone take the time to so completely trash the place?"

"Got me," said Billy. "I'm still shocked how much stuff is still in here."

"Maybe they thrashed everything because it was fun?" Elizabeth said while shining her light on a cascade of glass shards spilled across the floor.

Billy and I both stopped to look at each other. "Should I be worried that the idea of destroying the place in the name of fun makes sense to me?" I asked.

"Nah," said Billy. "I always hated these joints when the world was still sane. Works for me."

We rounded the outside corner and turned onto the front expanse of the store. I sighted down the aisle, lighting up an array of abandoned check-out stands and self-service kiosks.

"When you think about it, it kind of makes sense," I said. "There was a lot of crap in these places…a lot of stuff that people wanted but probably didn't need. Once everything went crazy, most of this stuff was rendered pointless. People don't need game consoles and picture frames right now; they need food and water—survival supplies, the essentials. The window for the kind of rampant merchandise looting we used to see back in the world was short. I remember hearing about people raiding electronics stores after the Flare when the grid failed. By the time the Plague hit, all of that was over. People were just trying to survive; not score Blu-ray players. And it killed everyone so fast once it really spread…people were too sick to venture out."

As if to emphasize my point, we began to pass what was left of the food aisles, which were absent of anything useful at all. Water, dry goods, any kind of canned food—even cereal boxes were all gone. What little was left of the perishable items like dairy products, fruits, and vegetables sat on the shelves and behind glass in isolated, rotting pockets.

We finished our rounds of the interior without event or further comment. Whoever it was that trashed the place was long gone by the time we got there. Billy located a couple of shopping carts and passed one over to Elizabeth. Pushing one cart himself, he was unable to handle his shotgun properly, so he put the safety on and rested the barrel on his shoulder such that the muzzle pointed at the ceiling behind him. He set the stock on the handle of his cart, resting his right hand over it to keep it secure, and steered the cart with his left.

"You're on point, Little Sis. Eyes open."

"On point?" I asked.

"Push out in front of us and keep your rifle ready."

"Oh, yeah. Sure thing."

We made our way to the electronics section first because we assumed the packaged CDs would take up the most space in the carts. I started to pick my way through the CDs that had been left on the racks as well as those strewn across the floor. Billy, on the other hand, began to grab everything in great, sweeping armloads and dumped it all in his cart. He must have felt my eyes on him throughout the racket he made because he stopped and looked back at me.

"Chop, chop," he said, clapping his hands together lightly. "We can sort all this stuff out on the road." He continued to scoop piles of cellophane-wrapped music unceremoniously into his shopping cart.

"Makes sense, I suppose," I sighed, and followed suit.

It turned out he had the right idea—we had just about everything but the preschool toddler music loaded up into two mountainous piles inside of five minutes. As Billy finished arranging the piles before they could overbalance, I moved through the aisles on my own until I located a portable CD player and an AC power inverter that would plug into the Jeep's cigarette lighter. Billy was good to go; his truck was old enough that it came with a CD player as standard equipment.

"You guys ready?" I asked when I came back to them with my two new finds tucked under my arm.

"Just about," Billy said. "It's a long shot, but I want to go look at where they kept the batteries. If there are any left, we should grab them."

"Good idea," I said. I placed the boxes for the CD player and power inverter into Lizzy's cart; it wasn't filled as high as Billy's.

There were none of the standard batteries to be had in any capacity, but we did manage to find a few of the more uncommon items. We found a few six and twelve volt universal lead-acid batteries, a few rechargeable battery packs (which looked suspiciously like a couple of AA's that had been shrink-wrapped together and attached to a sophisticated cable), and literally fistfuls of alkaline button and lithium coin batteries (the last of which Billy said could be used to power our rifle optics, which would need a replacement sometime after two to four years—he was always thinking ahead). At one point, I saw Billy's hand shoot out from the corner of my eye; when I looked in his direction, I saw that he was picking up a cheap Timex watch.

The toy section was next. The area was just as thrashed as the rest of the store but we managed to find a selection of coloring books that Lizzy liked the look of as well as a large box of Crayons and one of the more expensive containers of markers. When I told her she could pick out whatever toys we could fit in the cart, she looked around herself for a few moments, face solemn. She finally reached out and selected a Barbie doll, causing me to suppress a gag reflex (my parents had not been able to afford Barbie dolls when I was little, which I think contributed to the fact that I've always loathed them).

"Is that all you want, Mija? There's so much more in here," I said.

"Just this," she said with her small voice. "I don't like it in here."

I nodded and rubbed her back. "C'mon, baby. Almost done."

We stopped by the feminine products area (Billy standing well outside of the aisle as though he was a vampire avoiding a church) and I executed a repeat performance of the CD shopping spree. I grabbed everything I could get my hands on including boxes of pads and tampons, razors, lotions, cleaning products, and deodorant. Whatever space was left in the remaining cart was quickly occupied and then some, with a mound of female paraphernalia that towered over the edges of the cart walls.

"Okay," I said. "Are we good? I know this is my idea, but this place is really starting to get to me."

"Yeah, let's call it," Billy agreed.

We retraced our steps to the back of the store, through the customer service desk, and out the rear storage area. As we moved through the storage racks, I could see Billy's inner packrat perk up as his head swung around to look at the various boxes that were still left on the pallets. I'll bet that guy was a serious antique store hound in a previous life; his two favorite things to do were to relax by a fire at the end of a long day and scavenge.

Jake was where we left him outside, rifle couched in his elbow and scanning over the lip of the loading dock walls. "You guys find anything good?" he asked without looking back.

"Yes, come over and give us a hand," I said back.

He turned and saw us waiting in line with two overfilled shopping carts at the top of the steps. "Holy…" he said and hurried over to help carry them down. "I didn't think you'd be bringing back the entire store."

"It felt really exposed in there," Billy offered by way of an explanation. "I wanted to get out as fast as possible; we weren't exactly discerning in our selection."

"Well, let's get these unloaded. We'll throw them on the floor of the back seat in the jeep and sort through them as we go," said Jake.

"You take that cart," Billy said, pointing at the one Lizzy was leaning on. "I'll take this one to the truck." Unspoken was Billy's desire to also listen to music as he drove; Jake and I hid smiles behind his back as he pushed the cart over to the rear door of the Dodge.

I started moving handfuls of items into the Jeep and Jake came over to help. "Mija, go help Billy please," I said to Elizabeth.

She said: "Okie-dokie," and trotted over to him. She had evidently forgotten to be angry with me, for which I was thankful.

We finished unloading everything into the back row and stashed the batteries and toiletries in the back. Jake walked over to where Billy and Elizabeth were just finishing up and said, "You can't be sifting through those while you drive. Someone better ride with you."

"Oh, that's nonsense," Billy said. "I'll be fine."

"The truck is a manual, man. You don't have enough hands. There's no such thing as roadside assistance or emergency services.

Let's don't get cocky and wreck a vehicle needlessly. We have a long way to go yet."

"I'll ride with you, Billy," Lizzy said. She smiled at him and took his hand, which I truly believe put an end to any further protest. Billy could be a pushover for the girls.

I realized then how perfectly natural it seemed to me that she should be riding along with him in his truck. We had only been with these two men for a matter of days, and I already trusted them both completely. They had both risked their lives more than once to protect us, had both killed for us, and I had done the same for them. I found myself amazed at how quickly we were forming into a family. I think the heightened danger, risk, and sheer adrenaline of what we had been through together certainly played a part in accelerating the process but it was definitely real. We had begun to find a home in these people. Billy said that we were "building community" between us and even knew a word in his people's ancestral language, though I'm ashamed to say that I can't remember its pronunciation anymore. I remember that it sounded like "Taxlis-something." I really wish I had written it down now; I don't think anyone can speak that language anymore.

Billy fished around in his jacket pocket, pulled out the Timex, and handed it to Jake. "Here, I bought this for you."

"Well, thank you. That's very thoughtful."

"Yeah, well, let's not start taking long, hot showers together just yet. Just put the thing on, and we'll call it even."

Jake leaned his AK against the wall of the dock and put the watch on, fiddling with the plastic strap until it was secure. He retrieved his rifle with a nod and walked around to the driver's side of the Jeep, at which point Billy stopped him. "Yo! You think you're ready for that?"

"I do. I haven't really felt fuzzy or dizzy since waking up this morning and moving around."

Billy didn't move and only gave Jake his best disapproving poker face.

"I'll have Amanda with me," he said. "If I feel wrong, I'll stop, and she can take over. You saw me catch those keys, right?"

"Excuse me," I interrupted. "I don't recall you asking if you could drive my Jeep, fella."

The look on his face was priceless: shock shifted to horror shifted to embarrassment in one fluid display. There are very few times I can think of since then where his face was so expressive. It was rendered both comical and pitiful from the bruising still evident around his eyes. He began to stammer, "Oh... crap... look, I... hey, I'm sorry..."

I couldn't help myself; I burst out laughing at him. I was secretly proud at getting such a reaction out of him as he was usually so unreadable. I found it comforting to be able to crack through that armor.

"Calm down, Lancelot," I coughed after the laughing fit had subsided. I threw him my keys across the hood. "I'm not angry. Just maybe a bit less assumptions going forward, huh?"

"Yes, ma'am," he said seriously.

We all climbed into our respective vehicles. Billy hung his arm out the driver's side window to give his door panel two solid slaps with his open palm, put the truck in gear, and pulled away. Jake started the Jeep and followed behind him.

"Keep that rifle handy until we get moving along the 15, okay?" Jake said. I nodded and positioned the muzzle so that it pointed out my window. The whole affair felt a bit clumsy with my left hand on the grip, but I was at least confident enough to spray a few rounds in the general direction of danger if required. We drove on in silence with tension building in our backs and shoulders as we passed buildings. My own back felt like it was trying to fold double onto itself by the time we reached the turnoff to the freeway; I spent every minute of that drive waiting to hear a gunshot signaling that we were under attack.

As we swung north up the 15 and left the largest of the buildings, houses, and stores behind us, I finally loosened up enough to talk.

"So, I'm pretty convinced now that this whole excursion was a horrible idea. At least that's what my nerves are telling me."

"I don't think so," said Jake. "Look, we're going to have to get good at this kind of thing. It's not like we get to Billy's cabin and we're suddenly done. We'll still have to go out on a regular basis and scrounge for supplies. The more opportunities we get to practice, the better we'll get. Think of today as a trial run."

I contemplated diving into the experiences of that day on a regular basis. "Ugh. We'd better start collecting hard liquor. I'll need to take up drinking just to keep my nerves steady."

"Oh, you'll see," Jake said, waving my statement away with a hand. "You're only saying that because you're still keyed up from yesterday. It'll get routine, I'm sure. You can get used to anything given enough iterations."

"Iterations?" I said. I was wondering what kind of person used the word 'iterations' as part of their everyday conversation. "Jake, what did you do for a living?" It struck me that I knew next to nothing about him.

"This and that," he said without offering elaboration. "So, what do we have in the way of music?"

"You name it," I said. I noticed his obvious deflection but chose not to pursue it. "Bowie, Skynyrd, Taylor Swift, Eminem…there's Prince, Starboy…"

"Starboy?" he interrupted. "What exactly is a Starboy?"

"R&B singer," I said. "Let's see… I'm not seeing any Cash in here. Oh, here's some Elvis! Uh, Beatles… Radiohead, Mastodon, AC/DC…"

"Why don't you just pick something?"

"Well," I said while I thumbed through a few more cases. "Can't go wrong with Black Keys, I suppose."

"Yeah, they're good," Jake agreed. "Spin it!"

"Spin…it?" I asked.

"Never mind."

I pulled the power inverter out of its packaging and loaded it into the cigarette lighter in the dashboard. Following that, I got out the CD player, unwrapped the CD (struggling to get all of the annoying cellophane into an orderly ball) and loaded it up. The slow, distorted growl of Dan Auerbach's guitar began to claw its way out of the speakers not long after I hit the play button and "All You Ever Wanted" filled the cab of the Jeep as we rolled up the 15. I had no idea what was coming next, but the simple act of riding in a car with music playing helped to inject the illusion of normalcy back into my life for at least a little while. I looked over at Jake and caught him grinning out of the corner of my eye. I could almost forget the rifle I had wedged between my seat and the door.

# 11

# SWAP MEET

## Amanda

We drove a steady and consistent pace for the next three and a half hours before Billy's truck was pulling off toward an exit. Rather than taking the exit outright, he pulled over and slowed to a crawl in the middle of the highway. He stuck his arm out of the window and waved us forward. Jake complied, and I rolled down my window so we could talk to him.

"What's up?" Jake asked.

"I want to make a stop at this place here," he said, hooking his thumb toward a large, square looking building a few hundred feet to the East of us. It stood by itself, alone in a vast field—about as middle of nowhere as you'd please. It had large, red letters on the front of it that read "*BARNES.*"

"What is it?" I asked. I felt my stomach tighten at the prospect of another building sweep. I had convinced myself we wouldn't be doing this again until after we made it to Wyoming. My discussion with Jake had suggested that we may be at it again before we got there. I was utterly unprepared for the prospect of doing it only a few hours after the last excursion.

"They sold ammo and reloading supplies. I had this marked as a stop on my route since day one, just like the Vegas stop."

I put my eyes forward and cursed under my breath. Ammunition of any kind was simply too important to pass up. I think Jake must have known what was going through my head because he said, "What do you think about sitting this one out? You got the last building. I'll take this one. Gets boring standing outside, yes?"

I looked at him, trying to decide if I should be annoyed. The look in his eyes was perfectly serious and without guile; I decided to be touched instead. "You did say that I would have to get used to this," I reminded him.

"Well, I did, but this is a bit much," he told me. He nodded to Billy and waved him on, signaling that we would follow. "I figure we can spell each other. Billy has to go every time if he's going to insist on stopping every few miles..." he trailed off as we took the 300 North Street exit.

I considered his offer but ultimately decided to reject it. "No," I said, "you get the next one. Like you said, this probably gets easier the more I do it. I'd prefer 'easy' to happen sooner rather than later."

"Well, I can respect that," he said. "You're on. I'll take the next one."

"Do you mind if Lizzy stays with you?" I asked. "It didn't seem like a big deal last time until we got into the building. Once we were in there, it became clear how dangerous it actually was."

Jake scratched his chin and was silent a moment. "You sure you're comfortable with that? I failed miserably the last time we tried-"

"No. No, you didn't," I interrupted. "You went and got her back. At great risk to your own life, you got her back. You fought for her as hard as her own father would have." I stopped talking as his whole demeanor changed. Any bit of latent expression sloughed from his face completely, leaving a half-lidded, dead stare in its place. It was the kind of look actors assumed in movies when they had to pretend to be hypnotized. This was the first time I had witnessed this change in him, but it would not be the last; I would later learn that this is the exact same expression he wears when he decides to kill someone. I had forgotten to be afraid of him as I became used to his manner and company, even enjoyed having him around. This look reminded me why I had feared him when we first met.

I looked away from him and suppressed a shudder. "Anyway, I know she's as safe with you as she'd be with me," I said and let the matter drop.

"Yeah..." I heard him say from about a hundred miles away.

Billy attempted to lead us around the back of the building as we had done earlier that morning, but there was actually no "back" to drive around to. There was a firing range immediately behind the building, which they must have used to test the ammunition that was made on site. He drove us around to the south side of the building as a compromise, and we backed in there.

We all got out of the vehicles and Billy promptly came over to throw a monkey wrench into our planning.

"Listen," he said, "I don't like how visible we are from the road. All three of you hang out here by the vehicles, and I'll go through this place myself. You have good visibility; if you see anything coming lay on the horn and I'll come out."

"Are you sure?" Jake asked. "One of us can lay on the horn just as well as three."

"I am. I want you guys to be able to support each other if a group comes along. I'll be quick, I promise."

We checked our rifles and leaned them against the truck. He opened a rear door on the Jeep for Lizzy to hop into and then leaned against the bed of the truck to eyeball the road. Billy tried the side door and found it unlocked this time. "Well, that's not a hopeful sign," he muttered. "Be right back." He disappeared into the door, shotgun and flashlight in tow.

We weren't waiting out there very long, maybe only five or ten minutes. Jake and Lizzy chatted about the music selection that had ended up in the truck. She had apparently been schooling Billy on some of the very best Lady Gaga had to offer all afternoon. Their conversation was interrupted by Billy bursting from the building.

Jake and I both swung back around toward him with our rifles leveled. We both lifted the muzzles high when we saw it was him. He had the wild-eyed look of a prospector too long in the hills away from humanity who had stumbled across a massive gold strike. He walked directly up to us and said in a very low voice, "Let's start moving the food and water back over to the truck." I couldn't be sure, but I thought I saw his eye twitching. "We hit the god damned jackpot!"

————

We made Spanish Fork just after four in the afternoon. This was the next in a series of planned refueling stops that Billy had mapped out on our route to Jackson, Wyoming. Our vehicles had become an integral part of our survival so the intent was to not push things. We would stop for top-offs whenever our tanks were at half empty or less, assuming the area looked hopeful (meaning there were enough cars to tap with good visibility in the surrounding area). Spanish Fork was a town dense with housing along with the businesses to support that housing; there were vehicles aplenty for us to exploit.

We exited the freeway at Main Street and only had to proceed south for a block or two before we started passing vehicles stopped in the middle of the road. Rather than getting in too deep, we opted to stop there just in sight of the freeway and begin what I was already thinking of as our topping-off operation. I had engaged in this activity once before with Billy when we first picked up the Jeep, but I didn't see the particulars at the time; my job at that point had been to stand as a look-out for Billy while he worked under the cars.

"Come on," Billy said as he hefted the jack from the truck bed, "Jake can keep a look out for us this time. You can watch me and learn how to do this. It's really easy."

Hearing this, Jake positioned himself between the truck and the Jeep just between their front bumpers, his AK-47 held at the ready. He started scanning back and forth over the horizon like some kind of automated sentinel. Billy positioned the jack toward the rear wheel of our first target (a grey sedan), showing me how to find a strong jack point as he did. He lifted the end of the car up just high enough that he could wriggle under on his back. I lowered down onto the ground and lay on my side to see what he was doing.

"Okay, just stay out there and watch what I do. At some point, I'll find a jack stand, and this process will actually be safe…" His hand reached out, snagged the lip of one of his drip pans, and swung it back up over his head in an arc like he was making a one-winged snow angel. He pulled out a mallet and punch to go to work on the tank.

The first drip pan was nearly filled when the flow of gas began to die out. Billy tsked to himself and said, "Eh, maybe the next one has more."

"Guys," Jake called from his position as Billy wiggled out from under the car. "Company."

Billy and I locked eyes. I could see the gears turning in his head; an ambush with two-thirds of the adults in such a vulnerable position was bad news. "How many?" he asked without moving.

"I only see the one right now. He's keeping his distance."

"Let's get out there and see," Billy said to me and started to scoot back out from the car. From my position, all I had to do was roll to my back and sit up. I was walking back toward the Jeep while Billy was still in the process of achieving an upright position, looking over Jake's shoulder as I opened the door, told Lizzy to stay down, and pulled out my rifle. There was indeed a single person a quarter of a mile distant— far enough away that I could see only basic details. He stood unmoving, watching us.

"How long has he been there?" I asked as I came to stand beside Jake.

"Not sure. I called out to you as soon as I noticed him."

"He's just been standing there watching?"

"Uh-huh."

"So, what do we do?"

"Not…sure."

I looked at Jake and saw that this was true. His expression was focused; the unconscious look he assumed whenever in the process of solving a puzzle. He looked out over the distance between us and the stranger, unblinking.

"We have a choice, here," Billy said from behind us. "We can pack up and move on or approach. Either option comes with its risks."

"Leaving has risks?" I asked.

"Yes," Jake answered. "Right now, we can see him. If we leave, we'll lose sight of him, but he'll probably be able to keep an eye on us. Means he can follow us. In fact…" he trailed off as he started looking out in all other directions, "there could be friends of his closing in right now while he stands there distracting us."

"Look!" Billy said.

The stranger put one hand above his head and began to wave at us in large, sweeping arcs. He then lifted what was clearly a rifle over his head and held it aloft for several seconds, giving us all plenty of time to see it. Finally, he let the barrel drop toward the ground where it swung back and forth (there must have been a two-point sling on it), holding it out away from himself in that position, pointing down at the ground. He turned his back on us and began walking due north back toward the 15. He continued to hold the rifle out away from himself in the same fashion as he walked away.

"What the hell…" Billy muttered.

"I think we're being invited to a meeting," I said.

"Yeah," Jake said, nodding slowly. "I believe you're right, Amanda."

"Sure, a meeting. Or luring us into a *damned trap*," grated Billy.

"I'll go," Jake said. "I want to see."

"This ain't firewood, Jake," said Billy, making no sense at all to me. "We know there's something out there this time. The smart bet is to just move on."

Jake sighed, a sound that was so worn and exhausted that I almost felt by way of premonition the person he would eventually become. I have read about hindsight bias and know how it works, but I would almost swear to you that I saw into his future in that moment; saw the weight he would one day place voluntarily on his own shoulders. It made me feel tired to think of it.

"Billy," he said with the sound of someone repeating an old argument, "I'm not going to live in a world where the first instinct is always 'shoot them in the face.' If they prove out to be bad people, then fine."

"That'll get you killed," Billy answered.

"That's fine, too," Jake said. "It's why I'll go alone and see." He handed his rifle over to me. "There is no sensible reason we all have to turn into a bunch of pirates. We managed to function as a society before all this. The only thing that keeps us from continuing to do so is our decision to stop."

With that, he began to walk in the direction of the stranger.

"Yeah, well I just hope the rest of the population got the damned memo!" Billy called from behind him. He watched Jake walk away, clearly indecisive about what he should be doing. He finally scoffed and said, "Shit. C'mon, Little Sis. Let's go after him. You follow behind in the Jeep. I'll get this gas into a can and catch you up. Won't take long."

The stranger led us all off Main Street in a northeast direction along a narrow patch of dirt that ran just along the freeway interchange connecting the 15 to the 6. Billy and I had to drive up over the curb on the right and navigate through a small, landscaped patch of earth past the sidewalk. Beyond this was a narrow corridor walled in by the freeway on the left and a row of trees acting as a windbreak on the right. The corridor was narrow enough that we had to drive single file behind Jake; the branches of the trees would reach out occasionally and scrape along our door panels. I remember worrying about the Jeep's paint job like a moron.

We continued on along this narrow track for close to four hundred yards. Towards the end, the wall on the left lowered, disappearing into the ground and the track itself opened up into a large dirt triangle that was around the size of a professional baseball field; the exit point of our little path made up the South West corner. The triangle itself was bisected by the long, sweeping curve of the interchange as it wrapped back around on itself and provided South-bound access to the 6. In the top half of this triangular dirt area just off the highway 6 awaited our stranger as well as a minivan and what looked like a small campsite.

There was an easy-up sun shade close by with some chairs positioned beneath it.

We spread out wide to either side of Jake and remained twenty feet behind him; far enough to keep a good field of vision but close enough to swing around in front of him to provide cover if things became violent. For his part, Jake walked deliberately toward the camp, never wavering or hesitating. We moved at a steady four or five mile per hour pace, which is actually a pretty good walking speed but was painfully slow for me as a driver. I instinctively understood the purpose of doing it this way; giving the stranger time to look Jake over and become comfortable to his presence. Unfortunately for me, it had the side effect of making my nerves feel like frayed cables. I stole a glance over at Billy and saw he was doing little better—he was bent over the wheel of the truck trying to choke the life out of it with a death grip.

One hundred feet out from the minivan, Jake extended his palms to us and fanned his hands slightly, telling us to wait there. I applied the brake but did not put the Jeep in park so that I could slam down on the gas instantly if I had to. Jake continued on his path to meet the stranger with his hands extended far out to either side of him. I saw the stranger nod and put his hands out as well. I noticed now that he was a black man, probably around the same age as Billy if not a tad younger, judging by the grey in his thinning hair. He was wearing brown cargo pants and a grey T-shirt with a button collar. Jake walked to within a few feet of him. They both dropped their hands and began to talk.

Both of them looked incredibly stiff during this exchange. Having been in close company with Jake for the past few days, I had become used to his body language and was to a point where I could read his basic moods through those cues fairly well. His arms hung long at his sides without fidgeting, his back was upright, and his head was thrust forward slightly; it was the way the cowboys always stood in the old spaghetti westerns just before having a shootout, only Jake didn't have any guns. He was playing nice right now, but it was easy for me to see he was ready to get nasty very fast.

In the case of the other man, he held himself stiff and rested his weight on his rear foot with his thumbs looped into his front pockets.

His expression was guarded, but he looked Jake directly in the eyes as they talked to each other, which I felt was reassuring. He struck me as a man who was both confident and not in the habit of hiding things.

Presently, the black man gestured back toward the minivan, where I could just make out the silhouette of a head in the passenger window. The sun was low, now, and to my back, throwing a glare and making it hard to see.

Jake nodded and extended his hand to the man, who accepted it while smiling. Jake nodded again to him, released his hand, and walked back in our direction. He positioned himself between our vehicles and spoke to us through our open windows.

"This man has people with him: his son and two others that they picked up on the road. He was out foraging for supplies when he saw us come off the freeway. They would like to trade and exchange news."

Billy asked: "They seem okay to you?"

"Yes," Jake said. "Pull up close in a circle around the camp. They have water they can part with. Bullets are the main thing they're in need of."

Billy and I both perked up at this; our water supply was getting low enough that we would have to stop soon to find more—not dangerously low but enough that we began to think nervously of the shape we would be in if we suffered a vehicle failure and had to go back to walking. If a trade was successful, we might be able to push all the way through without having to stop for any.

"There's a kid!" Lizzy said from the back seat.

A boy had exited from the minivan and now stood by the man's side; his son, I assumed. Billy pulled the truck forward in an arc and drove it around to the side of the easy-up opposite the minivan, parking in the opposing direction while obscuring my view. I swung out left and then made a large U-turn to pull up behind his truck.

The black man waved at me and nodded as I killed the engine. I nodded back and smiled. Smiles were cheap. I sat in the Jeep for an indecisive moment and finally opened my door halfway to speak to him. "I have a rifle here with me. Are we getting off on the wrong foot if I bring it out of the car?"

"No, ma'am. I've a rifle here, too. Just another tool we all have to carry, now, like a pocket knife." He had a good Southern drawl on him, pronouncing words like "anothah" and "carreh."

I thanked him, pulling the sling over my head and arm. I came out of the Jeep and heard the man chuckle. "What?" I asked as I looked back at him after closing my door.

"I was just thinking: that is *one hell* of a pocket knife," he said while pointing at the Tavor. I didn't know what to say to this, so I just waved for Elizabeth to get out of the Jeep. I walked over to the man with my left hand resting along the top spine of my rifle to keep it from swinging. I extended my right hand to shake.

"I'm Amanda," I said. "This is my daughter, Elizabeth."

"I am pleased to meet you, Amanda," he said as he took my hand. His hands were warm and soft; well cared for. He put his hand out for Elizabeth, who took it shyly. "Pleased to meet the both of you ladies." He shook with Billy as well, who had just approached (not carrying his shotgun, I noted). "My name is Otis; this here is my son Ben."

Ben put his hand out to shake each of ours in turn and said either "Sir" or "Ma'am" as he shook each, even to Elizabeth. He was a beautiful young man of maybe eleven or twelve years who very clearly favored his father. He was on a definite path to break hearts one day, assuming he could find any to break.

Billy gave his name belatedly and said, "Jake mentioned you had two others with you?"

"Yeah," Otis nodded and held his finger up in a wait-one-minute gesture. "They're a bit skittish. I'll have 'em out. Make yourselves at home!" This last was shot out over his shoulder as he went around to the far side of the minivan and slid open the side door. We heard him conversing with those hidden inside behind the tinted glass. I noted Jake was already pulling chairs out of the truck bed and setting them up in a lazy circle opposite to Otis's.

Presently, Otis came back out from around the minivan with two new people, clearly brother and sister. They looked to be either in their late teens or early twenties.

The girl was pretty in the way that all young people are pretty, with youthful skin, thick, lush hair, and a lean body; however it was clear that as she aged, her larger nose would become prominent if not distracting. Her brother featured the same nose but, with his stronger chin and masculine facial structure, the nose would serve only to add to his appeal in a Clive Owen kind of way as he aged. Any appeal he may have had right then was masked by an obviously sullen attitude. They were sandy-haired and Caucasian.

"This is Robert and Samantha," Otis offered, coming around to stand behind a chair. They both nodded and said "Hi" but stood well back, neither putting a handout. Otis gestured to the chairs and said, "Please..."

As we sat, Otis pulled his rifle off one of the chair seats—an old-fashioned looking, wooden, bolt-action weapon with a large telescopic scope—and placed it butt down in the dirt against the backrest. He looped the sling over the back of the chair and then held onto it as he sat down to ensure the weight of the rifle wouldn't pull it over. Ben sat down next to him on his left side, to his right were Robert followed by Samantha while on our end from right to left was Billy, Jake, myself, and Lizzy.

We all sat for a moment, silently awkward. I can't say for sure, but I think it may have been the first time any of us had been in such a situation. We've certainly been in plenty like it since that day. Finally, looking for a way to break the ice, I said, "Otis, is that a Southern accent I hear?" A Southern man always loves to talk about home, in my experience.

"Well, yes it is," he said, smiling. I was momentarily hypnotized by how a face so dark could appear so full of light by smiling. "We were living in New Mexico when Ben was born, but I'm originally from Atlanta."

No one brought up the absence of the mother, a fact which was entirely conspicuous for its lack of mention. Otis picked up on this, apparently, and said, "Oh, we didn't lose his mother recently. That was some time ago."

Our side of the lineup breathed in unison, and now Ben smiled as well, as though he wanted to put us at ease.

"You're a good ways out from New Mexico," Billy said. "Do you, uh, mind if I ask where you're headed?"

"Sure," Otis nodded, making the word sound like "shoo-wuh," "we're making our way to Oregon. My folks passed on years ago, but Ben's mother still had some family up that way. We're going to see if we can find them. We picked up our friends here along the way. They, uh, they weren't so lucky with their people." I saw Robert's hand clench into a fist as Otis said this; there was a lot of anger there. "How 'bout yourselves?"

Billy cleared his throat and shifted. Jake answered without hesitation: "We're on our way to Wyoming. There's some land up there. Fresh start, maybe."

"Fine. That sounds fine," said Otis.

"So," said Jake, "you flagged us down at great potential risk to yourselves. What can we do for you?"

"Well, like I told you, we're looking to trade supplies. Ammo is what we need the most, but we can talk over anything, really. Water is what we're doing well on right now—we came across several flats of it a few days ago."

"More water is always a good thing," Jake said.

"Yeah. Our problem right now is we're out of gas. We've been hopping from car to car as we go. It was easier with just Ben and me, but now we gotta make sure we have enough automobile to move four people plus all the supplies we need."

"You haven't worked out refueling, then?" Billy asked.

"I tried siphoning with a plastic hose I'd found but it didn't work out."

"Yeah, it's the anti-roll stuff they build into the tanks," Billy said and looked across Jake to me. "You know if there's anything like an auto parts store around here, Amanda?"

Before I could answer, Otis said, "We just passed an Auto Zone on the way in today. It's not far from here; just down the 6."

"Oh, there you go," Billy said. "You folks staying here tonight?"

"I reckon yes," said Otis. "Anyway, haven't found a way to get us moving again."

"Okay," Billy said and looked back over at us. "We done traveling for the day?"

"We can be," said Jake.

Billy looked back to Otis. "Let's you and I head out early tomorrow. I'll help you get your gas situation sorted out."

Otis nodded, clearly pleased. "That sounds like a plan, Billy. Thank you."

"Finally get that damned jack stand," Billy said and struck his knee lightly. I cough-snickered into my hand.

"So aside from that, sounds like ammo for water?" asked Jake. "What's that rifle there?""

"Thirty-aught six."

"Hell," said Billy. "We're not carrying any of that."

Otis nodded his head. He looked disappointed but also had the expression of one who was expecting the news. "I've had a hell of a time keeping this rifle loaded. It's not even mine—a good friend who didn't make it through had it. Had a whole collection of hunting rifles and revolvers in all manner of odd calibers. He even had a Smith and Wesson 500. Can you imagine trying to find bullets for that?" He shook his head and sighed. "I have twelve rounds left for this, and then we need to get serious about trading up."

Jake leaned over to Billy and whispered to him. They conferred for a few moments, gesturing back and forth. Finally, Billy shrugged and gestured over to me. Jake leaned in close to me, and I heaved over in his direction to put my head close to his.

"Water's going to be a big deal soon. We're talking about giving them the Bushmaster and a box of .223. Thoughts?"

"What, you're going to trade him for his rifle?"

"No, even trade for the water."

I wrinkled my nose at him. "Seems like a lot to avoid scavenging for water. You know we'll be able to find some. Plus, we're going to spend some time getting them refueled tomorrow, apparently," I whispered, looking across at Billy.

"Amanda," he said, pulling my eyes back to his. "You know what happens if they run into the wrong people. We have the AK, your

Tavor, the shotgun, the two AR's, and the pistols. Even giving him the Bushmaster we still have the extra AR." He didn't bother mentioning the bullets. After Barnes, the rear of the Jeep was sitting nearly six inches low from all the extra weight we were dragging. "There're more guns in this world now than there are good people, or any kind of people, really. We'll find more."

I nodded, knowing he was right. Jake put his hand out, and I dropped the keys into it.

"Just a moment, please," Jake said and got up.

"What's up, folks?" asked Otis, as Jake went to the rear of the Jeep.

"What the hell's going on? What the fuck's he doing??" asked an alarmed Robert, really speaking now for the first time. His face was flushed and angry. He was coming out of his chair, moving in front of his sister.

"Hey, calm down," Billy said.

"Boy, sit *down*," commanded Otis with the sound of someone now fully out of patience. Robert slammed back into his chair in a fury, not even bothering to conceal the mask of rage on his face. "You got to think, Robert! If these people wanted us dead, Amanda here could have drawn a line right across our bellies with whatever the hell that nasty lookin' thing is, ain't that right Amanda?"

I swallowed and nodded. I had been halfway to doing exactly that. I hoped it wasn't too obvious and pulled my hand away from the trigger while trying to avoid drawing any attention to it. I failed miserably.

Jake came walking back from the Jeep with a black rifle hanging from his right hand, index finger threaded through the front sight. From his left hand dangled a plastic ammunition case.

He came back to his chair and sat down. Billy said, "Thirty-aught six isn't exactly ultra-rare, but it's going to be harder to find than .223 or 5.56. It's probably just best if you trade up right now."

Jake pulled the handle back on the rifle to check the chamber and passed the rifle across to Otis, who accepted it with his mouth hanging open.

From the side, Billy said: "This here is a Bushmaster XM-15

MOE. It will fire both .223 and 5.56, which were probably the two most popular rounds in this country right before everything went under. It is a very nice rifle, and I'm going to insist that you treat it like a lady." Billy said this last part with the most serious of expressions. We knew he was joking, but Otis only coughed and said, "Yes, sir."

Jake picked up the plastic case and handed it across to Otis with both hands. Realizing that it must be heavy, Otis laid the rifle across his lap and received the offering with two hands.

"That's over four hundred rounds of .223 and two magazines," said Jake. "When we get you fueled up tomorrow, you folks are going to take a side trip."

"A side trip?" repeated a numb Otis.

"'Bout twenty miles south of here down the 15 is a building on the East side of the freeway standing by itself out in the middle of nowhere. It'll have "Barnes" across the front in big, red letters. They were an ammunition manufacturer. We came from that way, and there was more in that place than we could reasonably carry on our own. There's plenty still there. You'll find more .223, 5.56, and even some more .30-06 for that hunting rifle."

Otis sat dumbstruck for several seconds. He tried to speak once or twice, but the only sound that came was a slight grunt. Finally, he cleared his throat and said, "Uh...how much water do you think you need?" I was surprised to detect a quaver in his voice.

"Dude," Ben said before any of us could reply, "I'm saying give it all to them."

We burst out laughing uncontrollably, the kind of roaring, rib-cracking laughter that only comes on the tail of some tense, psychological trauma. The punchline doesn't even need to be that funny in these situations—on some level your body realizes it needs that release desperately and seizes control whether you want it or not. I laughed until my stomach muscles hurt and I was gasping for breath. I saw Otis wipe tears from his eyes more than once and even Robert and timid Samantha were smiling despite themselves. The only one of us not laughing and in control was Jake, of course, but his face carried perhaps the most unfiltered smile I'd ever seen from him. I'm almost positive his eyes were moist as well.

When we all came back under control, Otis put his hand on Ben's shoulder and said, "Let's get them three flats of the water, son." Ben jumped up and ran to the back of the minivan, pulling up the hatch. I heard him grunt and he backed away with a massive flat of bottled water. He carried it over to our truck where Billy was already waiting with the gate down.

"There's thirty-six of those to a package," Otis said. "Even if you have no water at all, that should get all of you to any point in Wyoming you want to be with some left over."

Jake reached out across the center to rest a hand on Otis's shoulder (an uncharacteristic familiarity that surprised me) and said, "Thank you. That's going to make a big difference to us."

"You folks are having dinner on me tonight as well," he continued. "Won't take no for an answer."

"That's much appreciated," I said.

"You have any more of those guns?" Robert asked out of nowhere.

Without missing a beat or hesitating in any way Jake's head rotated to him, any of the warmth his face held freezing over in that one fluid motion, and he said, "'Fraid not." He offered no further explanation but also did not look away.

After a few moments, the perpetually sour look melted from Robert's face and settled to an expression of uncertainty. He looked down at his lap and said, "Fine, then."

"Cheer up, Squirt," said Billy. "You can take the Remington, there. After tomorrow, you should be able to shoot it as well."

"My god damned name isn't Squirt," growled Robert. He got up from his chair and walked off on his own toward the overpass to the north of us.

"I'm sorry…about him," said Samantha. Listening to her speak, I thought I understood the true definition of a 'mousey voice.' "He's been really angry since our parents…" she trailed off.

Jake nodded. "Lost them on the road?"

"We…yes."

Jake nodded again and looked off at Robert's retreating back. "Yeah," he said to himself in a low voice.

———

As promised, dinner was provided that evening courtesy of Otis and what provisions his people had found on the road. Mostly this was canned food, some of it Chef Boyardee, some of it Campbell's, but he did produce a profound delicacy in the form of a nearly two foot long dry salami that he had been saving either for when they were feeling very low or very high. He said that he insisted on sharing it on account of our "extravagance and generosity." It was so delicious that I half wanted to offer him another rifle to see what other food he might have stashed away. We do a lot better these days with the subsistence farming and our hunting parties mean that meat is often available, if not plentiful. One tends to forget those early days before any of us had managed to establish a real toehold anywhere. All food was canned, dried goods, or MREs if you were really lucky to stumble across a cache—most of which tasted like "a wet bag of ass" (Gibs's words, not mine), to tell the truth. A regular old piece of salami cut fresh from the package was heaven.

We managed to produce a fire, get the food warmed up, and put the fire out before the sun went down. We were in an exposed position out in the open located next to two major highways and decided it would be best to avoid a fire during the evening. I recall there was no moon during that time; however the starlight has been forever strong since the lights went out—we couldn't rely on the night to obscure us from view, so part of the discussion during dinner involved arranging a watch schedule between us throughout the evening. The larger number of the group meant very short shifts even if we ran two people to a shift; one of the first of many benefits I would come to realize in living in greater numbers.

With the logistics of the evening out of the way, the conversation turned to the exchange of news between our two groups. Otis brought a good deal of information with him out of New Mexico.

"They started rounding us up and transporting us by vehicle to the tent cities outside of Albuquerque," Otis said. "School buses, Greyhound buses, Army trucks...hell, we even saw people getting pulled behind trucks on flatbed trailers and big shipping semis with containers full of people. Sick or healthy, minor symptoms or nothing at all. Didn't matter what your condition was; if they found you, they brought you."

Billy got up as Otis spoke; made his way to the truck and the container marked "pantry." Otis's story halted as he moved and Billy said, "Please go on. Don't mind me." He came back to his chair with a very familiar brown bottle and some Dixie cups.

"Hey," Otis said in appreciation. "Whatcha got, there, Billy?"

"Tellin' stories is thirsty work," Billy said as he offered a cup to Otis, who took it and nodded. He filled two other cups a third of the way full and passed them out to Jake and me. He looked to Robert (who had come back when the food came out) and Samantha to ask, "Will you share a drink with us?"

"Seems pretty stupid, honestly," said Robert. "What good does it do to stand watch if we're all going to do it drunk?"

Billy, who had just been getting ready to pour two more cups, betrayed a fleeting expression of hurt before he covered it up with a smile and said, "Well, no one's planning on getting drunk, kid. It's just to take the chill off, you know?"

"No, I don't know," Robert said. Samantha tried to lay a calming hand on his arm but he shrugged her off, and I could see that he was winding up for quite a tear. "Please explain to me how you take the chill off without drinking to a point of being numb. I mean, it seemed perfectly clear to me that the same thing is accomplished more easily by putting on a fucking sweater as opposed to intentionally thinning out your blood. Exactly what backwoods, shit-kicker, home remed..."

"Robert." It came from Jake. His voice was flat and low; I almost didn't hear him. Robert certainly did—the tone of Jake's voice stopped him in his tracks before he could truly unload.

"Yeah?" Robert asked. He looked less than pleased at being interrupted while in the process of building up momentum. His voice was impatient.

"Not a single thing that's come out of your mouth since we've arrived has been useful. It would be good if you thought about that and maybe see if you might be able to contribute something meaningful the next time you open it."

"Oh! Well, how abou…"

"Shut the fuck up, Robert."

I had only known Jake a few days by that point, but in that time, I don't think I can recall him ever using the word "fuck" in conversation. I have since learned that he can curse with some of the best (you should see him when he gets going with Gibs sometime) but he tends to be very polite with people he doesn't know well…at least until he gets a lock on them. You become attuned to his manner of speaking and assume that it's the only way he communicates. In reality, he's more of a vocal chameleon—changing expressions and speech patterns to suit his audience (another one of those behaviors that tends to draw people to him). Consequently, for those rare occasions when he does say "fuck" in strange company, the reaction in those around him is similar to what you see in animals when thunder cracks unexpectedly: they cringe and try to crawl under the nearest cover. Even with people who have only just met him, it's as though they sense that he pulls that word out only for special events.

In Robert's case, his mouth fell open, and he seemed to shrink about three inches in his chair.

"I'm sure you've had a long and stressful day," Jake continued as though nothing had happened. "Why don't you turn in? I'll take your watch for you so that you can be fully rested for tomorrow."

Samantha rose from her chair, eyes downcast, and pulled at her brother's hand. Inwardly, my heart ached for her embarrassment, but there was nothing any of us could say that wouldn't make it worse. He followed her, trying and failing to walk with some kind of dignity. They got into the minivan and were hidden behind the tinted windows.

"I'm sorry for that, Lizzy," Jake said.

"It's okay. He had it coming."

Jake looked at Ben and Otis in turn. "I apologize to the both of you for that."

Ben nodded at Jake, clearly shaken by the exchange. Otis nodded to Elizabeth and asked, "Do you know any card games, honey?"

"Mom taught me Crazy Eights," she said.

"Ben knows that one, don't you son?"

"Yeah!" Ben said. He pulled an old, beaten pack of Bicycle playing cards out of his jacket pocket. Looking at the rest of us, he asked, "Is it alright if we play on the tailgate of the truck?" I said, "Of course," so he took her off to the truck a few feet away, pulled down the gate, and helped her to climb up onto it. He jumped up beside her and started shuffling the deck.

"Been rough with him. Robert, I mean," Otis said quietly. "He gets like that. I don't know the details behind what happened to their parents, but I know it wasn't pretty. I'm not sure how strong to be with him. Don't know what's appropriate."

"He'll be a problem eventually," Jake said. "You'll want to get that handled or leave him behind soon."

Otis's heavy sigh indicated that this was a problem that had been troubling him. "Yeah," he agreed.

Billy took a sip of whiskey, coughed, and said, "You were saying about the tents?"

"Oh, sure," Otis said. "So, they were rounding us up, good bad, or indifferent. Not being mean about it but just making it clear that we were coming with them no matter what. Took us all down to the tent city and put us in these big old communal things with row on row of cots."

"Sounds familiar," I said. Otis nodded to me and lifted his cup in a little salute.

"From there, they shuffled us around some more," he continued. "As folks within a tent got sick, they were moved out into quarantine sub-areas; sick tents within the tent city, I guess you'd call it. In time, the number of sick equaled the number of healthy, and then the ratio overbalanced the other way. It became easier for them to move the healthy into their own sub-areas. It started getting crazy toward the end. Ben and I were moved sometimes two or three times a day. The following morning, there were always more people who had passed on in the night—more people that had to be hauled out to the pits. After a while, I figured out that no one was actually working on any kind of cure or medicine to make it right. They were just playing a giant human shell game with us until there were none left to move around anymore."

The sound of cards slapping down on the tailgate startled me. The kids giggled, and half-argued, half-joked about who won the last round. The sound of Lizzy laughing and playing with another child helped to take the chill off the story Otis shared.

"We were in those tents, oh, five…maybe six weeks? That's all it took for some three hundred thousand people from Albuquerque and the surrounding areas as well as another fifteen thousand Army, medical, and support staff to get whittled down to something approaching less than one percent. I have no idea how many were left when the dying finally stopped; Ben and I didn't stay around to find out."

Otis drained what was left of his cup and gasped. Billy offered more, which was accepted gratefully. I noticed a slight tremor in Otis's hand as he held out the cup.

He was silent a moment while looking off into the distance at nothing in particular. Suddenly, he sat up and asked, "You folks remember the National Dispatch?"

It didn't ring a bell for me. Billy, Jake, and I looked among ourselves, and it became clear that none of us had heard of it.

"Ah, must not have circulated out your way. You remember that all the private news networks were still trying to get back up and running after the Flare? Well, they never quite had the chance to get off the ground, and any traction they got was lost when everyone started getting sick. The Stars and Stripes created an offshoot service called The National Dispatch. Started using it as an interim service to deliver news updates and keep everyone informed. Nothing fancy—just basic newsprint, maybe five or six pages per issue, zero advertisements."

"Why the name change?" asked Jake.

"Had something to do with branding," Otis said. "I asked one of the soldiers about it in the tents. He said they were trying to minimize the appearance that the news media had been taken over by the government, which it essentially had. Wasn't like they were being shady; the government was literally the only organization left that was capable of getting the word out."

"Never saw it out my way," said Jake.

"Me either," I said. "And I was in a tent city a lot like the one you were in."

"Well, I'm not surprised. They were down to sending copies in on pallets with the supply trucks." Otis leaned forward and pitched his voice low. "I saw a story in one of the articles that said that some researchers thought the Plague was some kind of...uh...chimera, I think it said."

"No shit?" Billy said.

"What's that?" I asked.

"Nasty stuff," Billy told me. "I saw something on this sometime after all the Anthrax and dirty bomb scares. One of them doctors that seemed to make his whole living dreaming up shit to be worried about started talking about these manufactured vaccines that were made from two or more different viruses. He said the process could be adapted to combine some kind of killer cocktail virus. A new kind of bioweapon. This article *said* it was man-made?" this last question was directed back at Otis.

"Well, it said they suspected but I been thinking about it. You think of the timing of everything as it happened: first, the Flare comes and flattens the power grid and, not too long after that, everyone starts getting sick."

"I know where you're going," Billy said. "I had the same thought myself. I just never had the benefit of a newspaper to back me up. Damned sure didn't think of any kind of chimera..."

"So I figure, someone somewhere was getting up to some business in the lab that they probably shouldn't have. Don't even know if they were trying to make a weapon, you know? There were pharmaceutical companies and every other damned thing dreaming up all kinds of futuristic garbage across the whole country; growing noses in Petri dishes and grafting human ears onto mice. All kinds of Frankenstein type foolishness. Suppose the power went out at some critical moment while they was cooking up whatever nasty shit they were working on? Suppose whatever containment they'd put together was only as good as the electricity it was running on?"

"But they would have had backup systems...safety measures." Jake said.

"Sure. Fukushima had all kinds of backup systems and safety measures, too. Remember them?"

That shut us all up.

"Anyway," Otis said, "the timing of it all was such that I don't believe for a minute that the Plague was just something that popped up out of nowhere." He drained off his second cup and declined Billy's offer of more with a shake of the head and a "Thank you."

"None of which helps us today," Otis declared, raising slightly out of his chair and brushing off the tops of both legs with his hands. He settled down heavily into his chair and grunted. He giggled to himself and said, "That's good stuff," while pointing at Billy's bottle.

"Well, anyway, like I said I wasn't gonna hang around the place with Ben and watch everyone die off around us. When enough had passed on, the Army stopped trying to keep everyone from leaving. They became resigned. Their primary function became to keep the area sanitary, comfort folks as best as they could, and preserve human dignity as much as was reasonable. They were giving us a safe place to move on into the next world, see?"

I nodded. I had seen.

"I remember being surprised at that," Otis said as he looked off toward the freeway. "You think back to all the movies and TV shows where all the zombies broke loose: what did you always see the military doing? They was always becoming some evil, autonomous junta, weren't they? Seemed like every director or screenwriter involved in those damned things had to have that one gratuitous scene with soldiers shooting down a whole crowd of civilians—brutalizing them and whatnot. I didn't realize how much we'd all been conditioned to expect the worst out of the military until we saw everything fall apart for real. After a while, we all figured it out."

Otis shook his head and looked back at us. I could see tears running down his cheeks unchecked. He shook his head slowly.

"They was just American boys and girls like the rest of us. They took an oath at some point to protect the rest of the civilians; they families and loved ones. When the end came and they found they couldn't, they did their best to give us comfort, and then they finally died right alongside of us. Could have left to go looking for they own families—some of them may have, I guess. I heard of a few A.W.O.L. reports. But all the ones I knew by name were all there with us, and I passed by many of them lying in cots. I felt wretched and ashamed for leaving them there like that, but those of them that could still speak were all saying the same thing to me as I pulled Ben past."

Otis stopped talking and sighed. He wiped his eyes with his sleeve absently.

"What did they say to you?" Billy asked quietly.

"They said 'Run.'"

1 2

# PARTING

**Amanda**

We slept in our vehicles that night instead of the tents, due largely to our exposure and proximity to the freeway as well as our proximity to the city of Spanish Fork itself. Mainly we felt safer being encased within the hard cabs and liked the idea of being able to fire up the engines and evacuate without leaving any supplies behind. The flipside to our reasoning (I believe) was that we were also too tipsy to effectively set up the tents in the dark.

I took the first watch of the evening and, after roughly two hours, I tapped on Otis's window to let him know he was up. My last thought before passing out utterly was to wonder how long it would take to go to sleep in a reclined car seat; I was dead to the world from that point until morning.

I was awakened by the light of the sun shining in through the Jeep's windows and the heat that it was beginning to generate. Elizabeth was still asleep in the passenger seat, so I quietly pulled on my shoes, slipped out of the Jeep, and saw to my usual morning routine.

The truck was gone; something I had noted when I first stepped out of the Jeep, but Jake was out in a chair between the Jeep and the minivan nursing a smoldering fire. The easy-up was packaged away and strapped to the minivan's roof. I came over and pulled another chair off a stack that was leaning against the Jeep's front bumper, opened it up, and sat down beside Jake.

"No rifle this morning, huh?" he asked.

"No. It's a pain to always be carrying around. It's hard to pee with it strapped to the front of me."

"Well…yeah. I imagine it would be." He sounded embarrassed.

"So Billy and Otis are already out there?"

"Yes. Billy took the last watch of the morning, so when he was done, he roused Otis and me. Just before sun-up, that was. They went off in the truck a couple of hours ago. Shouldn't be too long, I think. Breakfast?"

"God, please. I'm starving like there's no tomorrow."

"How do some eggs sound?" he asked.

"They sound fantastic. Any of that sausage left?"

"Sure, sure," he said, walking over to the stack of chairs. Next to these were the ever-present pantry and kitchen bins. He popped the lids off both, pulled a camping skillet out of one, and a can of freeze dried sausage and a bag of powdered eggs from the other. He read the back of the bag for a moment, grunted, and then pulled a bowl and spoon out of the pantry bin. He brought these items over to the little cook fire and went back to the bins. Retrieving a bottle of water, he closed both bins and returned to the fire.

"Never made these before," he warned me. "Bear with me…"

He opened the bag, dumped out about a cup of the yellowish-white powder into the bowl and then poured in some water until it was all fully immersed. He began stirring the whole mixture with the spoon. After all of the powder was mixed in well enough, he began to work the spoon fast, clanging the sides of the bowl.

"How long are you supposed to stir it?" I asked. The whole thing seemed dubious to me; it became runnier and runnier as he stirred it. I was expecting the mixture to thicken up and look like eggs at some point, but it just stayed watery.

"The instructions just said to beat the eggs. It suggested using a mixer or blender, but since we're short of both, I figure I need to just smack it around for five minutes or so."

I settled in to watch that transpire. He was already breathing heavy.

As expected, he stopped halfway through to let go of the spoon and shake out his arm. "Here, let me take that a bit," I offered. He passed the bowl to me with a "Thanks" and went to go get a little camping grill to set across the rocks encircling the fire. I worked the spoon for another few minutes before giving up and saying, "These aren't getting any thicker...or any more mixed for that matter."

"I think you're right," he said looking into the bowl. "Oh well; in for a penny, in for a pound, right?"

He deposited a dab of oil into the skillet, swirled it around inside, and placed it over the fire. I offered him the bowl, which he took and upended into the skillet, stirring the result with the spoon as he passed the empty bowl back to me.

Two things happened at this point: the mixture began to take on an orange tint, and the texture looked nothing like improving.

"I think it's getting worse," I muttered.

"It is doing that..." he said.

I began laughing as he struggled with the mixture. "Are we really going to eat this?"

"Oh, I think we must try. Look how far we've come."

This comment surprised more snickers out of me, and I struggled to respond. "But what if...whoo! What if we end up shitting ourselves to d-death?"

I was done in by this point, laughing like a mad idiot. Jake stoically continued to stir the concoction with his spoon, smiling his serene smile. Occasionally, he would lift up a spoonful to smell and give me a thumbs-up, which sent me off laughing again. Over time, however, the eggs went from looking all wrong to looking maybe okay. The smell coming from them was more than okay.

"Hey," he said. "Maybe this is coming out right, huh?" The eggs were starting to fall over each other appropriately as he stirred.

"Well, don't just stand there, man, throw in some of that sausage!" I urged. My stomach was beginning to growl painfully.

He smiled and did so. He cooked the whole thing for a little while longer before he pulled it smoking from the fire and dumped it all onto a plastic plate. He divided the pile, spooned one half onto another plate, and passed it to me along with a fork.

We sat there facing each other in two chairs looking down at our plates. I finally said, "Well, are you going to try it?"

"I'm a little afraid to. Shitting myself to death sounds like a horrible way to go."

"Don't start that up again," I said while suppressing a fresh round of the giggles. I lifted the plate up and breathed deep, taking in the aromatic heaven. The smell was too good to ignore, so I shoveled in a mouthful.

I'm not going to pretend that the stuff tasted exactly like eggs ought to taste, but it was certainly close enough that my eyes rolled back in my head and I moaned involuntarily.

"Good?" asked Jake.

"Oh, man. All it needs is a little Tapatio."

"Yeah, think we have some. Hang on…"

"If you find any, you're my new bestest friend," I called to his back.

When he returned he said, "No luck, unfortunately. There was just this Pico Pica stuff."

I held my hand out. "It's not the same, but it will do fine in a pinch —you can still be my friend. Thanks!"

"Sure thing," he said and took a bite from his plate. He coughed and looked up surprised. "Wow! That's not bad."

"Right?"

I wolfed half of my portion down before I realized what was happening. I stopped suddenly, thinking about Lizzy.

"What's wrong?" asked Jake.

"I should save some of this for Lizzy."

"No," Jake said. "Eat it all if you're still hungry. The best thing you can do is keep your strength up. You can't protect her if you're starving. I can make more for her."

What he suggested went against years of conditioning on my part, but it made sense. We ate the rest of it in silence, enjoying the feeling of the cold morning air and hot food in our bellies. That's one of the things I always appreciated about him; he didn't insist on small talk. He was just perfectly happy to sit quietly in your company if that's what the situation felt like. I asked him about that once, in fact, and he said that he always thought of small talk as "one of those needless constructs we all inflict on each other to reinforce the idea that we belong."

He opened up the bag of powdered eggs again, poured double the previous amount into the bowl, and said, "You want to wake the others? I'll get some more going for them all."

We were all finishing up by the time Billy and Otis returned in the truck (even Robert, whose attitude went from sullen to confused when Jake handed him a plate of food with a "good morning" and a smile— he's always been pretty easy to forgive most things for as long as I've known him). I saw there were a few more gas cans than before in the back of the truck and suspected that the morning excursion was successful. They were stacked precariously on top of all the other gear, tools, and backup supplies, shifting around as the truck rolled toward us over the dirt.

Billy parked the truck nose to nose with the Jeep, and they both hopped out to come join us. "How'd you do?" Jake asked while whipping up a fresh batch of egg snot in the bowl.

"Really good," said Billy. He sat down in a chair by the fire and looked over at what Jake had going. "Oh, you got the eggs figured out, huh? Nice."

Otis hauled two five-gallon gas cans out of the truck bed and carried them over to the minivan. "Billy got us all setup, guys. We got the tools, and we got the talent."

"I caught that reference. Winston Zeddemore, right?" asked Jake.

Otis pointed in Jake's direction and laughed. "There you go!" He walked back to the truck to retrieve a jack and some drip pans.

"Not just that," Billy said. "I finally got some jack stands. We can refuel safely now. Hey, is that coming out alright? It looks awful…" He was looking at the concoction Jake was whipping up.

"No, it's fine. Trust me; I'm getting the hang of this now. It's my third batch."

"It definitely does not suck, you guys," said Ben, throwing out a thumbs-up to emphasize the point.

Jake finished up the third batch of breakfast and shared it around. Billy and Otis took their portions, followed by the kids coming in for seconds. I began to scold my daughter for taking a second round (those habits we learn growing up tend to die hard), but everyone assured me it was fine and that the food would go to waste otherwise. I relented, and she happily tucked in, reinforcing that age-old lesson that all Hispanic children eventually pick up on: Mom is much nicer around company.

We loitered around as the last of the food was eaten. Jake kicked out the fire, bustled about the area packing up the "kitchen," and ensured that all gear was stowed for when it was time to depart. I noticed he was moving slower than usual—stalling. We all seemed to be stalling in our own way. It was yet another lesson of change in this new world that I was coming to understand. Every experience was now more intense; more extreme. I believe we were all uniquely aware that there was a chance that each thing we did could end up being the last time we did it. People had been rendered a rarity by the events of the world and relationships with good people had become rarer still. This would not be the last time I experienced a long, lingering goodbye.

With nothing left to put away, Jake called over to Robert and asked him to come away from the camp for a bit. Samantha tensed up at this, but Jake put out a reassuring hand to calm her. They went to a distance of fifty yards out and stood toe to toe, talking. Jake looked serious but not unkind. Robert started the conversation with arms crossed over his chest and a stony face. I was distracted by Billy speaking over to my right and looked in his direction. He was talking with Otis.

"Here," Billy said and handed Otis a folded up piece of paper. "That address is in Jackson, Wyoming. It's right on the border with Idaho. If you don't find the folks you're looking for in Oregon... or, hell, even if you do find them—you can find us there at that address.

There's plenty of room, I have a well, good hunting. It's an option, anyway," he trailed off.

"Thank you, Billy. Thank you for everything." They shook hands.

Further out from Billy and Otis, Ben and Lizzy were having a goodbye of their own. I saw Ben reach into his pocket and pull out the deck of cards. He handed them to Elizabeth and then hugged her.

I wiped my eyes and looked back over in Jake's direction. Robert's posture had changed now. His hands were down on his hips with his head bowed, nodding sometimes and, at other times, unmoving. Jake had a hand rested on Robert's left shoulder. Presently, Jake extended his right hand between them and Robert took it. They shook, and Jake lightly slapped him on the shoulder; I saw Robert smile for the first time. They both nodded and began to walk back in our direction. I saw Robert surreptitiously wipe at his eyes as they came. Jake advanced just behind Robert with his hands in his pockets. His face was calm and serene.

It was the last goodbye before we all climbed into our vehicles to go our separate ways, perhaps never to see each other again. We stood in a circle between the Jeep, the Dodge, and the minivan.

"I can't thank you people enough," Otis said. "You may have saved us with all you've given."

"Well, the water will definitely help us," Jake said, "but I think this was good for us despite the water. It's good to be reminded that not everyone we see is trying to kill us. I think we needed that reminder."

"We did," Billy agreed and looked at Jake. "I know I did. I admit it. You were right."

"There's another tent city not far from here," I said. "It's where I started." I was surprised at how hard it was for me to say that. I almost had to force the words out—I can remember literally having to brace my stomach muscles to get the air moving. It had been only a few weeks since I was last there, but it might as well have been one hundred years ago, given how I felt now. I thought about who I had become as I stood there looking at Otis; all the time spent moving through unknown areas carrying a rifle that felt more familiar and comfortable every day, that I could operate by touch alone. I recalled

210 | JOSHUA GAYOU

back to the firefight in the warehouse; how I shot a man to wound him and expose more vital areas. How I shot him in the head without hesitation. I thought about what I had done to James out of simple vengeance and how, even now, I felt absolutely zero guilt or remorse for it; there were things over which I lost sleep, but James wasn't one of them. I had changed so much from the woman who came stumbling out of the quarantine tents on the way to Cedar Fort. Elizabeth and I had both changed so much.

Looking at Otis, I saw several things. I saw a good, loving father; a man of warmth, compassion, and good humor. I also saw a man who had yet to make the same evolutionary leaps that I had. He was close, I knew, but there were still lines for him to cross. I realized I had been silently assessing them all from the moment we met. Otis and Robert both were larger and physically stronger than me. Even so, I had little doubt in my mind that I could kill them if the need arose—perhaps not both at the same time; size and strength count for a lot. I knew, however, what my chances were if we went one on one: better than theirs. The fact that I thought about such things unconsciously also did not worry me. It occurred to me that the strange woman I had once been would not be missed.

Presently, I continued my explanation to Otis. "Continue on the 15 north from here, and then take highway 145 toward Cedar Fort just north of the lake. Stay on that road a few miles, and you'll see the tents spread all across the countryside. There were many soldiers there when I left, National Guard and the like. They had weapons, supplies. There's probably still MRE crates and medicine out there, ammunition too."

"Thank you," Otis said again. He counted off on two fingers, "Barnes and Cedar Fort. We'll look into that."

"And keep an eye on your fuel level," said Billy. "Don't let it get too far below half a tank before you start looking to top off. You never know when you're going to run into a big stretch with no viable vehicles to plunder. It used to be easy to judge with Google Maps and such; Thomas Guides don't offer the same detail."

Otis nodded to indicate he understood. We all hugged and said goodbye one last time, quietly grateful to each other, I think, that we had all taken a chance. We drove across several lanes of highway to find our way back onto the 15 headed north. Otis drove up the overpass that spanned the freeway in order to pick up the southbound side. I could see Elizabeth in the rearview mirror watching them as they drove away. She stayed that way, watching after them until they were lost from sight.

# ARRIVAL

## Amanda

It took one full day of driving and one last refueling stop to get us to Jackson, Wyoming. It was very clear by this time that Billy was no longer interested in spending any further unnecessary time out on the road. He kept us moving forward like a man possessed, slowing down for only one rest break and advising us to eat on the road.

The drive took longer than it would have once upon a time for all the obvious reasons: we had to take less traveled roads to avoid traffic pile-ups, weaving back and forth between Wyoming and Utah as we advanced North. In some cases we left the road entirely, rolling slowly over unpaved ground for miles at a time to get around the worst snarls. The road became a mountain pass as we hit the National Forest on the way to Jackson, slowing us down even more as we made our way uphill, downhill, and through various switchbacks. The road was treacherous in places as we drove along Snake River, following it for several miles until I began to think it would never end. We carved our way through the center of an immense valley with vast, tree-covered mountains walling us in on either side. For a girl who had grown up in the Utah deserts (or anyone for that matter, I suppose), the view was stunning, and I had to remind myself more than once to concentrate on the road.

I started seeing signs for Jackson as the sun was just beginning its descent in the sky and I estimated three or four hours of daylight left to us. Billy led us off the main road before we encountered the town itself and led us off on a smaller two-lane highway that seemed to cut a line straight toward the mountains a few miles distant. As we came closer, I saw that the road actually swung out to the left and then turned back to the right to weave into a natural valley at the foot of the mountain range, which was all but obscured from view when it was approached at an angle perpendicular to the range itself. We continued on, passing through the entry and driving into the narrow pass before us. On the other side of the pass, mountain walls densely covered in fir trees climbed to either side of us. The distance across the pass was anywhere from fifty yards to half a mile, depending on your position when you measured. It was impossible to tell for how long it ran; it folded back on itself several times, so that forward viewing distance was occluded by overlapping ridgelines.

Not long after our entry, I sensed an upward grade in the road; the engine started working a bit harder, running at a higher RPM. It couldn't seem to decide if it wanted to stay in its current gear or shift up and I played around with the gas pedal, attempting to force a decision out of the transmission.

Billy turned off on a dirt road about another three miles into the valley, which took us into deeper forested area and advanced our grade of climb a bit more. This leveled off not long after. Without warning, the trees opened up into a wide glen. Directly across from us at great distance, I could just barely make out two buildings peeking out at us from the tree line; the mountain itself appeared to jut straight up into the sky immediately behind them. The entire glen was ringed by trees; a sprawling encircled landscape that looked as though it might have been a lake once upon a time but had naturally run dry long ago. The dirt road ran us right through the center of the clearing and took us directly to the buildings.

One of these buildings turned out to be a large and rustic log home;

the kind that had been built to look like an old world settler design and yet could not disguise the fact that it had taken some serious money to produce. The two-level building belied a complex floor plan, with portions of it pushing out in all directions suggesting rooms of all shapes and sizes. Shuttered windows were visible throughout the home.

The second building was situated to the rear of the home on the right and was as unlike the home as it could have been. It was large, half again as high as the house. I couldn't see how far back it went as we drove up because it was partially buried in and obscured by the surrounding trees, but I learned later that it was three times the length of the log home. Billy called it a "Butler Building." It was a prefabricated construction that he used as a general garage and main storage area.

We parked out in front of the house's main entryway. The area was unpaved dirt. Exiting his truck, Billy walked to the center of the dirt patch in front of his house where he looked down at an old and untended fire pit surrounded by a rocking chair, three folding chairs, and a log. He stared at it all, hands on his hips, as though he was waiting for the scene to explain itself. He looked up at his house and then began turning his head slowly about the area, scanning the tree line.

From the passenger seat, Jake said, "Elizabeth, stay here. Lock the doors when we get out." He lifted the Tavor out of his footwell and handed it over to me. I took it, and he lifted out his AK-47 for himself.

"What's going on?" she asked.

"Nothing yet," he said. "I want you locked up and safe in case something starts."

We exited the Jeep (I heard the doors lock behind us immediately) and walked over to join Billy.

"I'm guessing you didn't leave all this here the last time you were out this way," Jake stated.

"Nope," Billy said. "Think I've had some unannounced company."

Jake sighed. "Well, get your shotgun. We'd better clear the house. Amanda, get your vest on. Keep an eye on things out here, please."

I went to the back door of the Jeep and opened it to retrieve the vest. I pulled out the second one and threw it to Jake. "Are you sure Billy shouldn't take this one?"

"No, I'm good," Billy called back from the truck. "I'd rather you wear it."

They ascended the three steps up to the front porch of the cabin, both bent over their weapons. Billy pointed over to a window to the left of the door that had been boarded up with a scrap of plywood; I assumed this was how entry had been gained. Billy tried the handle on the front door and, finding it locked, extracted a bundle of keys from his pocket, and inserted one of them into the lock. He looked up to Jake, who nodded. Billy swung open the door and pulled back to make way for Jake, who stormed into the house muzzle first. Billy went in directly behind him with his shotgun out in front.

I spent the next several minutes outside next to the Jeep straining my ears for the sound of gunfire. At one point I turned to look at Elizabeth who stared back out at me through the window with her saucer eyes. I mouthed the words "lay down" to her while motioning with my hand. She threw herself down on the back seat like she was hiding from a grenade.

My attention was pulled back by the sound of the front door opening; Jake and Billy had exited the house and were making their way over to the other building. They stopped at the front and examined both sides of the giant roll-up door that spanned the structure. Billy shrugged, and they came back to meet with me.

"We all good?" I asked as they came back.

"Someone's been through here for sure," said Billy. "They're gone now, though. Can't say how long since they were here, but that fire pit is pretty old. Maybe they were just passing through."

"Did it look like they left anything behind?" I asked. "Any new stuff lying around in there that you didn't recognize? Anything someone might come back for?"

"Hard to say but not that I could tell," answered Billy. "The beds were slept in, and some of the trash cans were stacked pretty high. A lot of stuff has been moved around. Much of it looks like it had just been left in place. I suppose that could mean someone meant to come back but I just don't know. I don't know if I'd tidy up a place that I had just spent some time in for a few nights while passing through."

"I sure would," I said. "Rude assholes."

"Well, we probably just keep our eyes open a few weeks. If anyone does come through, we'll deal with it then," said Jake.

"Good news is they didn't get into the garage. That's where the important stuff is," Billy said, turning to look back that way. He heaved a sigh that rolled through his whole body, clearly relieved to have arrived. "I think we're good. Why don't you guys pull the cars around the side and I'll give you all the tour?"

He met us out on the front porch by the door: Lizzy standing between Jake and me with our rifles slung over our shoulders. "Come on in," he said and opened the large door wide.

The log home, which looked impressive from the outside, looked even more so from the inside. Everything about the place screamed "Mountain Man." It was all log and beam construction with wood floors spreading out in all directions with thick, rich rugs laid out at various intervals. A staircase led upstairs immediately off the entryway. To the right of the stairs was a hallway leading past what appeared to be one or more bedrooms; to the left of the stairs was a great room appointed with dark leather seating and a large stone fireplace. Past the front room and entryway, a dining area could be seen all the way toward the rear of the house; I presumed the kitchen would be located there as well.

"There are two bedrooms upstairs, a loft, and a couple of bathrooms," he said. "Down here are the common areas, kitchen, another couple of bedrooms with a shared bathroom, and a den at the back of that hallway."

"Quite a few bedrooms for one, no?" asked Jake.

"Well, it was all part of the floor plan when I had the place built," Billy said as he leaned on the staircase rail. "I wanted the extra space because I would often bring friends or family and their children up here on vacation. You'll see—one of the downstairs rooms has a row of bunks rather than a standard bed."

"So... den?" I asked. "Is that the library?"

"Yes, that would be the same thing, you smart aleck. Why—you want to see it?"

"Oh, I don't know. It's been built up so much in my mind now. I sure would hate for it to fall short," I said while poking him in the bicep.

He curled his arm up in defense of my index finger, tucking it in tight to his side like a chicken wing. He stared at me a moment with a mock-offended expression and then began to laugh despite his best efforts to restrain himself. "You... you really are a little smartass, aren't you?"

"C'mon, Pops," I said. "Let's go have a look at it. Lizzy, come see. Make sure you have your library card!"

"Damned relentless..." Billy muttered as he led the way down the hall. Elizabeth and I followed with Jake bringing up the rear. "This is good," Billy said as he entered the room and turned around. "There are some things in here that I wanted you to see."

The room was not what I expected at all. I was expecting something like a converted bedroom with a few bookcases lining the walls, maybe a corner desk, but it was nothing like that. The space itself was larger than the family room in our old apartment back in Sandy. Shelves spanning from floor to ceiling wrapped around the entire room, broken only by two large vertical windows on the outside wall and another stone fireplace that was one third the size of the one in the great room. A wooden executive desk dominated the rear of the den, positioned directly in front of the windows. The best example I can bring to mind that describes the feel of the room was Don Corleone's office in The Godfather—only filled with books.

"So what do you guys see in here?" asked Billy.

"How much did this place cost, anyway?" asked Lizzy, looking around the room. The outburst was a bit embarrassing, and I *may* have given her a swat on the shoulder.

"That's... that's actually not what I meant," said Billy. "Take a close look at some of these titles."

Jake went over to one of the shelves and started browsing through the books. He stared at the spine of one for several seconds, his mouth working silently, and then said, "I'll be..."

"What is it?" I asked. He waved me over and pointed at a row of books. I started to read the titles out loud. "Bushcraft 1... How to Stay Alive in the Woods... Build the Perfect Bug Out Bag... Survival Medicine Handbook. Holy crap, all of this is about survival?"

"No," said Billy. "Just that section. I've been collecting for years now. How-to guides, manuals, references. This stuff covers everything from electrical repair to engine rebuilding. There are books on tanning animal hide—hell, several books on processing the whole damned animal. One of those even tells you how to make glue out of animal hide. There are books on subsistence farming, carpentry, welding. I even have guides on primitive blacksmithing. I'm not saying I thought of everything, of course, but this is a good start. Anything we discover that needs to be done; there's a good chance I've put a book in here that will give us some ideas."

"Is all of this just a bunch of reference material?" Jake asked. "Don't you have anything that you read for pleasure?"

"Oh, sure," Billy said. "Those two sections there behind the desk are loaded with novels. Also on the other side of the window are a lot of classics and antiques. Here, look," he said, walking over to a shelf to the right of the desk. He tipped out a book about four inches thick. "See? The Iliad."

"Oh, man. I think that's a little heavy for me," Jake said while patting his legs lightly.

"You should read this sometime, Jake," said Billy. He sounded serious enough that we both looked at him intently. "I mean it. It's very good."

"Okay, okay," said Jake. He sounded as confused as I felt at Billy's sincerity. "I'll see if I can plow through it sometime. Might take me a while. I tend to be a bit of a slow reader."

"Who's this in the picture with you, Billy?" asked Lizzy. She was pointing to one in a series of framed pictures on the fireplace mantle. "He looks familiar."

"Hey, wow!" I said, coming closer to look. "When did you meet Arnold?"

"That was back when he was the governor. Had to meet with him to discuss taxes at the time. He was going around running his mouth over how all the tribes needed to 'pay their fair share' in state taxes. Obviously, the state government had spent itself into a giant hole, so the clear answer was to go after small, deep-pocketed groups with little comparative clout to make up the difference on their stupidity. Damned clown."

"Why do you have a picture with him if he was such a buffoon?" Jake asked with a subtle grin.

"Well... I mean... the guy was still Conan, after all."

"I thought his name was Arnold," said Lizzy.

"Never mind, Mija."

"Anyway," Billy said, resetting our attention, "with Google and Wikipedia being nothing but a forlorn memory, this is what we have now." He made his way toward the doorway. "You guys make yourselves at home. Pick the bedrooms you want and such—just stay away from the one on the left upstairs; that's mine. Once you get it all figured out, you can come help me unload the cars."

Jake looked over at us. "Okay, then. Either of you prefer upstairs? I don't care either way."

"Can I have the room with the bunk beds?" asked Elizabeth.

Jake smiled at her. "I'm good with it if your mom is."

"You...you go ahead, Mija."

"Hey," said Jake as Lizzy bounded out of the room. "You okay? What's up?"

I cleared my throat and shook my head. "It was just something Eddie used to say. Whenever Elizabeth asked permission on things—if he didn't mind he would always check with me first to be sure. He would say 'If Mom's happy, I'm good.' It was just a shock to hear it."

"I'm sorry," said Jake.

I was a moment answering, lost in my own thought. Finally, I said, "Don't be. We can't all be walking on eggshells around here. This just happens from time to time. I was just doing some math in my head there. It feels like ages, but I only lost him like three or four months ago now? I honestly don't know for sure. Most of the time I'm numb to it or I'm too busy dealing with a problem in the moment. Every so often, though, something unexpected jumps out and reminds me how badly I miss him."

"Yeah," Jake agreed. He took a deep breath; let it out. "I'll take the upstairs room," he said as he walked to the door. "I suppose you'll want to be close to your daughter. I'll go give Billy a hand unloading."

His voice trailed off as he walked down the hallway toward the front of the cabin. I felt as though he had escaped from the room.

I left the den and followed his path, stopping at the first door on the left to look in on Elizabeth. She was sitting on the top bunk in the center of the room (there were six bunks throughout—two on the left wall, two in the center, and two on the right wall) dangling her feet off the side. "What do you think?" I asked her.

"This is great!" she said with a smile that nearly cracked her face in half.

"You just be careful up there, okay? Don't fall off."

"I won't, Mom," she called after me as I walked down to the next bedroom and looked in. The décor of the room was very much in line with the rest of the house with rich wood furniture and earth tones in all of the coloring. There was a queen sized bed on the left wall with a lovely Native American painting of some women sitting together at a river bank; they appeared to be making baskets or pottery—it was hard to tell because it was a stylized piece. On the wall opposite of the painting hung a Jackalope head mounted on a board. It was obvious that Billy had done all of his own decorating.

I exited the front of the cabin to find some of the plastic bins from the truck already stacked outside the door. Worried that they might finish unpacking without me, I rushed down the steps and trotted around the side of the house. They were over by the roll-up door of the Butler Building. I slowed to an energetic walk and joined them.

"I like the bit of taxidermy," I said to Billy. "You shoot that thing yourself?"

"Oh, you found Jacky," Billy said absently. He had a key ring out and was thumbing through various keys.

"We were just praying that Billy didn't leave his garage key back home in California," said Jake.

"Oh, crap," I laughed and then looked down at the roll-up door. There was a half-inch thick steel plate on either side of the door at the bottom. These plates appeared to be welded to the wall of the building frame itself. Rather than being secured to the door with some form of padlock or chain, there was a heavy duty keyhole lock embedded in the center of the plate. "Oh, crap!" I repeated. "Can we actually get in there without a key?"

"Not without a torch," Billy muttered. "Ha! I told you I brought it!" he said, holding the bundle of keys up to Jake's face with one of them extended out between thumb and forefinger.

He unlocked both sides of the door and then grabbed a handle mounted to the bottom center. He lifted, and the door glided up easily, rolling up some twenty feet overhead. When the door was too high for him to push with his hands, he grabbed a chain to the right of the inside frame and pulled it up a few more feet. He anchored the chain to a metal hook on the wall and walked in.

The inside space of the building felt more like a warehouse than a garage. The ceiling was set high overhead, and the space stretched back far enough that I couldn't see the wall on the other side. I was straining my eyes to see better and contemplating going back to the Jeep for my flashlight when the sound of a switch being thrown came from behind me. The interior was illuminated by hanging lights spread throughout the area.

"What the hell?" I asked.

"Solar panels," said Billy. "Lining the whole roof. They charge an array of batteries along the back wall, which will keep the LED lights going all day and night or run the power tools in the back for a few hours straight before drying out."

"Does the main house have solar?" asked Jake.

"Unfortunately not," Billy said. "It was on my list of things to do, but I never got around to it. It was important to get this building online first—all of the critical stuff is here."

The first thing to grab my attention after the lights were turned on was a truck out in the middle of the floor. I couldn't tell what kind of truck it was because it was under a tarp. The only thing I could see for sure was that it was big.

"This will be our fall back when all the gas stops working," said Billy as he rested his hand on the hood. "It's a diesel, four-wheel drive Ford Super Duty. It makes about one thousand foot-pounds of torque and will happily pull the ass out of a T-rex without even slowing down. I've also added a one-hundred-gallon reserve fuel tank up in the truck bed with a transfer pump wired into the truck's electrical system and a full sized ball hitch on the back. There is a twenty-foot utility trailer back in the corner of the shop by the drums. We'll be able to push out over a significant distance in this thing without having to refuel."

I stood up on my toes to look over the bed of the truck to the rear corner of the garage. Next to the trailer Billy mentioned, there were six steel drums stacked in a rack on their sides with three on the bottom and three more on the top. Jake was walking back there to look at them.

"Fifty-five gallons a piece, right?" he asked.

"Yes," Billy said as he joined him. "I started stockpiling diesel as well as some other items not too long ago. Half of those are empty, which works out for us. I hadn't counted on prioritizing gas, but we'll need to start collecting gas as part of our regular activities so we can get the most use out of your vehicles while they'll still run. The steel drums will help. They're a nice clean environment which will help to maximize the life of the gas we salvage. If we get lucky, we may be able to find some long life additives in surrounding auto shops and the like. It's possible we'll be able to extend the useful life out of the gas vehicles by a year or more."

"What will you do with the diesel?" I asked.

"We'll find something else to keep it in. Diesel will keep for a decade whether you baby it or treat it like shit. It's a big reason I got the Ford over there; a decade of useful life, assuming you can keep it fueled and in good repair. The problem is finding more. Diesel wasn't terribly popular so it won't be as abundant as gas—it will take longer to find it and stock up a meaningful supply. Being in Wyoming will help, though. A lot of people up this way preferred nice diesel trucks. Also, any shipping trucks we can find should be a minor bonanza. Giant fuel tanks in those semis."

"You have your own little auto shop back here, don't you?" Jake asked, looking at the tool boxes and racks.

"More like a combination garage/woodshop."

Jake looked up a set of wooden stairs that ran to a smaller second level suspended over the rear of the main floor. "What's up there?"

"Additional storage, a pool table and an old couch, my reloading bench and gun safes, that kind of thing."

"I can't believe all this," I said. "It's like you were planning on the world falling apart. I'm not complaining now since it all paid off in the end, but what inspires someone to dig in this hard?"

Billy nodded and smiled. "Come on, Little Sis. Let's get all the stuff from Barnes stacked up in the garage. After that, I'll see about getting some dinner going and explain while I'm cooking. Hopefully whoever was here left a little food in the pantry."

After several trips between the Jeep and the garage, Billy shut off the lights and rolled the door back down. He locked both sides and accompanied us back to the truck. There were only a couple of plastic bins left in the bed aside from the spare tires, gas cans, and extra tools. He took a bin, handed the other to Jake, and advised us to leave the rest for the next morning. The bins we carried back to the house were deposited in the main entryway along with the others that had been left by the front door from earlier. With that, Billy slapped his hands together a few times and made for the kitchen.

Jake followed him into the back area, but I made a detour to the bedroom recently claimed by Elizabeth. She was going through the drawers of a highboy dresser along the far wall.

"Hey, what are you doing?" I blurted. We were clearly operating from different assumptions; to me, we were guests in Billy's home and to her, she was surveying her new domain.

She looked up at me with no hint of guilt or concern, showing that she actually hadn't been snooping around. "I thought I could put some of my things in these drawers," she said. "There's nothing in them, see?"

"Okay," I said. "Let's ask Billy about it. I suppose we'll have to get you some more clothes too. You're only going to get bigger."

"I'm pretty big already," she said proudly.

"Okay, Little Miss Big Girl. We're getting dinner ready in the kitchen. You wanna come hang out?"

"Maybe later," she said. "I want to see what else my room has."

"Ugh, okay. Just…try not to get into anything that looks like you should stay away from it."

I left her room and went back to the kitchen. I saw that the rear of the house opened up into another common area, more private than the front room. To the left was a good-sized kitchen (not enormous but plenty of room for four people to move around in it) with an island. The coloring followed what I had already seen through the rest of the house, with rich woods everywhere. To the right was a family room-style living area with couches and a now useless TV as the dominant focal point.

Jake and Billy were standing over by the kitchen island; the latter had a little propane grill set up on the island over which a pot of water was set. Next to the pot were a small box of pasta and a jar of red sauce.

"OH, holy crap, spaghetti? I don't think I'd planned on seeing that again, ever." I said as he ground salt into the water.

"Yeah, don't get used to it, probably," Billy said, stirring the pot with a large spoon. "Longer shelf life food is still good right now, but that won't last. Think of it like the gasoline: best to just consume as much of it as we can right now before it all goes bad." He leaned back against the counter and crossed his arms over his chest. "So, I believe you wanted an explanation as to how a seemingly rational man goes bugnuts and starts preparing for the world to explode."

"Something like that," I chuckled.

"Well, Jake got a part of this explanation, but I don't think even he realized the lengths I'd gone to—"

"I did not," Jake chimed in while nodding.

"—but the simple answer is: it was all a hobby."

"A... hobby?" I asked.

"Sure. One that creeps up on you." Billy walked over to a pantry, retrieved a bottle of water, and had a drink. "Like I told Jake, I was always preaching self-reliance with my people back home, which was an attitude that bled over into my personal life. At first, it started with the normal stuff, right? I was out in California, so first I had earthquake kits in my house and vehicles. The kit in my house had food and water enough to last three days, or just long enough for emergency services to come in and bail me out if we got a really nasty shaker, right?"

I nodded.

"Right, well, then I witnessed how well emergency services did bailing people out of Hurricane Katrina. A few years later I saw them get it wrong again in New York with Hurricane Sandy. The point was that three days (the common doctrine I had been raised on) clearly wouldn't get the job done. During the time I was coming to this revelation, I was also thinking about my retirement."

"Huh," muttered Jake. "You don't look old enough to retire."

Billy raised his bottle to Jake in a mock salute. "Younger than most but I've still been working my ass off in one form or another since I was thirteen. I was looking forward to slowing down. Anyway, I began work on this place here, oh, I guess four years ago now. A significant wad of my life savings went into this place, even at Wyoming prices, and as I was building it, those ideas of self-reliance were carried forward, resulting in the Butler building off the side of the house." He stopped talking long enough to dump the pasta in and stir the pot some more. "I was following Mormon principles by this point."

"Mormon?" Jake asked.

"A year's worth of everything, huh?" I asked.

Billy pointed at me. "She's got it." He looked over to Jake. "The Mormons were a big inspiration in what I was trying to do. The concept of self-reliance is encoded into their faith. They counseled their own to be ready for anything, with supplies laid by for various contingencies starting with the typical three-day kits—essentially the bug-out bag concept. On top of that, they kept a three month supply of everyday necessities and a one year supply of long life dried goods like grains, beans, dried milk, and so on. They also stockpiled things like gasoline, tools, and clothes, basically any of the stuff that you can't easily make for yourself under reasonable circumstances."

"That's quite a thing," said an impressed Jake. "You're saying all of them were doing that?"

"Oh, well, they were *supposed* to," Billy shrugged. "I'm sure you had your sandbaggers in their group just the same as you have in any other. But again, this idea of preparedness is baked into their cultural identity, you see? By and large, these people were just about ready for anything."

"Weren't ready for the Plague," I said.

"Okay, almost anything. Be fair: no one was ready for that." He turned off the grill and retrieved a colander from an overhead cabinet, which he placed in the sink. Protecting his hands with a dish towel, he poured the spaghetti in to drain.

"Sorry, there's no butter for this," he said almost to himself. "Still deciding if I leave the fridge where it is or get rid of it. Takes up a ton of space to not be doing anything."

He transferred the spaghetti to another bowl, opened the jar of sauce, and poured half of it in. He then looked up, shrugged to himself, and poured in the rest, most likely realizing that he had no cold storage for the opened jar.

He began to stir the bowl. "Anyway, I followed their lead and ended up here. This was all over time, you understand. I did pretty well for myself. I wasn't rolling in millions' worth of cash or anything...in fact, most of the money we made at the casino either went straight for the betterment of the tribe and our lands or was just reinvested back into the casino itself. I did earn a comfortable salary during my time running the place, though. Had some luck with my investments. Even so," he gestured all around at the house with a hand, "doing all of this at once would have hurt. What you're seeing is the result of several years' worth of planning, saving, and building."

"Billy," I said while placing a hand on his shoulder.

He looked surprised at the gesture. "Yes?"

"On behalf of Jake and myself, I want to thank and congratulate you for being an obsessive doomsday prepper. It turns out the lunatics were right. We concede."

He rolled his eyes and smiled. Lifting the bowl, he moved over to the dinner table dividing up the space between the kitchen and the family room. "Hey, Girly!" he called. "Come have some dinner!"

"Silverware?" Jake asked.

"The drawer to the left of the sink," answered Billy. The sound of metallic jangling came from Jake's direction while I looked into the pantry for more water. The pantry itself was looking bare—there was a half-empty flat of bottled water on the floor, some jarred and canned goods interspersed throughout, and an opened box of crackers. I grabbed some water bottles and went to sit at the table as Elizabeth came wandering in. Billy pulled a handful of plates from a cabinet and set them out at one end of the table. We sat down, and he began to serve out spaghetti to all of us.

"Like I was saying," Billy continued, "the hobby started with this concept of food supplies, but the more I did, the more I thought of that I could be doing. Suppose I needed something while basic services and infrastructure was down? I could survive here on the food I'd packed in for plenty of time, but I might not be able to get my hands on new things that I needed, so I added a woodshop. It had the added benefit that I'd be able to fix things that broke as well."

He stopped talking to have a bite. I was shocked to see that a significant portion of the food on my plate had disappeared down my mouth. After weeks of nothing but MREs, canned goods, and prepackaged foods like protein bars, a simple plate of pasta was gourmet eating.

"Adding in a new feature or capability always exposed another area I was lacking. I added a woodshop but that really only covered the ability to work with wooden things. I should add a machine or metal shop, right? Well, I never got to that—it was just on the list of things to do. I put solar on the Butler Building so that I could power everything in the event of a grid failure, which made me realize that the main house would be S.O.L. I had planned to put some solar on this house as well but just didn't get to that in time. I had to compromise."

"Compromise how?" Jake asked.

"Propane generator. There are ten, one hundred pound propane tanks lined up along the wall out in that garage; I'll point them out to you the next time we're in there. You store propane as a liquid, and one tank holds almost twenty-four gallons. It's something like two-hundred-seventy times more compact as a liquid, so there's a ton of gas out there. I don't recall the math to determine how many joules of energy are stored in one full tank, but the answer is *a lot*. The very best thing is that propane won't decay like gasoline or diesel will. The stuff will last forever. Our only challenge is finding more when we run out. Our limitation there is that we have to count on all the tanks and storage facilities failing over time, leaking it all away into the atmosphere. I don't know when that will happen but, when it does, we won't be getting any more of the stuff until someone figures out how to pull it out of the ground and bottle it again."

"Does that mean we could watch movies on the TV in here?" asked Elizabeth.

"Well, yes, but I don't think we want to burn up our emergency energy watching movies," Billy said. At her disappointed expression, he quickly amended: "Hey, maybe we have movie nights every so often, though. We can't be running stuff around the clock, but we'll have special nights sometimes for movies, okay?"

Elizabeth seemed to think about this compromise for a moment; finally smiled and gave him a thumbs-up.

"Is it alright if I have some more?" I asked, gesturing at the bowl.

Jake sat up and looked over the bowl at my plate. "Damn, dude."

"It's *good*!" I barked defensively.

"We should eat it all. Anything we don't finish will just go to waste," Billy said. Everyone spooned up a second helping.

After a few more bites, Billy spoke while chewing, unable to contain himself long enough to swallow first. "You know, the other thing about the solar on the garage: it's not getting the best efficiency. Too many trees around it. Another one of my projects was going to be to take down the trees closest to it. This has the added benefit of providing fresh lumber for anything that may need to be built."

"Oh, what do we need to build?" I asked.

"Anything really. Another building, tanning racks, livestock pens, and fences... we'll think of more over time. A new project always starts with someone saying 'You know what would make things better around here?'"

"Sounds like you've got your work cut out for you," Jake said.

Conversation around the table stopped at the implied meaning behind Jake's statement. Finally, Billy put his fork down and looked at Jake. "We do. Think you might stick around to help?"

Jake chewed for a moment while he considered this. "Well, I did help you get here, but there's obviously still much to do. I can stick around for a while to help you get settled in."

"Okay," Billy said as he wrapped another bundle of pasta around his fork. "I can work with that."

# GOOD TIMES

## Amanda

I'd love to report that the next few days were happy ones, but life is rarely a simple, single-emotion experience. There were definitely periods of happiness but, more importantly, it was also the first time Elizabeth and I had felt truly safe in months. Now that I wasn't constantly on edge all the time, I finally had the opportunity to get inside my own head to process the grief over everything we had lost, everything we had been through, and (perhaps the worst) some of the things I'd done to survive. The others seemed to sense the need I had to work through these things and gave me a wide berth when there wasn't work to be done. I spent a lot of time walking by myself around the property within the vicinity of The Bowl (the term I had begun to use for the grounds on which the cabin was built and the surrounding valley almost completely encircled by mountains). Billy told me that the area contained within the valley was a very rough and irregular square mile—he had purchased only a portion of the area when he acquired the land, but the concepts of such things like property lines seemed to lack relevance anymore; we just looked at the whole thing as our territory.

During my walks, the guys both insisted that I go armed as we were all still thinking about the squatters who had been here before us and wondering if they would return. I didn't want to lug my rifle around, bullpup or not, so we compromised: I wore a Glock at all times, taking it off only to sleep at night but keeping it at my bedside. Billy had a Glock 17 in one of his safes in the garage that I preferred to the 19 we had out on the road. It felt a lot more solid and substantial in my hands, and it also had some kind of fancy glow in the dark sights that Billy had installed after he purchased it. He said they were tritium, which meant about as much to me as if he had said they were super awesome unobtanium—all I knew was that I could see them in the dark and they were a lot easier for me to line up than the 19 with its flat, white dot sights. It also came with a belt and molded Kydex holster that rode comfortably on my thigh, putting it right under my hand when my arm hung naturally at my side.

Those walks were a big part of what helped me to work through my issues, and they are a practice that I continue to this day. Communal living is *close* living, and I've found that a regular dose of solitude plays a large role in keeping folks from clawing each other's eyes out. Gibs likes to say that I'm "going out past the wire," the old jarhead.

In the evenings I would spend a bit of time sitting on the porch while the sun went down. The others always detected when I was back, indicating that they were keeping a steady eye out for me, which made me feel good. Lizzy would come to join me around this time. Shortly after she arrived, Billy usually came out to bring us both a mug of hot chocolate like an old grandmother. He would then light some candles for us to see in the failing light and ask to join us, to which we always agreed. We would chat about nothing particularly important and sometimes plan out the following day.

The days themselves were not just filled with idle soul searching; there was plenty of work to keep us busy. Every day brought a new scavenging run of the surrounding areas, with the rarity of what we were going after dictating how far we would have to push out. Priority one was to get ourselves a decent gasoline reserve. We could all feel the clock ticking on unleaded gas, and we wanted to make as much use of those vehicles as we could while they would still run. I personally wanted to drive my vehicle as much as possible. I really loved that Jeep; it was my first new, truly nice car and I only got to use it for that first year after the fall of everything before the gas expired (we managed to extend the life of gasoline with the use of fuel stabilizers—we found box after box of the stuff on one of our earliest runs to an auto shop).

Before we could go out for gas, we needed containers to store it all in, so our very first run involved heading down to the hardware store and other home improvement stores to get as many plastic fifty-five-gallon drums as we could get our hands on. Jake and Billy made that run in the Super Duty with the trailer while I stayed home with Lizzy. We were learning that our small number was going to pose a challenge to our ability to effectively gather supplies in an efficient manner. The evidence of the squatters on the property cemented into our minds that concepts like enforceable property rights were a thing of the past. Our "ownership" of a thing depended completely on our ability to defend that thing from other people. If we left any of it unattended, there was nothing at all to stop others from coming in and taking it. This was, in fact, the very thing we were doing as we ventured out to gather supplies. We didn't know if we were taking anything that someone else was depending on to be there when they returned to it. We saw some-thing we needed, and there was nobody there to claim it; we took it.

After the plastic barrels were secured with the surplus diesel supply transferred into them, Jake and I went out hunting for gas the following day in the truck while Billy stayed home with Elizabeth. The truck bed was empty of everything at this point with the exception of one of the now cleaned steel barrels, every gas can we owned, the drip pans, the jack and jack stands, and the mallet and taper punch. The mission here was to get as much gas as we could as fast as we could.

"Fast" turned out to be a relative concept in this case. Finding areas congested with cars was easy; accessing them all as they became bunched up and stacked bumper to bumper less so. The fastest approach by far was to park the Dodge up as close to the target vehi-cles as possible, which often meant driving onto curbs or sidewalks. In those cases where we couldn't do that, there was no choice but to walk gas cans into the tangle of vehicles and walk them back out to the truck to empty into the barrel; a trip that got a little further with each gas tank that we tapped.

We had a fifty-five-gallon drum to fill. The average car gas tank holds between ten and fifteen gallons, but the cars never had full tanks. Sometimes we got lucky and pulled as much as five gallons out of one car, but most of the time it was one gallon here, two there, and so on. Very rarely did it take more than one gas can to empty a tank—we were far more likely to get a tank that was bone dry.

Dry tanks were particularly frustrating. We could tell if a tank had anything in it by banging on it but, unless we were dealing with a truck or SUV, we sometimes had to go to the trouble to jack the vehicle up onto stands so that we could crawl underneath and give the tank a whack. All of this work added to the total time we had to spend out there. It took us some time to figure out that a vehicle with a corpse in the driver's seat was more likely than others to have a dry tank; many people seemed to have died in their cars while trying to leave the city. Their cars just stayed in park and idled down to nothing after the driver expired.

All things considered, getting that fifty-five-gallon drum filled took all freaking day.

The next trip was all about clothes. Specifically, Billy didn't have any clothes for women or little girls and all the stuff he did have wouldn't fit Jake because it was too big for him. I was also specifically on the lookout for feminine supplies of all varieties (razors, sanitary items, lotions, and such). This was a bit easier to handle and required less drudgery.

Jake and I took the Jeep on that trip. There were several good options for clothing stores in Jackson that Billy was able to mark out for us on a map; all of which were, unfortunately, in the heart of the town where traffic pileups began to make the roads impassable. Even so, we managed to find a workable path near enough to Teton Kids that we didn't feel like we would be leaving the Jeep in a completely unguarded situation. We also learned that going house to house was a very viable solution that had the added benefit of allowing us to scavenge other goods while we were there (in one house we even found a nice bolt action hunting rifle, a few boxes of ammunition, and a heavy compound bow with broadhead arrows). Going house to house did have the drawback, however, of putting us face to face with the very unsavory remains of the former residents; many of these incidents were heartbreaking. I remember one particular house in which I found my way into a bedroom with the remains of a child laying in his or her bed. Next to this, an adult corpse sat in a chair, bent over with its head resting on its hands on the edge of the bed. The child was very close to Elizabeth in size. It was unclear who had died first: child or parent.

I left the house and Jake had me spend the rest of the day standing watch outside with the Jeep while he went room to room in subsequent homes, for which I was grateful.

The next trip out focused on food. Water was thankfully under control due to both the well out behind the house and the stream running through the bowl, but food became a constant concern for us. Our current stores (partly what we had brought with us on the road but mostly the provisions Billy had stashed away before we ever met him) would carry us through six months if we were careful, but we knew we wouldn't be able to keep this up forever. We could only go out to scavenge food so many times before we completely exhausted anything that was left over. Our plan was to stockpile as much long life provisions as we could up front in a frenzy of concentrated gathering. This would provide us with the breathing room we needed to come up with a more permanent solution.

Billy spent a lot of time pouring through his books on the subject. For all of his interest in self-reliance and preparation, it seems he had never counted on things going so far south that basic services never came back. There was always this inner belief that infrastructure, agriculture, shipping, and emergency services would make a comeback after some reasonable period of time (the concept of "reasonable" being relative to the severity of the disaster that had preceded it). Though he had purchased books on the subject due to a broad interest in the content, he never really believed long-term survival would depend on the ability to maintain a subsistence farm indefinitely. He suddenly found himself needing to play catch-up with regard to such problems as production area per person, crop rotation, irrigation, and seasonal crops. Foods like potatoes and beets were planned to be our mainstays but we weren't convinced that these were crops we could keep going all year round without first building some sort of enclosed greenhouse; the winters in Wyoming were bitter and, unfortunately, the growing season in our area was one of the shortest in the state. Billy spent hours reading through several books, taking notes, and devising planting schedules in a notebook.

An additional problem to all of this was the fact that we actually needed something to plant. We couldn't just point at a section of ground and decree that "here there shall grow carrots." We actually needed some carrots to stick in the ground. When Jake mentioned this at one point, Billy responded by digging a big whiteboard out of a corner in the garage (which had become our staging area for mission-based tasks like scavenging or work projects in the immediate area), hung it up on the wall, and began to divide it into sections with a dry erase marker. Within each section, he added a heading such as "Clothes," "Shelter," "Food," "Weapons," "Building," and so on. In the square for food, he began to write entries like "Potatoes," "Carrots," "Beets," and "Corn."

He turned back to us and said, "The fundamental problem is that to plant a crop of something, you need a bit of that something to start with. That means we've got to go out and find this stuff to get started. Now, we can grow just about anything from seeds if we can find the seeds, but we may also be able to just find and transplant living vegetation. There are farms all around the area which may still have viable sources right in the ground. I say "may" because I don't know where this state was in the harvest cycle when the Plague hit critical mass. Either way, we'll need to scout and see what we can find. We'll also be able to look for packets of dried seeds in places like home improvement stores. The people who lived in this state tended toward a self-sufficient nature; there will be all sorts of businesses out there that catered to the home farmer. Keep your eyes open for anything that says "Hydroponics" in the sign. Places like those should be goldmines."

Jake snorted humorlessly to himself. "Out in California, 'hydroponics' was just code for 'weed growing supplies'."

Billy paused and seemed to contemplate this for a moment, looking up at the high ceiling of the garage. "The climate here for pot is all wrong but if you happen to find any, bring it back here certainly. I'd hate to think I've already smoked my last joint."

I laughed at this and Billy hastened to add, "I'd never do that in front of Lizzy, of course."

I laughed even harder. "Billy, after everything we've been through —after what that kid has seen, you think I care about you taking a hit? Just do it outside is all I ask; the stuff smells like a skunk's business end."

Billy nodded, turned around, and wrote in "cannabis" under "corn." He looked at this for two seconds and then added a question mark next to it. Behind his back, Jake glanced in my direction and gave me a "do you think he's messing with us?" look. I smiled and shrugged.

In the absence of easily renewable power, our evenings began to feel like Family Fun Night. When the light failed, we would light candles and spend time together in the front room. Most evenings found Billy in his favorite leather chair by the fireplace (not lit during this time; the log home was surprisingly good at holding in the day's heat) with a bright LED lantern propped over his head on a wall shelf. He usually had about five or six books stacked next to him on a side table with a notebook in his lap, switching between reading various volumes and scribbling in the notebook, often times muttering to himself. I spent some time in Billy's library trying to find books to read but his taste in novels skewed in a direction different to mine. He tended to favor a lot of classics and various flavors of what I thought of as "Manly Fiction"—many sci-fi, military, and thriller titles with a lot of historical fiction sprinkled throughout. My tastes swung toward romance and supernatural stories, so there was little for me in his collection. I made a mental note to have Jake pull over the next time we passed a bookstore.

Billy also had a good collection of board games, which we used to play often in the evenings. We would spread the game of the night out on the low coffee table between the couches and chairs in the house's main front room. There were plenty of the standard games that everyone in the world knows like Monopoly, Sorry, The Game of Life, and even Battleship but he also had some games that I never heard of like Stratego, Risk, Forbidden Island, and more. He also had a chess set, to Jake's delight, which would sometimes be set up on the table so he could teach Elizabeth to play. To my surprise, she was eager to learn. The game might as well have been Greek Calculus to me, so I had a hard time following some of the concepts he went over with her. Even so, after a few nights of listening to him go over the rules of the game, I found myself picking up more than I intended.

I recall the first evening he just focused on how each piece moved. Some of them were simple, like the bishops and rooks but others seemed like a pain, like the knights. When I said as much to him, he said, "Knights are horribly undervalued in this game. The nature of their movement makes it harder for your opponent to anticipate your intention; I've won several games because the person I played against made a simple blunder—they basically forgot that my knight was covering a key square. I'd personally take two knights over a queen in any game, really."

"Get out of here," said Billy from his chair, looking at Jake around the edge of his book. "Over a queen?"

"Sure," said Jake.

"Think I want to play you some time. Might be an easy win."

Jake sat back and smiled. "I'd like that."

On the following evening, Jake discussed how there were essentially three phases to any real game of chess: an opening, middle, and end game. "The opening is where the players position their pieces, planning their attacks and defenses. The middle game is where all the plans you set up in the opening are executed, which typically results in a bunch of pieces getting captured on both sides. The end game is where you have a reduced number of pieces, sometimes only a couple, and someone is actively pursuing a mating move."

On the third evening of play, Jake focused on the opening phase of the game and how Lizzy could get herself into the best position of strength to maximize her chances of beating her opponent. "See these four squares?" he asked while pointing at the exact center of the board. "This is the most important area during the opening phase. You want absolute control of this terrain by the time the middle game phase begins. The ability to gain superiority over these four squares can often times determine who will maintain an advantage throughout the game."

"So if I do it right, I'll win?" asked Elizabeth.

"Oh, no, it's not guaranteed," said Jake. "It only helps. Situations always change. Your ability to win is defined by your ability to adapt to the board as it changes. Control of the center early on is just a way to put the odds in your favor."

"So how do I get control?"

"Basically," Jake answered, "you try to cover as many center squares as you can with as many pieces as you can and then, at some point, you decide which single square you're going to target. That square will be occupied by your opponent, and you'll attack it. You need to have enough pieces targeting that square so that when you and your opponent are done fighting over that square, you'll come out with more pieces left than him."

Every evening they played, he covered a new key concept with her and then they would play through a game exercising what they had discussed. He never played to win during these games. He spent most of his time asking her why she made such and such a move, not telling her that the move was right or wrong but just asking her to explain the reasoning behind it. In the process of doing so, she would soon discover whether the move she had made was wise; if it was not, he allowed her to take it back and try another direction. Through this process, I began to understand what an outstanding teacher Jake could be and wondered, not for the first or last time, if teaching had been some aspect of his previous life in any capacity.

Billy and I both also began to learn how devious Jake could be.

After several nights of Jake working through the basics with Elizabeth, Billy finally challenged him to a game. To my surprise, Lizzy happily set the board up for them and then moved to the side to watch them play (I thought she would be annoyed at having her game preempted, but she seemed more eager to watch the two men play a game).

"White or black?" Billy asked. Jake responded by picking up a pawn from each side of the board. He put his hands behind his back, and we heard the sound of the plastic pieces clicking around in his hands. He then put both hands out in front of Billy, both of them closed into fists around the pieces. "Pick one," he offered.

Billy tapped a hand, which Jake rolled over and opened, revealing a white pawn. Both pieces were replaced on the board, and Jake said, "After you."

The next series of moves were slightly disconcerting to watch. Billy started by moving one of his center pawns two spaces out into the middle of the board, which Jake met instantly by moving out his opposing pawn. Billy pushed another pawn next to his initial piece, this time only one square forward. As soon as his hand came off the second pawn, Jake had a knight moved out from the rear and placed down in front. As they went another five or six moves into the game, Billy's choices came slower and slower, requiring more consideration as the board developed. In contrast, Jake countered instantaneously each time, his hand already hovering over his selected piece and waiting for Billy to release his own (I noticed Jake would never touch one of his pieces until Billy had let go of his).

It wasn't very long before the board resembled the last possible second before a major car wreck. I had at least learned the basics of the game over the last few nights just being in the same room and listening to Jake teach Lizzy; I could see how much tension was built up on the center of that board. Every piece was threatening an opposing piece or protecting one of its own. The only thing I can bring to mind that really describes what the board looked like was the closing scene in Reservoir Dogs where the characters all held guns on each other in that giant Mexican Standoff. I didn't see how it could get any worse—neither one of them could move another piece outside of pushing a random pawn out along the edges of the board. Evidently, Billy agreed and pulled the trigger.

An exchange of six moves followed quickly, each of them resulting in a capture for the other side. They happened so fast that I couldn't keep up with which pieces were being taken and had to bring myself up to speed by looking at them lined up along the sides of the board. I could see that Jake had captured two pawns and one bishop while Billy had two pawns and one knight.

The center of the board was now a shambles as far as I could tell. The balanced aggression that had existed only a moment ago was now obliterated with only a few survivors left out in the center. This fact seemed to deter Jake and Billy not at all; they began to bring out more pieces in a second wave to the first skirmish. I wasn't knowledgeable enough to know who was ahead at the time, but if I remember correctly now, a bishop and knight are considered equal in value so they would have been at a draw by this point. This slowly began to change as Billy pressed his advantage.

He proceeded to cut down pawns while Jake seemed only to divide his responses by either running away or attempting to block Billy's advance. Jake pulled a bizarre move that I had never seen where his king and rook suddenly swapped places; Elizabeth spoke up at this, wanting to know what just happened. Billy assured her that the move was perfectly legal and referred to as "castling."

Billy reached out and captured a bishop with his knight in a seeming sacrifice of the knight (one of Jake's pawns was guarding the bishop). Rather than capturing the knight, Jake ignored it and moved his own bishop from its starting position out to the middle of the board on Billy's right side. Shrugging, Billy pulled his knight back out of harm's way. Jake responded by moving his own remaining knight forward into the middle of the board in support of his bishop, which Billy promptly captured with his queen. He grunted when he did so, mildly surprising me. Both of Jake's knights were captured, and now Billy's queen was out in play, threatening to make an even worse mess of Jake's defenses.

I feel like I need to explain something about Jake at this point.

242 | JOSHUA GAYOU

Thinking back on the game he played with Billy, I don't believe there was a single instance where he wasn't in complete control—of either himself or the game. I honestly believe that the entire game went exactly as he wanted, including every piece he lost. Even when it looked like he was being beaten, I really think it was by his design. At no point throughout all of this did he betray a single ounce of emotion or indecision. I would call it a poker face, but this was something else entirely. It's a misconception that high stakes poker players show no expression or emotion during play—they show plenty of both, realizing that a complete absence of any human behavior is unnatural, cannot be maintained indefinitely, and betrays just as much about the player as any number of tells or ticks. Due to this understanding, the poker face of a high stakes player is really just an exquisitely practiced performance of choreographed expressions, positions, and statements that are in line with the player's own normal behavior. The trick for them is not to hide all emotion; the goal is only to camouflage deeper intent.

Jake was no poker player and had no poker face at all. In situations such as these, you could feel his insides thrumming. He became a package of hyperactivity concealed in an unmoving shell. His face, already muted in expression in his everyday life, became barren of all expression and articulation. Not a single muscle on his face twitched or moved unnecessarily. His eyelids even ceased to blink as though their only purpose had become the accumulation of data and blinking would create intolerable gaps in the stream of input. At no point throughout the entire game did he ever show signs of satisfaction, annoyance, confusion, or uncertainty. There was never a time where any of us could tell if he was winning or losing—there was simply no way to gauge if the game was going the way he desired or if his plans were being thwarted irrevocably. He only absorbed information and produced none. I am exaggerating in no way when I say the man was a void.

We all sat around the table wondering what he would do next when he reached out, took his queen, and moved it all the way across the board into Billy's back rank and said, "Check."

Billy froze in place, staring at what had just happened. He reached out toward the board, stopped, and pulled his hand back. Finally, he moved his king over a space to get it out of danger. Jake's bishop came forward, flattening a pawn at its final destination.

"Check."

Billy shook his head and moved the King again.

Jake moved his queen, to which Billy responded by growling, "Son of a…"

"Check."

Billy sat now for a long time staring at the board. He leaned in several directions looking at things from all angles, agonizing over what he would do next. I couldn't see what the big deal was; it seemed clear to me that he had to move his king again. It took me perhaps two minutes or more while Billy deliberated before I realized the problem: both Billy's king and queen were now threatened by Jake's queen. Billy couldn't capture the queen with his king because Jake's queen was guarded by a pawn deep in Billy's territory as well as a rook all the way across the board in Jake's area—Billy would have been moving his king into check, which is illegal. If Billy captured the queen with his own queen, his piece would be lost. He finally muttered, "Damn it…" and captured Jake's queen with his own, which Jake promptly captured with the rook.

"Check."

Billy sighed and shook his head, clearly disgusted with the entire situation. He moved his king out of check. Jake pushed the rook to the final rank, trapping the enemy king behind a wall of its own pawns.

"Mate," said Jake.

Billy sat back in his chair. "What happened to you liking your knights more than your queen?"

"Nothing. I still do," said Jake. "But you were also in the room when I said that."

"What?"

"You heard me say that I would take two knights over one queen so I figured you would go after them. You did, but you developed a case of tunnel vision while you pursued them, sacrificing good formation of your pieces to capture them both. Your desire to get my knights caused you to rush the opening, resulting in many of your pieces remaining underdeveloped. I helped this along by bringing both knights out to attack the center early instead of pushing more pawns to support d5, leaving the knights vulnerable. You were so focused on getting those knights that you didn't see the check and subsequent king/queen fork coming."

"Jesus," said Billy. "You're one of *those* guys, aren't you? All Bobby Fischer and calculating fifteen moves ahead and everything?"

"Thinking that many moves ahead is a pointless exercise," said Jake. "All it takes to wreck a sequence of that length is a single move. I never think ahead more than four."

"But you literally went into the game knowing he would go after your knights," I said. "You set that up, it happened, and you used it to win. That whole game was a lot longer than four moves."

"I had a general plan," replied Jake. "I knew what situation I wanted to create and waited for opportunities to do so. Not the same."

"So next time, don't go straight for his knights, Billy," said Elizabeth.

"Except next time I'll know that we had this experience and adjust my plans accordingly," Jake told her.

Billy was waving a finger at Jake and laughing. "You're a dirty player, Whitey."

Jake raised his eyebrows. "Have you ever heard the expression 'play the board'?"

Billy nodded, "Sure. It means you make your best poker hand without using any of the hole cards."

Jake nodded. "It means something different in Chess. It refers to planning your strategy based only on the position of the pieces rather than what the opponent is likely to do. It's how you want to learn to play when you're a beginner. Later on, as you better understand the game, you play the player. The pieces on the board are only an expression of your opponent's personality; therefore the opponent is your problem. The pieces on the board are only incidental."

# BAD TIMES

### Amanda

The time we spent together at the cabin includes some of my happiest memories since the world toppled over. As I mentioned, there were times during this period in which I experienced discontent with bouts of depression, however Lizzy, Jake, and Billy were always there for me when I needed them or ready to back away when I needed my own space. Even my daughter, who was so young at the time, could tell that I needed the leeway to work through the dark things inside of me, displaying the poise and the wisdom beyond her years to grant it. My family circle, which had collapsed under the weight of the Plague, had expanded again to include Jake and Billy, who transcended the position of simple friendship. They became necessary.

"I want to thank you both," I told them one night. We were all sitting on the front porch enjoying the last light of the day before the sun went down completely. "I don't know what inspires a person to invite a total stranger to come live with him, but you've saved my life in more ways than I can express."

"Well, we weren't just going to leave you," Billy said and cleared his throat.

"Yeah, I know," I said. "But you extended that same invitation to Jake at some point and then to Otis later. What is it that makes that seem normal to you? I'm not complaining, but that wouldn't have been anything you did before, right? People don't just invite strangers they meet to come live with them."

"Well, they actually did," Jake said from his spot on my left. "People used to put ads for roommates in the paper or online all the time, which was essentially inviting strangers to move in, just as you say."

"Aside from that," Billy said. "It's something I think I picked up from Jake."

"Me?" Jake asked.

"Yap. I can't say why I really invited you to come along for the ride outside of the fact that you made a good drinking buddy and generally weren't a horse's ass. I think I was also lonely too. But I didn't set out to start collecting strays. The original plan when I left California was to avoid strangers at all costs. Just figured it was safer that way."

"So what changed?" I asked him.

"Jake's refusal to live in an evil world. He made it clear to me early on that he wasn't willing to avoid people just on the chance that they could be dangerous. He simply wasn't interested in living that way. When I explained that this was an excellent way to get killed, he said that was fine. I realized that he meant what he said. The point he was making was that he would choose how to live in the world on his own terms and, if the world had truly become a collection of evil people, he really had no interest in living in it, therefore choosing to die on his own terms."

I looked at Jake, not knowing what to say. I could think of nothing appropriate. He only looked out across the glen, at peace.

"His attitude helped me to realize that there isn't so very much worth holding onto anymore if we don't hold onto that core aspect of ourselves. We've all lost nearly everyone; our friends, loved ones, and families. What we're left with—what we have to look forward to is a life harder than anything we've ever known. What the hell would be the point of gutting it out if the only people left in the world are those you either won't trust or must actively try to kill?"

Billy took a pull from his coffee mug (which was absent any coffee). "I learned this from Jake, and I agree. I'm not doing it."

"Guys," Jake said, sitting forward in his chair.

Far across the valley, we saw headlights emerge from the overlapping tree lines of the cleft entrance. The vehicle slowly rolled into the valley over the dirt road. When it had advanced fifty feet, a second set of headlights appeared behind it.

Billy jumped up from his chair while pulling his keyring from his pocket. "Elizabeth, you come with me right now." He looked at Jake and me as he passed. "You two get your rifles but keep them low."

Jake was already moving for the front door as Billy and Lizzy disappeared off the side of the porch. He came back with my rifle, his AK, and Billy's shotgun. He laid each on the table and then handed me the Tavor. As I checked the chambers of first the rifle and then my pistol, I heard the roll-up door of the garage cycle up and then back down again. Jake had gone back inside the house.

Billy hurried back up onto the porch and picked up the shotgun to check it. He racked the pump to load a shell into the chamber, then pulled one off the sidesaddle and thumbed it into the tube magazine to top it off.

"You locked the garage?" I asked.

"Yeah. I left the keys inside with her. The locks can be opened from the inside without the key. She's safe for now."

Jake emerged from the front door carrying the two protective vests. He handed one to me, which I pulled on hastily, and offered the other to Billy, who turned it down. "You wear it, Jake," he said. "Shit happens to you more often anyway."

The vehicles were about halfway to the house by this point. The light had been low since before they entered the valley with the sunset hidden behind the rim; it was now downright dark.

Billy looked over to me: "Get inside the house and see what kind of vantage you can get in the front room. Keep it dark in there and crack a window for your barrel."

I complied, grabbing my mag pouch hanging by the front door as I went and breathing deep to calm my nerves. I could feel my heart hammering away. I picked a window that gave me a wide viewing angle of the whole entryway and porch and then slid it open just far enough to give my rifle a good range of motion. I pulled over a foot-stool to sit on so that I wouldn't have to shift around while crouched, which could cause movement that might be seen.

"Think it's the squatters?" I heard Jake ask through the window.

"No way to tell but I'd say likely so," Billy said.

"How do you want to do this?"

"Play it by ear," answered Billy. "Keep that thing handy but keep it muzzle-down for now. No reason to think they're not friendly until they prove otherwise."

"Very well," said Jake and I heard him work the action on his rifle. The sound of slow footsteps across the planks of the porch told me he was spreading himself out from Billy's position.

Billy stood within my field of view off to the left, waiting. The vehicles (two full sized trucks) were just pulling up to a stop. They left the headlights on, bathing the porch and house in a harsh light that washed out all color. It was hard to see them when they got out, but I counted seven as they came to stand in front of the trucks. Positioned in front of the light as they were, it was impossible to make out any feature, build, dress, or attitude. I *could* see that they were armed.

Everyone regarded each other silently for a few moments before Billy said, "Well, hi there!"

I heard the sound of someone scoffing from their general direction. A disembodied voice said, "Uh...evening."

Without missing a beat, Billy continued, "I'm guessing you were the fellas who came through this way about a week or so ago?"

"Yeah, that was us."

"Thought so." Billy shifted his weight over to his other leg. He was holding his shotgun out in front of him though it wasn't pointed at anyone in particular. I couldn't see Jake at all. I swept my rifle barrel over the entire group to make sure I could get all of them from my position (it required me swinging the butt of the weapon rather than moving the muzzle) and then put the red dot on the one in the middle. "Didn't know if you guys would be coming back or not. Been a while."

"We were out hunting up supplies. Didn't occur to us that someone would find their way back here and make themselves at home. We figured it was well hidden."

"Well, as to that," Billy said apologetically, "I knew this place was here because it's actually my home."

"Say what, now?"

"This is my home. From before. I bought the land and built the place from the ground up. Been working on it for years. I was planning on retiring here. You guys must have just stumbled across it."

"Hey, what the fuck is this?" another voice from the group spoke up. It was hard to tell where from, but he sounded like he was on my left. "Any asshole could claim that shit—how do we know this particular asshole..."

The original speaker of their group interrupted, "Hold on, Doug. Just calm down. Ain't no call to go there just yet." Addressing Billy, he said, "My rude friend does have a point, though, right? You *could* just be some random couple of guys, couldn't you?"

"You fellas have spent some time in the house, haven't you?"

"Yes, yes we have."

"Get a good look at any of the pictures in there?"

"Gawd damn!" a third voice said from the right of the group. "I knew I recognized him; he's that guy that was in the picture with the Terminator!" A few other voices muttered at this, betraying recognition.

The first speaker was silent a while before he said, "Emmet, kill those lights." They did so, placing the porch in sudden darkness. Off to the left, Jake turned on an electric lantern we had hanging off a nail from one of the eaves. Everyone was bathed in a soft, muted glow and the men before us were suddenly a lot less menacing. They looked like a group of regular people that had been living hard on the road, just like us, with various layers of all-weather clothing and a motley assortment of firearms. Some of them didn't even have decent rifles; they stood there with revolvers or whatever else they had managed to pick up on the road.

"Well…shit," said the original speaker, who I could now confirm was in the middle of the group. "Look, what's your name?"

"Billy. This is Jake."

The man nodded and gave a small wave to both. "I'm Howard. Look, uh, I'm not quite sure where to go from here. We never really counted on the original owner of this place coming back for it, you know? The problem is we were all counting on this place for our survival. It's not just the house; the location was a big piece of this. Being set back and hidden the way it is in this valley, I figure it will escape the notice of any passersby."

"Yap, I getcha," said Billy but offered no more.

"Yeah, well, right now things are kind of quiet with the exception of the odd evil asshole you run into on the road, but I have a feeling things aren't going to stay that way. Just look at my group, here."

"You guys are a bunch of evil…?"

"No, no, that's not what I mean," said Howard, waving his hands. "What I meant is that we all sort of gravitated to each other over time, see? I was on my own when this whole thing kicked off. Then I ran into Emmet, Trey, and Paul. Later, after that, we picked up Doug and his boys. Point is, people were scattered for a bit, but they're going to start collecting back into groups again, building up their strength and such, like we did. I have a feeling we have some serious Mad Max shit in store when some of these groups get bigger. All depends on who ends up in charge."

"And your point is you'd just as soon wait the whole process out in a secluded area to see if your theory is right or not," Billy finished for him.

"Well, yes. More or less."

There was a beat of silence as Billy processed this and I noticed something during this space of time. There was a subtle gap of space in the group of men down by the trucks, as though there were actually two groups instead of one. The group on the right were standing behind

Howard, and the group on the left seemed to be crowded around who I assumed was Doug. I also noticed that, as Howard discussed their reasons for choosing the valley with Billy, the people in Doug's group fidgeted, sighed, and rolled their eyes. These people had a rift, and it looked like blossoming into something ugly.

On top of this, I disliked the fact that there were no women with them. With a woman in their company, I would have been better able to gauge what kind of men they were; if the woman or women looked healthy, relatively happy, and unharmed, there was a good chance that the men were okay. Without that indicator, I wasn't excited about Lizzy and I suddenly becoming the only females in such a large group of strange men, some of whom appeared hostile. I prayed silently that Billy could see all this and that he had reached the same conclusions as me.

Billy finally said, "The thing is this: you all seem well enough, but we don't actually know you. I get where you're going; you're suggesting we partner up. We're not opposed to that, but I don't think we'll be jumping in head first without looking either. I think it's best if we get to know each other."

More sullen muttering from Doug and his group.

"I understand," Howard said. "What do you suggest?"

"This isn't the only house in Jackson," Billy said. "There are hundreds out here in these hills that are open to any who happen by, many of them nicer than my place—I wasn't the only guy interested in retiring in this backcountry. Why don't you boys go set up at one of these places for the next little while? I can mark a few nice ones out on a map for you. We'll meet back here next morning, maybe have some breakfast, and talk it over some more. Kind of work things out over time and see what happens."

Howard was nodding his head at this like it made sense, but Doug wasn't having any of it, apparently. Unable to contain himself, he finally burst forth.

"Can anyone explain to me why we're standing around discussing this bullshit? It's late. We've been driving all fucking day..."

"God damn it, Doug, will you shut your fucking mouth for once?" Howard shouted.

"Hey, fuck *you*, Howie. I'm about over this. I'm in no God damned mood to go out looking for another bed in the middle of the motherfucking night when I know good, and God damned well that we have some right here." The divide between the two groups of men began to widen during this exchange. "Now, I see two assholes on that porch and seven of us. Someone explain that fucking math to me. Someone explain to me why we don't just subtract these dickheads right now."

"God damn it, Doug, you fuckwit…"

Jake chose this time to break his silence. "I really think it best if you all head out of here."

One of the men in Doug's group swiveled and pointed a handgun toward the house off to my left and said, "Hey, put that fucking rifle up, asshole!"

Billy leveled his shotgun at the man holding the pistol. In response, the rest of the men had their guns up with the muzzles jerking between Billy and Jake…all of them except Howard.

"GOD DAMN IT, STOP!" he shouted, standing between his group and ours with his palms extended out toward both. "We don't have to do this! You just be patient for a bit, and no one has to get shot up."

"Been plenty patient with you so far," said someone next to Doug in a deep voice. "Not much to show for it." This seemed to puff Doug up even more.

"What does it end up being tomorrow, huh, Howie? We have to go out to collect food for these pricks to offer up in tribute so we can join their secret fucking faggot society? There're only…fucking…two of them."

"I said to lower that fucking rifle!" a man barked, sounding as though he was on the edge of panic.

My heart was slamming against my chest. I had held out hope that the situation would either stay calm or get back under control, but things didn't look like getting calm any time soon. The fatal flaw in this whole group appeared to be a weak leader…a weak leader that was going to be relieved of command within the next few seconds if someone didn't do something fast.

Intuiting this fact for himself, Billy lowered his shotgun and said, "Okay, look, let's all calm down, guys…"

"Oh, fuck all of this," said Doug. He shot Howard in the back of the head.

Gunfire erupted instantly from all directions. Doug was the first man in the group that I killed; I had kept my dot on his chest as soon as I understood how the balance of power was distributed among them. I put several rounds in his chest, but I can't remember the exact number anymore; at least three. I killed another man standing next to him as well before the group realized that they were dealing with more than two men and started to scatter.

At some point during my shooting, I heard and felt two grunting explosions from Billy's shotgun, one of which caved in a man's chest; the other blew his neighbor's leg off at the knee. The shotgun ceased firing abruptly after that and I saw Billy slump, falling backward into the front door, which rattled it on its hinges. Gunfire of varying intensities continued, belching clouds of smoke out into the air and obscuring the view in the light of the lantern. Out on the edges of the smoke, I saw the shadowed form of two men running off in opposite directions around either side of the house. The sound of Jake's AK-47 followed after them and then ceased.

Presently, I heard his footsteps rush across the porch and low, urgent talking, all of which sounded like it was coming to me through packed cotton. I realized my ears were ringing. Slapping sounded at the front door, and I could hear Jake call, "Let us in, Amanda! Hurry!"

I rushed to the door, unlocked the bolt, and wrenched it open. I was met with the sight of Jake's back, so slender in those early days, bent over Billy's huge burden of a body and straining as he struggled to haul him back into the house. As he pulled him back over the threshold, I saw Billy's hands were clutching at his abdomen and covered in dark black blood. They were shaking, and I thought he might be going into shock. I noticed he also had wounds in his right thigh and shoulder.

Jake dropped him onto the entry rug and ripped off his own over shirt while I slammed and locked the door behind him. He pulled out his Ka-Bar from behind his back, cut the shirt in half down the middle, and wadded one half up to jam into Billy's gut. Billy half groaned/half growled at this and snarled, "God damned rednecks…"

Jake looked up at me with wide eyes. "I have to keep this packed on him; he's not strong enough to hold it. There are two left. They ran around the back of the house."

"Don't worry," I said. I shouldered my rifle and had a moment's hesitation. The right hallway leading to the bedrooms all had windows that could be accessed from outside, but so did the rear living area of the house; the dining area even had a sliding glass door that opened out to the rear of the property. There was no way to get to the rear common area through the bedroom hallway; the hallway went to a dead end at Billy's library. I could choose one direction or the other but not both easily.

I heard a noise from the rear of the house, which made my decision for me. "Keep an eye on that hallway," I said. He nodded to me as I made my way toward the kitchen. When I reached the entryway, I looked all around but saw no obvious movement anywhere. The curtains were drawn across all but the sliding door, and there was no light out back; any available moon or starlight being obscured by the tree cover at the rear of the home. There was no way to see any silhouetted shadow moving behind those curtains.

I debated opening the slider and stepping outside but soon discarded the idea. It sounded like an excellent way to broadcast my position and provide a target to whoever was out there. I finally settled on taking up a position crouched behind the kitchen island and waiting.

The sound of breaking glass came from one of the bedrooms on the side of the house. A few seconds later, a large rock flew through the sliding glass door, sending shards of glass all throughout the combined rooms of kitchen, dining room, and TV common area. The island behind which I hid protected me from the worst of it.

A shadow appeared in the wreckage of the door frame even while glass was still falling to the floor. It was hunched over and moving fast. I followed the shape with my rifle and fired off several shots, all of which missed (I hadn't yet learned at this point how hard it was to shoot something moving laterally across my field of view) but the sound of shots fired coming from his right startled the intruder, who drew up suddenly and swung in my direction. This was all I needed to line a bead up on him, and I put rounds into him until he fell.

I recalled hearing the window of the bedroom shatter, but I stayed where I was with the barrel pointed back out the frame of the obliterated glass door, wondering if the window had just been a diversion. My answer came when a single gunshot sounded from the direction of the front door, followed by grunting and snarling. I heard the sound of furniture being displaced and the thin, high pitched tinkle of small glass breaking. I rushed around the useless refrigerator and back into the main hall leading to the entryway, only to see Jake in his original position over Billy where I had left him. I could just make out a pair of boots extending from the bedroom hall behind him. They were on their heels with the toes pointed up. I grabbed one of the many flashlights that we kept throughout the house and thumbed it on as I ran over.

The last man to have broken into the house lay on his back with Jake's Ka-Bar sticking out of his throat. It was buried to the hilt.

Jake looked up at me with an expression of complete hopelessness hanging on his face. "He's going, Amanda. I can't stop him—he's fucking going!"

I ran over and kneeled by Billy. His eyes were shut tight, and he was breathing shallow as if it hurt him to take in any air at all. He reached up with a shaking left hand and wrapped it up in the collar of Jake's T-shirt. He growled and said, "I need you to read the Iliad."

"What?" Jake barked. He laughed, sounding hysterical. "What the hell are you talking about, you crazy old..."

Billy's hand twisted in Jake's collar and pulled hard. Half of the front of Jake's shirt tore away from his chest. "Don't argue with me, God damn you. You promise."

"I promise!" Jake blurted, not wanting to deny him anything. "You have my word. Immediately."

Billy sighed and let his hand go loose. It stayed tangled up in Jake's shirt, limply hanging off the ground. "Good. That's good, Whitey." He rolled his head over to the right, looking up at me. "You...you take ca..."

The last of his breath escaped in a sigh as he died.

———

The next few days were spent recovering from the fight. On the night that Billy died Jake drug all those we had killed from Howard's group around the back of the house out of sight and hauled Billy out on the porch, covering him with a sheet. He did this while I opened the garage to find Elizabeth, who had been crying and near panic. I did my best to calm her fears before trying to find a way to explain the unexplainable to her. She became even worse at that point, running out of the garage and toward the house to her room. When she got there, she screamed in horror; it was her window which had been broken by the intruder. I caught up to her, collected her, and took her up to Jake's room. I finished the night by helping Jake drag an old sheet of plywood out of the garage and to the back of the house, which we used to board up the broken glass door. It wasn't a very good job (we knew we'd have to clean it up later) but it would do to keep animals out of the house overnight.

When we were done, we both cleaned the blood from our hands using some rain barrel water and a five-gallon bucket outside. I went numbly upstairs to Jake's room to sleep with Lizzy. I believe he spent the night on a couch downstairs, not willing to claim Billy's room.

Jake spent the following morning digging graves while I went through Howard's trucks to see what they had. Among the usual supplies was an acetylene torch and igniter which I suspected they had planned to use in gaining entry to the garage. There was also a dead buck in one of the truck beds, most of which would go to waste as none of us knew how to properly dress a deer or preserve the meat without any cold storage at the time. I stored the various supplies in piled sections in the garage, to stash later in more permanent areas. The firearms and ammunition from the group were collected and deposited on the upstairs level of the garage by the safe.

With this done, I went outside to find Jake, who was just finishing the mass grave he had excavated for Howard and his six men two hundred yards away from the house. It was not terribly large, but it was deep enough and would accommodate them all when stacked in on top of each other. I pulled down the tailgate of the truck in which Jake had transported the bodies, took one of them by the shoulders, and began to pull. He came up next to me to help.

We had them all covered with tamped down dirt within an hour. "Thanks," Jake said. "Ready to go say goodbye?"

"No, but let's do it anyway."

We drove back to the house and parked next to our growing collection of vehicles (the hulking Ford was still stored in the garage), and I helped Jake dig a grave for Billy close by under a large fir tree. We laid him into the ground; covered him over.

Jake briefly rested a hand on my shoulder and said, "I'll go get Lizzy." I worried for her as he left, fearing that she would regress into silence again the same way she had done when Eddie died. To my surprise, she emerged from the house with Jake not long after. She was holding his hand; in her other hand, she was clutching something fiercely. As she came closer, I could just make out the brass end of Billy's old folding pocket knife peeking out of her fist. I realized Jake must have gone through Billy's pockets and, finding this one personal item, gave it to Elizabeth to remember him by. I met his eyes and mouthed the words, "Thank you," to him. He nodded and came to stand beside her before the tree.

"This tree is where Billy has come to rest," he told her. "If you ever feel like you need to talk to him, you come out here, sit under this tree, and talk."

"Will he hear me?" she asked. She was crying silently and just able to control her voice enough to speak.

"I honestly don't know," answered Jake. "But it's what I intend to do whenever I'm missing him. If there's a chance, he can hear I figure it's worth trying."

I will never forget how they looked when he bent and kissed her softly on the top of her head: my new broken family. He left her there alone and came back to stand next to me.

"She'll be okay," he said. "You both will."

*When?* I thought but didn't say.

As though reading my mind, he said, "Tomorrow or the next day. Eventually. There's much to do. Plenty to keep occupied. There's always another problem to solve in this world."

"Jake," I said. The tone of my voice caused him to look over at me. "Don't leave us. I know you were planning on it at some point... whenever it was that you thought we would all be settled in and safe, I guess. I don't know why or what it is that's driving you but just... don't, okay? I'm too exhausted to come up with an argument. Just stay here. We need you."

Jake looked back at Elizabeth standing under Billy's tree. He drew in a heavy breath and blew it out through pursed lips. I made ready to repeat myself, trying to conjure up in my mind the magic combination of words that would make him understand. Make him see. I was distracted by the thought of the protective vest that I wore the night before and how it had been unnecessary; no one had gotten off a single shot in my direction. I thought about how it would have saved Billy's life and fought back my own tears. I began to panic inside. I thought: *I can't convince him. I can't even string two sentences together right now.*

Finally, he surprised me by nodding.

"Yeah," he said. "I can do that."

# EPILOGUE

## Gibs

Blake Gibson ("Gibs" to his friends) wiped a forearm across his eyes and blinked as he hauled on the oversized wheel of the school bus, navigating a path up the cluttered debris of garbage and derelict vehicles on Wyoming's Northbound 191. He hated that God damned bus. It was a big pain in his chapped, finely aged ass to maneuver, was ridiculously loud, and keeping the tank topped off was about as easy as keeping his unreasonable cow of a second ex-wife satisfied to any reasonable degree. He would have given anything to trade down to something more manageable; one of those Fiat clown cars, a motorcycle, even a fucking go-kart. Anything would have been preferable to a massive, fuel guzzling, bright-ass yellow, "Hey-You-Guys!" school bus.

Unfortunately, the damned thing had ended up being a bit of a necessity. No less than fifteen people had barnacled themselves to his hide (man, woman, and child of every age) and this had turned out to be the most efficient way to transport them. They had initially attempted a convoy of several vehicles but that had only worked about half as well as a dick sandwich. It turned out that the time required for the activity of refueling vehicles actually scaled up when the number of vehicles increased – they had eventually spent more time topping off tanks than they had making progress. A compromise was found: this fucking bus. Sure, it was a whore to weave around through all the pileups and the gas tank was virtually bottomless but the benefits seemed to outweigh the negatives in the long run.

Gibs looked up in the long overhead rearview mirror after getting around a particularly nasty knot, having rolled his left rear wheel off the pavement and into the dirt to do so. The bus had lurched sickeningly in that direction, threatening to topple and roll down a shallow hill into a ditch. "We all good back there?" he called.

He was met with one or two smiles. Even Barbara, a little old grandmotherly type, met him with a thumbs-up and a wink.

He nodded and put his attention back on the road. "Rah," he muttered to himself.

He didn't know where the hell he was going nor did he have any clue what he was looking for. They had been on the road for weeks now, looking for somewhere to settle down, always finding some reason to flee hopeful looking places. He had lost two of his people in the process of escaping Denver; picked up three new ones not long after. Every day they pushed out a little further looking for that green grass on the other side of the fence, all the while their diminishing food and water a constant worry on Gibs's tired, overburdened mind. As it happened, the time required in the process of scavenging supplies also scaled up with the number of people for which he had to provide, and some of his people were too infirm to get out there and dig with him.

Sixteen people including him, two rifles, a pistol, and a couple of boxes of bullets between them all. Fuck.

Gibs wiped his forearm across his eyes and blinked again, shaking his head to combat a lack of sleep. Off to the side, a sign approached on his right. It was as blurry as if he had killed off a bottle of Jack that morning, which he hadn't. Good sweet Christ but he'd butter up a chimpanzee's nuts for a cup of coffee. He'd even drink that shitty Folger's crystals garbage.

He focused hard enough that a headache bloomed in the center of his forehead, forcing the sign to resolve.

"Jackson, 65 miles"

"Jackson," he thought. He liked the sound of that. It brought to mind a favorite Johnny Cash song of his. "Screw it," he thought. "Jackson it is."

He repositioned himself in his seat and sat up straight. He lifted up his right hand and waved forward, which conjured his friend Tom Davidson at his side, who he insisted on referring to only as Davidson.

"Think we'll have a look at this Jackson town coming up, see what we find. Maybe we hunker in there."

Davidson slapped him on the shoulder and nodded. "Right on. I'll let the others know." He turned and made his way back down the aisle, holding onto the seat backs as he went.

Gibs smiled to himself; never much of a singer, he began to tunelessly chant:

"We got married in a fever, hotter than a pepper sprout. We've been talkin' 'bout Jackson, ever since the fire went out. I'm go-in' to Jackson, I'm gonna mess around. Yeah, I'm go-in' to Jacks-DAH, sonofa-fuckbitchcocksucker!"

He hauled on the wheel again, narrowly missing a washout on the road by scant inches. He got the bus straightened out on the other side miraculously with only a minor squealing of tires, the backend fishtailing in sickening fashion. He coughed and took several deep breaths to calm himself. Jesus!

Having thus regained control, he couldn't help but finish his initial thought: "Look out Jackson town."

# A NOTE ON THE NARRATIVE

This completes the first volume of the history of the Jackson Commune, comprising the early days of its founders, how they found each other, and how they came to settle there.

I have taken some small liberty in the narrative flow of this document for the purposes of grammar and readability. This was done mostly to help obscure the usual ticks and placeholders that people employ in common spoken language (Jake Martin tends to make frequent use of the words "right?" and "you know?" in his conversation, whereas Amanda uses variations of "like" or "I was like" often). In transcribing my notes into a final written form, I found early on that such usage would have to be cleaned up and elected to do so in favor of readability, accepting the minor hit to accuracy. I have secured the approval from my interview subjects before making any changes to their narrative; the initial intent and feeling behind their words has, I feel, been carried forward into the final product.

—**B.C.**

# FROM THE PUBLISHER

Thank you so much for reading *Commune Book One* by Joshua Gayou. We hope you enjoyed it as much as we enjoyed bringing it to you. We just wanted to take a moment to encourage you to review the book on Amazon and Goodreads. Every review helps further the author's reach and, ultimately, helps them continue writing fantastic books for us all to enjoy.

If you liked *Commune Book One*, check out the rest of our catalogue at www.aethonbooks.com. To sign up to receive updates regarding all new releases, visit www.aethonbooks.com/sign-up

JOSHUA GAYOU lives in Southern California with his wife Jennifer and son Anthony.

When he isn't writing, he divides his time between being a senior engineer at a prominent In Flight Entertainment (IFE) company, accomplishing tasks around the house as assigned by his wife (The Boss), building stuff out in his wood shop, playing board games with his kid, and whatever else his twisted little mind takes an interest in.

Visit joshuagayouauthor.com

CPSIA information can be obtained
at www.ICGtesting.com
Printed in the USA
LVHW092303111119
637079LV00009B/295/P